**"Well, look at you."** Sydney stopped right in front of him, planted the base of her surfboard on the ground and kicked out a hip. **"I never would have imagined I'd see this."**

"See what? Me?" Theo asked.

"No, this." She reached up and flicked a finger against the buttons on his polo shirt. "They're unbuttoned."

"Oh," he laughed, shoved his hands in his pockets and ducked his head. "Yeah, well, it's more comfortable being able to breathe in the heat, right?"

"Uh-huh. I see you got a sunburn, too. Forget your sunscreen yesterday?"

"Not at first. Just forgot to reapply it."

"We're no sooner going to get you acclimated than it'll be time for you to go home," Sydney said, a teasing grin on her face. Droplets of water dotted her face. "Hope you took a long soak after that horseback trail yesterday."

"I did indeed take that advice to heart." It was probably the only reason he could walk today, now that he thought about it. He could get used to this, he thought. He could also get used to seeing Sydney smile, too.

Dear Reader,

There are some places that, when you arrive, make one feel as if you've come home. Hawai'i has always been that place for me. Growing up, I heard stories of the branches of the family that migrated there from Tasmania, and I remember visiting some of those elderly relatives on my first trip to the islands. It was the Christmas when I was eight and so much of that journey remains clear in my mind: the mountains of poinsettias, the ukulele strumming Christmas music, waking up on Christmas morning to the sounds of the ocean and the sight of brilliant sunshine.

Those memories and the affection they evoke have been my inspiration as I begin this new series for Harlequin Heartwarming. Every word I've written so far has come from such a place of love and affection it's almost overwhelming. Creating the small town of Nalani is most definitely a labor of love and I'm so grateful for the opportunity to go back—in my mind at least—any time I want. Rest assured, I will be making a return trip to the islands. Sooner, I hope, than later. But until I step foot on those glistening beaches and hear the waves spilling up and over themselves once more, Nalani will suffice.

I hope it will for you as well.

Aloha,

*Anna J.*

# HEARTWARMING

## Her Island Homecoming

—

*Anna J. Stewart*

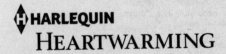

**HARLEQUIN**
**HEARTWARMING**

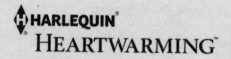

ISBN-13: 978-1-335-58498-4

Recycling programs
for this product may
not exist in your area.

Her Island Homecoming

Copyright © 2023 by Anna J. Stewart

For questions and comments about the quality of this book, please contact us at CustomerService@Harlequin.com.

Harlequin Enterprises ULC
22 Adelaide St. West, 41st Floor
Toronto, Ontario M5H 4E3, Canada
www.Harlequin.com

Printed in U.S.A.

Bestselling author **Anna J. Stewart** can barely remember a time she didn't want to write romances. She's been a bookaholic for her whole life, and stories of action and adventure have always topped her list, especially if said books also include a spunky, independent heroine and a well-earned happily-ever-after. With Wonder Woman and Princess Leia as her earliest influences, she now writes for Harlequin's Heartwarming and Romantic Suspense lines and, when she's not cooking or baking, attempts to wrangle her two cats, Rosie and Sherlock, into some semblance of proper behavior (yeah, that's not happening).

## Books by Anna J. Stewart

### Harlequin Heartwarming

#### *Butterfly Harbor Stories*

*The Bad Boy of Butterfly Harbor*
*Recipe for Redemption*
*A Dad for Charlie*
*Always the Hero*
*Holiday Kisses*
*Safe in His Arms*
*The Firefighter's Thanksgiving Wish*
*A Match Made Perfect*
*Bride on the Run*
*Building a Surprise Family*
*Worth the Risk*
*The Mayor's Baby Surprise*

Visit the Author Profile page
at Harlequin.com for more titles.

For my friends and family.

My *ohana*.

With love.

# CHAPTER ONE

*April*

"REMY ALWAYS CONSIDERED the sunrise to be his own personal show." Bare toes scrunching in the damp morning sand, Sydney Calvert stood on the shoreline and tried once again to swallow the lump of grief she'd been carrying around since she'd gotten the call. It wasn't possible her big brother was gone. Not so soon. Dying without warning at thirty-four? She drew in a trembling breath and dug deep for the strength she needed.

The tropical-tinted air kissed the white-capped waves drifting onto the shore of Nalani, Hawai'i. They'd been born here, in this tiny little cap of a town on the east shore of the Big Island. A town that now offered the promise of a new day. A new beginning.

A breeze wound its way through the maze of coconut palms, rustling the leaves in an early-morning wake-up call. It had been too long since she'd stood here. Too long since she'd come home. Years had passed, and yet coming back now didn't feel as if she'd been away. Didn't feel as if anything was different. And yet?

And yet. Sydney blew out a long, controlled breath. Everything had changed.

The time would come when the thought of her brother wouldn't bring a tear to her eye but a smile to her lips. She just had to hold on long enough to get there. Today she'd embrace the otherworldly quality of black-sand beaches and uninterrupted vistas of tumbling waves and surf. Surf Remy had made his own by riding it every chance he got. Surf that, today, would serve as the site of his memorial.

Progress and time might have left their stamps on the islands as a whole, but there were pockets—so many perfect, pristine pockets—of utter and complete…paradise.

Sydney closed her eyes, inhaled the familiar intoxicating scent of hibiscus and jasmine, and accepted what was to come.

"I keep expecting him to run out of the house and say this was all some horrible practical joke." Smiling, she tucked her wind-caught hair behind one ear and turned, waiting for the morning sun to dry her tears as she looked at her late-brother's longtime girlfriend. "Instead, it's the day we'll all say goodbye."

Tears glistened in Tehani Iokepa's eyes, her black hair long and straight down her back and set off by a solitary hibiscus blossom behind her ear. The same hibiscus flowers that made up the dozen or so leis Remy's girlfriend had spent the past few days crafting.

Leis that sat piled gently nearby, awaiting their final placement on the water.

Tehani stood straight and unbending as she looked beyond Sydney into the ocean around them as if she, too, expected Remy to magically reappear. "Nalani is giving us the perfect send-off for him." Her voice was thick with emotion, her eyes filled with longing for the man she'd loved. The man who, had they only a little more time, would have become her husband.

Sydney held out her hand, palm open, and Tehani stepped forward, and grabbed hold. "Remy always took paddle-outs very seriously." Sydney's recollection was an attempt to lighten the mood. They'd had three weeks to get used to the idea that Remy was gone; that life would never be the same for anyone who knew him, let alone loved him. Remembering what had made him so amazing was the best gift she and Tehani could give each other.

Remy Calvert had been the kind of man whose presence overwhelmed all others. But not with ego. Never with ego. With vivacity. With welcome. Love. There wasn't a friend he wouldn't help or a challenge he could refuse, and all of it was done with a gratitude and grace Sydney didn't possess.

For years Sydney had teased Remy that he could pull a smile out of a stone, but he'd taken it as a compliment and wore his charm and soul-deep love for his home on his smiling face. He'd loved their home, from the chain of islands to the simple little town of Nalani, to the two-story bungalow nestled in a thicket of coconut trees on the far end of the beach. Home.

He'd loved this place so much he'd rarely ever left. Sydney tried to find comfort in that—that he'd died where he'd been the happiest. But comfort was difficult to come by when, at the age of thirty, she'd now said goodbye to her entire family.

A familiar, gentle bell tinkled in the distance. "That sounds like Maru's malasada cart." Sydney's eyes went wide as she turned and spotted an older woman and a much younger one unloading a carload of trays and clear plastic boxes filled with sugary goodness. "Didn't Remy tell me she had a stroke last year?"

"It would take more than that to stop Maru," Tehani said. "Her granddaughter helps her to make them now, and she doesn't wheel that cart around anymore. Mano and Remy repurposed an old tiki bar as a mobile stall for her so she could stay out and be out of the sun. But the bell remained." A smile crossed her lips. "Everyone around here knows what that bell means."

"That bell means I'm going to gain five pounds by the time I head home." Even now, Sydney's stomach rumbled for the coconut pudding-stuffed doughnuts. "I swear I dream about those haupia-filled ones."

Tehani stepped back and pulled her hand free as cars began filing into the makeshift parking lot. Vans and open-air Jeeps and trucks unloaded by the dozen; people young and old yanked colorful surfboards free of their transport before heading to the beach. More cars transported more people carrying freshly made leis, which they draped over one another's necks.

Beyond the lot sat Nalani's main drag, a street that was filled with various shops, eateries, and stalls where locals offered their handmade crafts and homemade goods. A full-tropical one-stop hit of Hawaiian goodness.

A *tropical artist colony* was how Sydney had always referred to it, with homes situated in and around both the beach and village. Old and sturdy coconut, pine and banyan trees gave shelter and shade for those who called Nalani home while also allowing for climbing lessons for the young ones embracing outdoor life. Down the road, money trees mingled with eucalyptus in arching groves against the sun while framing perfect island scenes.

"I didn't think so many people would come." Sydney's whisper earned an arched brow from Tehani. "It's a weekday."

"You've been away too long if you've forgotten how important ohana is," Tehani scolded. "Family always comes first."

Absolutely, it did. It was why Remy had named his local tour-and-excursion company Ohana Odysseys. He wanted everyone who came here, who paid for his and his employees' services, to feel like family. No, not just *feel* like family—*become* family.

Become *oh-ha-na*.

"Remy always made time for them," Tehani said. "Of course they'll be here for him today. Mano made certain of it."

"Right." Sydney winced at her careless comment. "Sorry. You're right. I shouldn't be surprised."

Tehani nodded as they were approached by a familiar face.

"Mano." Sydney smiled, walked toward Tehani's brother and, after he plowed two surfboards into the sand, stepped straight into a hug. He was exactly as she remembered him, with his broad shoulders, tattooed arms and healthy physique. He was considered quite the island catch, but from what Remy had said, their old friend was firmly hooked on his ex. Not that Sydney had any thoughts other than friendship where Mano was concerned. Even now, as he held her tight, she knew it was as close to a brotherly hug as she'd ever get again. "I hear you're partially responsible for arranging the paddle-out."

"I put the word out, is all." Mano's voice carried the same tight grief Sydney had been trying to talk around. *"Kaikunane."* He reached for Tehani. "It's a good day, sister."

"We were just saying," Sydney interjected when tears jumped back into Tehani's eyes. "I'm sorry I didn't get here sooner to help plan—"

"Plans are taken care of," Mano assured her. "What's important is that you're here. Remy would be—"

"Irritated over all the fuss," Sydney said, trying to joke, "and wondering when the party was going to start."

"Mano!" Someone from a group of surfers called from the parking lot and headed over, some detouring over to Maru's stand for a jolt of breakfast sugar. "Brah, we'll give Remy a good send-off, yeah?" The young man at the front of the pack carried a surfboard under one arm. He wore brightly colored board shorts and a warm smile. "You must be Sydney. I recognize your picture from the office. I'm Kiri. Aloha."

"Aloha," Sydney responded.

"Kiri assisted with a lot of your brother's land tours and surfing lessons," Mano told her. "But Tehani can fill you in on all those details later. Shall we get this ceremony underway? Daphne. Good morning."

"Good morning." A tall, statuesque redhead had joined them, a yellow zip-up sweatshirt tugged around her. She wore her long red hair braided down her back and a cautious expression on her face. "Welcome back, Sydney. Glad you got in safely. How was your flight?"

"I'd have been happier flying the plane myself."

"Remy always said you were the worst passenger on a flight." Daphne's face brightened; Sydney bet it was from fond memories. "He couldn't stop bragging about his hotshot rescue-pilot sister."

"Yeah, well." Sydney had no response to that. She did the job she was good at. The job she loved. Being in the air, having her hands on the control instruments of anything with wings... There was nothing better in the world. Unless it was using her skills to help people.

The truth was, if she had been flying her plane last night, she wouldn't have had so much time to think. And wonder. And worry about what could have been. All pointless things that had only added to her grief and stress. By the time her flight had landed— three hours late—she opted to stay mostly right here on the beach, coming to terms with the fact she wouldn't ever be welcomed home by her brother again.

"You're looking great, Daphne," Sydney said. "Remy told me you'd moved out here a couple of years ago to work with him. Island life certainly seems to agree with you."

Daphne nodded. "I can't imagine it not agreeing with anyone."

Sydney wasn't so sure. She'd loved it here, but the rest of the world had called to her through one big bullhorn. This small town had never felt big enough to contain her dreams.

"Not going to paddle out with us, Daph?" Tehani asked as she stripped down to the floral bikini she wore under her shorts and T-shirt.

"Surfboards and I are not a good combination," Daphne said with a slight chuckle. "I'll stay on shore with the rest and hand out leis. Help set up the food and direct people."

Ah, the food. Sydney shook her head. She'd missed the pre-funeral feast, but she was hoping to make up for it with the post-ceremony celebration. Today was the first time in weeks she actually had an appetite.

"That'd be great. Thanks, Daphne," Tehani said. "Syd? You ready?"

*No*, Sydney thought as she took a deep breath. She wasn't ready. Not by a long shot. She glanced down at the gray urn containing her brother's ashes. But she had to be if any of them were going to move on.

"If you need some more time," Mano began, but Sydney shook her head and quickly stepped out of her skirt and blouse, shivering as her swimsuit-clad body adjusted to the morning air.

"Forgot how chilly it can feel." But even as she said it, a warm breeze wafted over the area.

Tehani raised her face to the sun, offered a smile. "I think maybe he heard you."

"Yeah." Sydney's voice broke as she bent to pick up the urn. ' I think maybe he did."

"You good paddling out with it?" Mano asked as she accepted one of the smaller boards he'd brought for her. "How long has it been since you were on the water?"

"Not that long." She'd found some good surf spots out in South Carolina. The water was different on that side of the country. Harsher. Sharper. But being in the water came in second only to being in the sky. "If I need help, I'll give a shout."

Mano and Tehani waded out into the ocean on their boards, using their arms to paddle a good distance from shore. As Sydney made her way through the water, she watched as countless others followed Mano and Tehani out. Every one of them was here because of Remy. Because they'd loved and respected him. She could get through this without losing it.

She owed them—and Remy—that much, at least.

Sydney kept the urn close to her chest as she paddled out, the cold water lapping up and over the board, splashing into her face. With every stroke, she could feel her pulse quicken, as if taking extra beats for her brother. Well out from shore, she saw the circle of boards and surfers forming, stretching into a large ring. Mano and Tehani shifted aside to make room for her. She came up, straddled the board, keeping one hand on the urn as she caught her balance.

In lieu of a eulogy, Mano had suggested a traditional Hawaiian blessing be sung, the sounds of which now rose up as Sydney lifted her eyes to the sky. Her tears mingled with the droplets of ocean water. Bright, fluffy clouds drifted by as the surfers joined in. They began placing or tossing their leis into the water and, as the song came to an end, Sydney lowered her chin and pried open the urn.

She turned the metal container over, poured most of Remy's ashes into the water, stopped and then offered the urn to Tehani. "'*O 'oe kāna hōkū.*' You were his star."

Tehani visibly swallowed, bowed her head and accepted the urn. "Mahalo," she whispered and, after a moment of quiet, poured out the rest of the ashes.

A whoop sounded from across the circle, and seconds later, hands and feet began splashing, creating waves of acceptance and transmittance as the ocean became Remy's final resting place. More flowers flew, soaring into the sky before dropping onto the water, petals falling loose and dotting the ocean with beautiful hibiscus, roses and orchids.

The cheers of celebration over honoring a friend, honoring family, echoed until Sydney could no longer see the ashes. Her feet dangled in the water, and she clasped the edge of the board as the circle broke apart and some paddled off to ride the waves farther down the beach. One final tributary ride for Remy.

"You okay?" Mano asked the two of them.

Tehani nodded but didn't say another word before she turned her board around and headed back to shore.

"Did you know?" Sydney asked Mano now that they were alone. "That he was sick?" She didn't have to look at him to know he had flinched at her question.

"I knew something was wrong. He'd been…off. Distracted. Not by much. But by enough to notice." He went silent for a moment. "Dwelling on it now won't change anything, Sydney. He wouldn't want it to."

"I know." She did know. But it didn't make it any easier. "He asked me to come back. A few months ago. He said he had this new idea he wanted to run past me, but he wanted to present it in person." Her smile contained nothing other than bitterness. "I told him if it was so important, he should come to me. It was a safe challenge, one I knew he'd never accept." She bent over to feel the ocean caress her face. "Nothing could ever make him leave this place."

"I don't have to tell you how much he loved you. Or how proud he was of you," Mano said.

"No," Sydney said, finally letting go of some of the guilt. "No, you don't." The flowers and leis bobbed and danced in the water as the sun rose higher. "I just hope I deserved it." She nodded, gave one last look out at the horizon and then looked to Mano. "I'm ready."

Together, they turned and rode the gentle waves into the shore.

"I HAD A feeling this was where you were hiding." Tehani faux-stumbled into the two-story office space that housed Ohana Odysseys and plopped into the chair on the other side of Remy's desk. She'd covered her bikini with a sarong the color of ripe peaches that set her dark skin to glowing. "I swear if I eat one more malasada, I'm going to explode."

"I needed some quiet." Sydney sat back in her brother's chair. The memorial celebration had been going on for hours, and Sydney was beyond exhausted. It was as if her body had been waiting for her mind to catch up. Only trouble was, with the funeral behind her, she had new things to worry about. "Business has been doing pretty well, it looks like, for you guys and the company."

Tehani shrugged. "Better than 'pretty well.' He was planning to expand."

"Yeah." She'd come across some sketched-out plans. "He definitely had ideas."

The building that housed the successful tour-and-excursion company sat smack-dab in the middle of Nalani's main stretch, its weatherproof modern-day structure covered in bamboo to give the authentic feel of a vacation in the tropics. The roof, a solid and sturdy tile, lay beneath a decorative thick layer of dried grass. The three-step porch on the outside led into an open office space on the ground floor, with wide, open windows overlooking the beach and a partial loft space that, at one time, had served as Remy's living quarters.

Those threadbare days were gone, as were most of the financial struggles that barely kept Odyssey afloat as Remy guided tourists and visitors all over the area. That wasn't to say tough times weren't ahead, especially with a planned expansion. Quirky, cartoony tourist posters hung framed on the wall. The front desk, Tehani's terrain, boasted an upscale computer booking system and information center, and the bulletin board behind displayed photographs of the locals with the positions they held: tour guides; catering for in-house meal delivery; private swimming, surfing or diving classes. Then there were the local experts, including Daphne, who was a botanist by trade but gave in-depth horticultural tours by request.

What had started out with simple Jeep outings had gradually grown into a pair of fifteen-seat vans that transported their customers to various land, water and hiking excursions. The zip line excursion had become one of the most popular activities, according to the financial records Sydney had pulled up. But the helicopter tours—courtesy of the rebuilt 2004 chopper Sydney had found for Remy through one of her pilot contacts—had been bringing in the most profit over the past eighteen months.

"I can't even wrap my brain around most of this," Sydney muttered.

Tehani looked at her for a good long moment, then pushed herself up and retrieved a key from her desk. "Scoot over." She nudged Sydney and the chair, then crouched to open the bottom-left drawer Sydney had given up hope of exploring. Inside, with the binders and folders, sat an envelope with Sydney's name on it. "No better time than now, I suppose."

"What is it?"

"You know what it is. Or at least, you're afraid you do." Tehani reclaimed her seat, rested her folded hands over her stomach as she watched Sydney open the envelope and read.

Was it possible for a heart to speed up and stop at the same time? Sydney's chest tightened as her eyes skimmed, then skimmed again. Then she slowed and read every single word.

"He left me the business." She lowered the papers. "He left me Ohana Odysseys."

"He did," Tehani said with a nod. Sydney blinked at her, looking for any hint of animosity or anger or resentment. But she didn't find anything other than curiosity over what Sydney might be thinking. "You can't be surprised."

"I can." Sydney shook her head, set the letter down, picked it back up. Stared at her brother's girlfriend. "Tehani, it should have been you. Or Mano. I thought there was some discussion about them partnering up to give Hibiscus Bay Resort its own private company."

"There was. Then Remy got…distracted." Tehani shook her head, a clear sign she didn't want to discuss that issue further. At least not yet. "Remy's plans, the ones he told you about when he called a few months ago— you were a big part of them. He wanted you to come home."

"Yeah, I got that message loud and clear."

"No, it was more than him wanting you

to visit. He wanted you to be a full partner in Ohana Odysseys. You and the others."

"The others. What others?" She really didn't think her mind could spin any faster.

"You, maybe Mano. Daphne was already here, so he figured he'd won her over. You guys, in this all together."

"I don't understand." Why was her mind so foggy? "Remy wanted us to buy in?"

Tehani nodded. "He wanted to make Ohana a true family business. And what better way to do that than with the people he considered family?"

It was a lovely idea, but… "What about you?"

"I was on board. It made good business sense, especially with the way we've been growing. Most of the money he brings in stays here in Nalani. He was able to fund the school repairs and get some new roofs on the city office buildings. Help people pay their rent or mortgages."

"No, I mean, that's all great, but what about you as a partner?"

Tehani's eyes were dry when she looked at Sydney. "That was going to happen after we got married."

Grief resurged, this time along with anger over the utter unfairness of her brother dying. Sydney shot to her feet, began pacing, as if she could outrun her brother's plans for her. Plans that in all rights, should have been for Tehani. "I can't do this. He expected me to come back here and help run the place?"

"I wouldn't say *expected*," Tehani said softly. "More like hoped. But things are different now. Expectations have definitely shifted."

"What does that even mean?"

"It means that without Ohana Odysseys, there's a very good chance Nalani will cease to exist. Oh, it won't happen overnight," Tehani added quickly but with more than a little heat. "But it'll be difficult to keep the stores running and the houses occupied without tourists filling the coffers. Hilo and Kona have always been huge draws. We've been pulling from that and expanding our reach. But without someone steady at the helm—"

"You. You should be at the helm."

Tehani shook her head. "If Remy wanted me to run Ohana, he would have made that plain. He didn't. He left this place to you.

There are more detailed business plans for you to follow at the house. I can show you where they are in his home office."

"I don't want to see more developed plans. I have..." *Plans of my own.* "I have to get home, Tehani. I'm this close to having enough money to start my own flight school. It's what I've been working toward for the past six years." She sank back into the chair and rested her face in her hands. "I can't just walk away from that."

"I understand." Tehani actually sounded as if she did. But her understanding did nothing to shake the panic descending like a tidal wave over Sydney. "It's not like you could take a sabbatical with your job and see if there's some way to actually make this work. Right?"

Sydney dropped her hands and glared. "My brother really did tell you everything."

Tehani's expression softened. "He mentioned you had a lot of vacation time saved up and that you'd been given the opportunity to do some traveling. What if you spent that time here? A couple of months, maybe six? Come back and see if you can make this work. I will help as much as I can, and you know everyone here will do the same. Please, Sydney. Remy's already gone. I don't think I could bear to see his dream die with him."

Sydney could feel herself caving, those pleading dark eyes of her almost-sister-in-law boring into her with a helpless defiance. "Tehani, I don't know." Was she really considering this? Thinking about giving up her own plans, her own dreams, to try to save her brother's?

"It wasn't just Ohana Remy left in your hands, Sydney." Tehani's voice quieted, then intensified, as if she'd formed her final argument. "It's Nalani's future as well. There's no telling who will come after the business if you put it up for sale. Certainly no one with Nalani's best interest at heart."

Now it was Sydney's turn to glare. "That's just playing dirty pool."

"Maybe it is," Tehani agreed. "But Nalani's my home. It was Remy's home and yours. I'm willing to do anything I have to in order to save it." She hesitated, then pounced. "The question is, are you?"

# CHAPTER TWO

*Three weeks later*

SYDNEY EASED BACK on the throttle and brought the five-seater tour chopper to a gentle landing. The headphones—while they facilitated communication with either occupants, nearby traffic or airports—did nothing to dilute the whap-whap-whapping of the overhead blades. One of her comfort sounds, Sydney thought with a smile as the engine wound down into a gentle whine.

She hung the headphones up and quickly unstrapped herself before shoving open the cockpit door and dropping to the ground. The second her feet hit solid earth, something shifted, and the unease that had settled inside her weeks before returned.

As much affection as she had for everyday life, nothing—absolutely nothing—compared to the sensation of soaring through the air under her own control. Up there, every worry and concern evaporated. All that she had to concentrate on was circling the sky and focusing on the glorious sights around her.

Some people belonged behind a desk. Others like Tehani or their friend Keane Harper were meant to ride the waves. Sydney? Give her the wide-open sky, something to pilot and endless time, and nothing could darken her day.

The late-morning wind kicked up as she closed up the chopper and headed across the raised landing pad, which had a view of the ocean on one side and the road leading into the heart of Nalani on the other. Lines of coconut trees in glistening white sand was the reminder she needed that despite being on solid ground, paradise still surrounded her.

The elevated platform had been a big deal, both investment-wise for the tour company and Nalani itself. Positive progress, Remy had called it when they'd last spoke. Progress that would solidify their hometown as a destination to be reckoned with when it came to exploring and experiencing small-town island life on the Big Island. Of course, in Remy's mind, he'd imagined an entire fleet of tour helicopters offering the best-possible views of the island.

As Sydney reached the short staircase, Tehani popped her head up over the railing and indicated the recently repainted chopper. "How'd she do on her first mission?"

"She flew like a dream." Sure she had. Sydney had picked out the aircraft herself when Remy asked for her help. She shook her head in amusement at the artistic custom addition of bright pink and orange flowers painted in homage to the Hibiscus Bay Resort less than two miles inland. "Her pilot, on the other hand," Sydney continued, "needs some time to get used to being back in these skies."

She reached up and pulled the band from her hair and shook it out into the warm April breeze. Who was she kidding? Flying around the island was second nature no matter how much time she'd been away. "Still, it was a good training run. You were right. Spencer will be a fine copilot, and he's got an amazing eye for the island." One thing with search and rescue was that there were never enough eyes on the ground. "We got a feel for how the other works. We'll make an effective team for local Search and Rescue."

"They're glad to get more backup," Tehani confirmed as they made their way to the side of the road and started the quarter mile back to Ohana Odysseys. "I'm grateful for the backup, too. Business is returning to what it was before...well, before. I booked five new clients for next week while you've been in the air. But only one chopper tour so far. On the bright side, we had a group buy one of our all-day snorkeling packages. If things keep up like this, you'll have to start hiring some new employees."

That doubt Sydney had been choking down quieted for a moment as she considered the money that would bring in. Ohana wasn't struggling by any means, but a booking like that would definitely propel them into the financial safety zone for a good few weeks. Between their land, water and air excursions, she was definitely getting reacquainted with every aspect of their little corner of the Big Island. But she'd be lying if she didn't admit the pressure was beginning to get to her.

With the town of Hilo located a mere ten

miles to the north, Nalani had found it difficult to stand out from one of its bigger sister towns. One of the things Remy had done with Ohana Odysseys was make the experiences small-group to private, no more than eight people, so as to focus on that personal island touch he'd prided himself on offering. Thankfully, their gang of friends and neighbors willing to take part-time gigs as guides and instructors was firmly in place.

"Guess we're going to be busy these next few weeks," Sydney said. "Might be time to put out a call for more help?"

"Or..." Tehani said in that *I've already solved your problem* kind of way that made her an invaluable asset to the business. "Wyatt Jenkins is up for overseeing the catamaran until we find someone permanent."

"Wyatt? Really?" Sydney immediately felt a weight lift. "I thought he was on O'ahu, working construction on that new hotel project?"

"He was," Tehani said in a way that reminded Sydney that Wyatt hadn't made it back for Remy's service. "He got home a couple of nights ago. Mano might have mentioned we could use some extra help with tours."

"Mano and Wyatt to the rescue, as always." Affection swelled in her chest.

As a teenager, Wyatt had moved to the island to live with his grandmother and became fast friends with both Mano and Remy. In addition to being one of the nicest guys Sydney had ever known, Wyatt was the epitome of *jump in to help with anything* kind of people. He was more than a jack-of-all-trades. He was a one-man contingency plan.

"If he's up for finding a crew for the *Kalei*, he'll be my hero for life." Ohana's forty-two-foot vessel, named *Happiness* in Hawaiian, had been one of the first major investments Remy made when Ohana was getting off the ground.

"He is. He also said he'd take care of the catering. Kiri's backing him up—but don't worry," Tehani added when she saw Sydney wince. "Those trips won't conflict with Kiri teaching the surfing classes."

"It's not the surfing lessons I'm concerned about," Sydney admitted.

One of the reasons she'd kept those lessons to early mornings only was because

Kiri was all of seventeen and still in high school. Given his determination and dreams of becoming a marine and environmental biologist, Sydney had made it clear when she hired him that she expected his primary focus to remain firmly on his education. If that meant sacrificing afternoon lessons, so be it.

But all this talk of covering tours and classes did raise an issue. Remy's death had left a void in more than their lives; it had left a huge opening in the business where aquatic excursions were concerned. Smaller tour operations had popped up in the past few years—nothing to be concerned about competition-wise, but if Ohana continued to cut down on their ocean-centric offerings to customers, it wouldn't be long before they lost that part of their business altogether.

Relying on Kiri and Wyatt alone wasn't going to cut it. What she—what Ohana Odysseys—really needed was a full-time aquatic instructor who could oversee all those water-specific activities and excursions. But that seemed like an impulsive investment, given the current circumstances. All this piling on meant Sydney definitely needed to get reacquainted with every aspect of their little corner of the Big Island.

"Things are getting back to normal," Tehani said. "Oh, and Daphne's putting together a new tour at the university's botanical garden." She shoved her hands into the pockets of the bright orange shorts that matched her loose-fitting tank. "She should have the details for us in a couple of days."

"Do we need a new tour?" Sydney caught her lip in her teeth. Making changes—any changes—still didn't sit right with her. It felt almost disrespectful to Remy and his vision. Decisions like that felt like a sledgehammer reminder that her brother was not coming back.

"New excursions appeal across the board," Tehani said. "We have to keep our customer base interested, right? New tours bring back old customers, as they offer different experiences." She hesitated. "Remy knew about Daphne's plans, if that's what's bothering you."

That wasn't all that was bothering her. "It's not that I disapprove." Sydney cringed. "I just—"

"You just keep expecting Remy to come

bursting through the door and protesting any changes you might make?"

Sydney sighed. It had been nearly two months and yet…

Grief circled with the ferocity of a tropical storm. She sighed. And yet. "You and Daphne and Mano have been here. You know what works and what doesn't for the people who visit. It doesn't seem right that I have the final say."

"Except that you do." It was the first time she heard something akin to disappointment in Tehani's voice. Sydney caught her arm and pulled the younger woman to a stop.

"What does that mean?"

Tehani shook her head, her long black hair sliding around her shoulders like a curtain of silk. "I'm sorry. I didn't mean to say anything. It's not my place."

"Oh, yes it is." Sydney stepped closer, unable to ignore the uncertainty in her friend's obsidian-dark eyes. "We're family, remember? We've known each other forever, T. And we had a deal. If we're going to make Ohana work—"

"Are we? Going to make it work?" Tehani folded her arms across her chest and looked anywhere other than at Sydney. "I thought that's why you came out here. I thought we agreed we were going to make Remy's dreams for his business, for our town, come true."

"I'm here, aren't I?" Unaccustomed to seeing Tehani this troubled unsettled her. "I know it took me a little longer than expected to rent out my house and put my stuff in storage, but—"

Tehani's look landed sharp and hot. "Golden Vistas Resorts."

"Oh." Sydney's stomach dropped. "Oh. That." Panic surged, and suddenly she didn't know what to do with her hands. She ended up shoving them into the back pockets of her cutoff shorts. "Tehani, that was just me trying to weigh my options. I haven't committed—"

"Committed to selling Ohana Odysseys to one of the biggest hotel-and-resort conglomerates in California? No. But you've talked to them about it." Tehani's voice broke as tears flooded her eyes. "Haven't you?"

Guilt and regret twisted around Sydney's heart and squeezed. "I said I'd consider their offer," Sydney admitted. Tehani didn't need to know that Sydney's relief at receiving the offer had finally allowed her to breathe. The responsibility of carrying Remy's dreams on her shoulders was driving her into the ground. "That's all we've discussed so far, T."

"You told them you'd be happy to host them at any time here in Nalani."

"Well, yeah." Sydney had been paying lip service to an unexpected and very generous buyout offer, but she didn't think that would help her case with Remy's girlfriend. "Nothing's been decided. Not by them and certainly not by me," she assured Tehani. "I wouldn't sell without talking to you and Mano. You and your brother have every right to be involved in whatever decisions I might make. And whatever opportunities arise."

A tear trickled down Tehani's face before she ducked her chin. "That's what I kept telling myself, but if that's true—"

"It is. It is true, I promise you." Sydney stepped forward, caught her friend's shoulders in her hands and squeezed. She wasn't lying. As for the future...? "I know what Ohana Odysseys means to you. To the entire town of Nalani. But I also couldn't ignore an offer that could, in a lot of ways, do more here than I ever could." She wasn't Remy. She wasn't someone who had the golden touch, spinning ideas into almost instant success. No, Sydney always seemed to struggle a good deal more for what she wanted to make happen.

"Ohana doesn't need some greedy company gobbling it up and turning it into just another tour business, Syd," Tehani accused. "Ohana is special. It needs—it requires—*mana pono*." She touched fingertips to her heart. "Life energy focused on good, beneficial work. Without that, this place will die. And so will its people."

Before losing her brother, Sydney had never realized guilt had so many sharp edges. Remy, along with the other residents of Nalani, had lived their entire lives focused on what Sydney had always interpreted and accepted as a kind of symbiotic and island-centric karma. It was an honor to live on the islands, but it was an honor that came with the responsibility of respect and care to that which provided all they had.

The representative from Golden Vistas

had assured her the company was well aware of the task they'd be taking on, but that didn't stop the doubt from circling inside her like a shark. Maybe she hadn't been thinking or hearing clearly through the fog of loss.

"Tehani, I promise you, I have not made any decisions other than to come back here for a few months—"

"Six!" Tehani cut her off. "You promised me six months, Sydney. I said I could prove how viable this business is. How we can keep building on our success. I thought you understood. I thought we'd settled on a trial run."

"It is settled." Sydney nodded even as she felt her own plans begin to slip through her grasp. "Six months. We agreed."

"Yeah?" Tehani's relief made Sydney's spine tingle. "Okay, then. I guess I just started freaking out when… Well, with that email from Golden Vistas about their accounting guy coming out here to evaluate—"

"Wait, what?" Sydney demanded. "What email? What accounting guy?"

Sydney reached into her back pocket and pulled out her cell and, after realizing GVI had emailed the general Ohana Odysseys account rather than her owner-dedicated one, felt a bubble of irritation burst. A multi-million-dollar business couldn't get the right email address? That didn't bode well for a successful relationship.

Sure enough, as a result of her last conversation with the CFO of Golden Vistas Incorporated last week, they were sending a man named Theo Fairfax to Nalani for an extensive financial and practical evaluation of Ohana Odysseys.

Sydney's eyes went wide. "It says here he's flying into Hilo today." She glanced at her watch. "He's landing in a few hours!"

"You should have told me, Sydney." Tehani swiped at the tears on her cheeks.

"About the accountant? I didn't know." Add another brick of grief to the wall Sydney was beginning to accept was under constant construction. "But you're right. I should have been open with you about the options I'm considering." She stopped herself from admitting to Tehani how overwhelmed she'd felt since learning Remy had left his lifelong dream of a business in her hands alone. Or that being back home in Nalani at times offered more pain than promise.

The fact she felt torn between her own plans and keeping her brother's dream alive had twisted her into knots. On the one hand, the decision to return home had been easy. But on the other...?

She'd put her life on hold. She couldn't help but fear that the more time passed, the more her own future would slip further and further away. "I'm sorry." She drew Tehani in for a hug and squeezed her eyes shut. "I promised you six months, and that's what I'm going to give you. No more secrets. I promise. Deal, T?"

Tehani stood stiff in her arms, as if she wasn't ready to believe her. "I'm sorry." She stepped back, shook her head and looked up trying to stop her tears. "I'm not being fair, I know. You didn't ask for this to happen."

"Neither of us did." They'd both lost someone important—the same someone—and yet it was times like this that Sydney understood Tehani had actually lost so much more. She'd lost the future she'd been planning with Remy.

"I don't want you to feel guilty—"

"Sure you do."

"Well." Tehani managed a small laugh. "Maybe a little."

"Hey." Sydney gave her arms a quick squeeze. "We're in this together, remember? I promise I won't pull the rug out from under you. You'll have a safe place to land, whatever I decide."

Tehani nodded. "I'll figure it out. Whether you sell or not…" She took a deep breath and sighed. "I guess I'd best prepare myself for you to do just that." Tehani smoothed both hands down the front of her shirt and offered a sad smile. "We'll be okay."

"Nothing's written in stone." *Not yet*, Sydney thought. But she couldn't quite bring herself to tell Tehani she was wrong to plan for the worst case scenario. Running Ohana Odysseys was a lifetime commitment, one Sydney simply wasn't willing to embrace. Not when her plans to open a flight-instruction school were nearly viable. She had a deal in place and a building purchase just waiting for her signature.

All that said, she had to consider her own *kuleana*, her responsibility not only to Remy's legacy but also to the island she called home.

"Did Remy keep up with the leases on the vacation huts on the beach?"

"He hadn't rented them out yet, but Rewa comes in and cleans every other week. Should I call her—"

"No, I'll run over and do a quick check, see if there's anything we need."

"The keys are in the lockbox in the top drawer of Remy's desk at the office. If you need the lease paperwork, that should be—"

"In his office at home?" Sydney sighed again. "I guess I can't avoid going in there any longer, can I?" Remy's office—once their father's—was the one part of the house she had yet to venture into. Everything else had felt like shared space, but that room overlooking the ocean? She shivered at the idea of opening those doors and not finding him there.

"Want some help with the hut?"

"No." If anything, Sydney needed some time to clear her head, and focusing on their unexpected guest's accommodations would be a good distraction. "No, we'll consider this penance for my lack of openness. I'll grab some cleaning supplies from the house and head on over." She slung an arm around

Tehani's shoulders as they resumed their path toward the office. "I hope our accountant guest likes semi-rustic with a view."

"How could he not?" Tehani countered. "It's one of the most beautiful spots on the island."

How could he not indeed.

THEO FAIRFAX WAS not made for the tropics. It didn't take him much longer than a walk through the airport on O'ahu on his way to grab a puddle jumper the size of an anemic flea to confirm that fact. He hadn't been on the islands for more than a few hours, and he was already anxious to get back home to the cool, fog-capped air of San Francisco.

It wasn't just the heat, which made him feel like an over-zapped microwave TV dinner. Or the humidity that coated his skin instantly with a thin film of sweat the second he exited the airport terminal on what, back home, had been a rather dreary Thursday. It wasn't even the gray clouds tumbling over each other as if in a race across the warm sky above Hilo International Airport.

No, his conclusion was reached logically by combining all three of those things and adding in his deep-seated acclimation to air-conditioning, his sixteen-story office in the heart of the city and his well-broken-in office chair.

With his carry-on garment bag slung over one shoulder, Theo stood at the curb, a bit unnerved at the lack of typical hustle and bustle at any big city airport. "Not a big city," he reminded himself as his hand tightened around his laptop bag.

The signs to the pickup area seemed clear enough, but the truth was he wasn't entirely certain where he was supposed to go. His fellow travelers were few, and what people he did see appeared to be used to their surroundings. The instructions he'd received from his interim boss had been as opaque as the cardboard container holding his paltry and expensive airplane lunch.

According to the online map, the town of Nalani was about a thirty-mile drive southish. He'd been obsessively checking his email throughout his flight from San Francisco to O'ahu, hoping to hear from the new owner of Ohana Odysseys as to what he could expect upon arrival on the Big Island. But there was nothing.

To confirm he hadn't missed a message, he checked his phone once more. No email. No text. He sighed.

No clue.

He poked a finger under his collar as anxiety settled in that empty space between his lungs. He was not a man accustomed to winging it, and so far this entire excursion was one big unknown. Plans. Schedules. Expectations firmly in place. These were the things that made the world go round and, as far as Theo was concerned, were the most efficient way to live a life. Doing so, however, allowed little—if any—room for the unexpected.

If only his usual supervisor hadn't broken her leg two days ago attempting to outrun an escalator at the mall, Theo wouldn't have found said schedule completely upended and himself on a plane less than twelve hours later.

Nope, if she'd won that particular sporting challenge, he'd be in his office right now, slugging down his third cup of coffee and closing out his second annual audit of the marketing division of GVI.

*Coffee.* Theo felt his system zing at the

mere thought. The promise of Kona coffee straight from the source had been the only selling point when he'd been substituted in as the primary contact for this acquisition evaluation. Paradise, as far as Theo was concerned, was subjective and overrated. Coffee? Not so much.

His nerves were already tingling, something that always happened when he was thrown off-balance. He took a deep breath, let it out and dropped his thoughts into the mantra he'd created back in college.

*Professionalism plus planning plus practicality equals success.*

The equation had yet to fail him. It had gotten him through college; into his first job; promoted into his second; and then, finally, just a few years ago, landed him on one of the higher rungs of the financial ladder of GVI.

Boarding that plane this morning, going along with what his bosses asked of him, could be a blessing in disguise and would, hopefully, put him firmly on the list to replace GVI's latest chief financial officer. Whenever the current one retired, of course.

As usual for Theo, opportunity had presented itself and he was prepared.

This major business acquisition was exactly what his résumé needed for him to begin the next phase of his life. GVI had survived a rough couple of years and, while it wasn't common knowledge, they needed a big boon of some sort to keep their heads above water and stave off a wave of layoffs. With layoffs came publicity, and in this case, publicity about a fifty-year-old company potentially circling the drain wouldn't help them gain that new foothold they were desperate for.

They needed a big win, something new and exciting to tout to their shareholders and solidify their faith. An investment with growth potential. Personally, Theo didn't see what a small tourist business was going to do to accomplish that, but, as he'd been reminded before he left, he was only a numbers guy. Analyze the data, create a statement and report back. He was not now, nor had he ever been, a creative thinker.

Theo rolled his shoulders beneath his dark blue blazer, smoothed one hand down the thin blue tie that seemed to be perpetually dancing in the muggy afternoon breeze. He could smell the sweet hint of flowers above the combination of gasoline and exhaust. In the distance, he heard an odd rumbling as he approached a line of three bright white cabs at the end of the walkway.

A short, dark-haired young man broke away from the group chatting and laughing by the taxi sign at the end of the walkway. "Aloha!" he called. Beige board shorts and a brightly flowered shirt screamed Hawai'i as he offered a smile filled with an exuberance Theo couldn't remember ever possessing. "Welcome to the islands. Where are you headed?"

"Ah, Nalani." Theo hoped he was pronouncing that correctly. He'd tried to read up on the area when he hadn't been working on the plane.

"Brah, that's my home!" The young man shouted a farewell to his friends, then held out his hand for Theo's garment bag. "I'm Hori."

"Theo." The ease and familiarity shouldn't have surprised him. The islands were notorious for their hospitality and warm welcome. "I'm here on business." Why he felt the need to explain escaped him.

"That's what they all say," Hori said with a hearty laugh as he led him to the first white cab in the line. "We'll get you acclimated to island life in no time. I'll give you the lowdown on all the goings-on while we drive, yeah?" He no sooner had the trunk open than a light brown Jeep circled around and came to a quick stop right in front of Hori's cab. The magnetic sign on the side door displayed an advertisement for Ohana Odysseys: Tour with Family, along with a website listing.

The quirky, amusing font seemed in keeping with the curvy, disheveled woman who popped up and out of the top of the car. "Theo Fairfax?" She rested her arms on the overhead bar and shoved thick sun-kissed blond hair out of her face.

Theo blinked. "Yes."

"Aloha. Caught you in time." She didn't bother to open her door; she simply grabbed hold of the bar and jumped out and over. "Hey, Hori."

"You stealing my fares now, cuz?" Rather than sounding irritated, as most cabbies Theo had ever encountered probably would have, the younger man seemed amused as he set Theo's garment bag into the back of the Jeep before giving the woman a quick fist bump. "Howzit? He one of yours?"

"All good, thanks. And yes, he is." She patted Hori on the shoulder before heading toward Theo. "Welcome to the islands, Mr. Fairfax. I'm Sydney Calvert." She stuck out her hand. "Okay to call you Theo?"

"Ah, sure." Theo blinked once more and accepted the greeting. *This* was Sydney Calvert? The Sydney Calvert who had inherited Ohana Odysseys from her late brother? The Sydney Calvert his bosses had tagged as a flighty pushover and easy sell? The Sydney Calvert Theo had imagined as being far older, more desperate and less…lively? He nodded, mainly because it was the only thing he could think to do. "Yeah, Theo's fine."

His voice squeaked, hadn't it?

She was quite possibly the most beautiful woman he'd ever seen. That thick, lush blond hair of hers hung loose around her shoulders and halfway down her back. She wore cute cutoff jeans and a loose-fitting tank the color of ripe mango; below the thin straps peeked out thinner turquoise ones, indicating a swimsuit underneath. Her skin wasn't as tan as he might have expected, but he could see where the heat of the sun had been getting to her.

The clips in her hair weren't doing much to keep it out of her face, as she caught a good portion in one hand and made his fingers itch to do the same.

"I've got him from here, cuz," Sydney said.

"If you say so." Hori stepped back. "See you next Wednesday night?"

"I've got my hula skirt warming up in the closet." She swung her hips in an advanced preview and ended on a laugh. "Might need to do a bit of practicing before the luau."

Not as far as Theo was concerned. He dragged his gaze back up to her face.

"Let's hit it, yeah?" She reached for his laptop bag, but he stepped back.

"That's okay."

"Your call." She batted her startling blue eyes at him and grinned. "Jump in. Let's see if we can beat the—" Thunder rumbled overhead as a new bank of gray clouds crested the edge of the horizon. She opened the passenger door and stood back so he could climb in. When she closed the door, she leaned in close enough that he could smell the ocean on her skin. "Top's busted on this baby. It'll be a wild ride. I've got a raincoat in the back if you—"

"I'll be fine." While he didn't embrace the unexpected, he liked to think he could adapt when necessary.

She shrugged. "Suit yourself. May as well christen you first off." She shouted to Hori once more and, in the side mirror, Theo watched the man return her enthusiastic goodbye. After she hopped into the driver's side, she slammed her foot on the gas and threw the car into Drive so fast, he nearly got whiplash. "Sorry for the late pickup." She sped past the terminal pickup area and circled around to the main highway, bumping along with the traffic. "I didn't get the email you were arriving until I got into the office a few hours ago."

"Is that what they call island time?" He hadn't meant to sound snarky but realized immediately his question could be taken that way.

"Not exactly." If she took offense, she didn't show it. Hair still blowing around her face as the wind picked up along with the Jeep's speed, she shot him a playful grin. "Tehani usually opens it up in the morning. I had a training exercise with the local search-and-rescue teams. Figured as long as I'm here, I might as well lend a hand doing what I'm good at."

"Search and rescue, as in water—"

"Air assistance," she hollered over the rushing wind. A new tumbler of thunder rattled and made Theo's ears twitch. "Hikers, kayakers, swimmers and boats. I'm a pilot. Been flying ever since my feet could touch the pedals."

"So you're in charge of the helicopter tours for Ohana Odysseys."

"Among other things, yes, sir." She shifted gears in a way that made Theo wonder if she thought she was in the air now. "There's no better way to see the islands, if you ask me. You ever take one?"

"A helicopter tour?" There he went, squeaking again. "No." He hoped his tone this time was unmistakable. Beneath the laptop bag he hugged against his chest, he gave a quick tug on the seat belt just to make sure it was functioning. "I'm not exactly adventurous. More of a homebody, really."

"That right?" Sydney gave him a side-eyed glance. "Could have fooled me. Blazer and tie? Buttons all the way to your throat? That all but screams *tourist* around these parts. Makes you stand out, just so you know."

His lips quirked. "My sister, Beth, calls me an acquired taste."

Sydney laughed and the sound sent a jolt racing along his spine. "Sisters have a way of keeping you down-to-earth." Her smile slipped—just a touch but enough to remind him she'd recently lost her brother. He glanced to his right, uncertainty coating his throat. He never knew what to say about loss, so more often than not, he said nothing.

"Can I assume this is your first trip to Hawai'i?" she yelled into the wind.

"You may and it is." He pressed his feet flat on the floorboard, hoping she'd take the hint and slow down as brake lights appeared ahead of them. "Sun, sea and sand aren't on the top of my list of things to experience." He neglected to add he didn't have an experience list at all.

"Well, we'll just have to see about changing your mind about that, won't we? The email your bosses sent didn't say how long you'd be staying."

"Normally, a financial examination of this type takes about a week."

She shook her head. "Nothing normal about Nalani or Ohana Odysseys." She glanced over her shoulder, then shot across two lanes of traffic. "There's more to the business than what's been recorded in data. Or is that all GVI is interested in? The financial bottom line?"

"That's what my primary job is." He frowned and gave up trying to keep his hair out of his eyes. "If Elise had been the one to come—"

"Elise?"

"Elise Barbera. She's my immediate supervisor in my department. She normally conducts these kinds of evaluations."

"Does that make me your first?"

The heat in his cheeks scorched his skin. "Ah—"

"That was a joke, Mr. Data Man. Or maybe I'll call you Abacus."

His lips twitched. "I've been called worse." A fat drop of water landed right on his nose. He swiped at it even as dozens more landed—

right on the windshield of the Jeep. "Is it really going to rain?"

"Yep." She lifted her chin. "Island time," she teased. "Kidding. We get a good soaking usually about once a day. Cools things off. Resets for the rest of the day." She shook her head. "Tried to warn you."

"I do better with specificity."

"You sound like a spring that needs to be sprung. You're wound a bit tight, aren't you?"

"If by *wound tight*, you mean professional—"

"Professional's one thing," she shouted as the rain pelted the highway, the car and them. "You look like you're getting ready for a meeting with the queen. Relax, Theo. You can't enjoy the islands if—"

"I'm not here to enjoy the islands. I'm here to work." And the sooner he got down to it, the sooner he could head home and back to his nice, air-conditioned, *dry* apartment. Plump drops of rain landed on his shoulders and face.

"Right." Her smile seemed to be gone for good, replaced by an odd twist to her mouth that noted irritation. "Work."

"I'd like to start auditing the books—"

"Auditing?" She gripped the steering wheel and cast him a sharp look. "It'll be that in-depth?"

"*Examining* is probably a better word." He needed to choose his phrasing more carefully, but he was distracted by the fact she'd finally reduced their speed now that the roads were slick. "I need to present a full reporting of the company's finances, along with my rec-ommendation to the board. That is what I've been sent here to do." He turned toward her slightly as the rain continued to fall. "You are interested in selling Ohana Odysseys, aren't you?"

"I'm interested in seeing what a final offer might be." She seemed to hesitate. "Beyond that, I am firmly in the undecided lane. I've got a lot to think about when it comes to the business, and I'm not taking any options off the table until I have a full accounting, so to speak," she added with a grinning glance, "of what's possible. Ohana means a lot to me, but it means even more to the people of Nalani. I'm not jumping into anything without looking at all the poten-tial outcomes."

So his trip here could be completely futile. Worse, his inability to seal this deal could tip GVI even further into the danger zone. He pinched his lips together. Well, that wasn't going to suit his future, was it? He needed a good showing here to earn him the standing in the company he wanted—no, where he *needed* to be. Climbing the financial corporate ladder wasn't just about ascending; it was about maintaining.

If Sydney Calvert was on the fence about selling her business, he needed to come up with a strategy to push her over to his side of things. If for no other reason than to ensure he didn't backslide.

"I'll start putting together what you need," she said. "Shouldn't take more than a day or two. I hope that won't be a problem."

It was, but he didn't think admitting that at the moment was going to win him congeniality points. "I've got other work to keep me occupied until then. And I can begin my cursory examination of business operations in the meantime." Being put in charge of the evaluation gave him access to company files and records he hadn't been privy to before. He'd have to examine GVI's information just as closely as Ohana Odysseys' if he was going to do a complete job. "I've got plenty to keep me occupied," he assured her.

"Sure, sure. Or…" She shrugged. "You could, you know, maybe experience Ohana Odysseys firsthand. Numbers won't tell you everything. Take a few tours. Jump in on a few excursions. See how we operate day to day. Off paper. You know, the personal-experience touch."

He didn't want to contemplate what kind of tour she might have in mind. Tours implied…outdoors and nature, neither of which he was on good terms with. "I wouldn't want to distract—"

"How about we talk to Tehani? She's great at putting packages together. We can spread it out over a few days. We've got an easy rain forest hike you might enjoy. Or a botanical excursion that includes lunch out by a waterfall. Surf lessons?" She laughed at his wide-eyed stare. "Kidding. Kinda. Don't worry, I'll leave plenty of time for you to work. I bet you're an early riser."

"You'd win that bet." As he swiped his damp hair out of his eyes, the clouds burst apart and the sun shone through, instantly warming his wet skin as the air thickened.

"Ah." She lifted her chin and smiled. "There it is. And look. Over there." She reached her arm across him and, beneath the scent of the ocean, he caught the trailing hint of coconut drifting off her damp skin. "I bet you've never seen a rainbow that bright before."

It took him a few blinks to bring the colorful arch into focus, but she was right. The rays of light seemed to glisten against the afternoon sun. "It's...lovely."

"Careful, or I'll think you're gushing," she teased. "I like you, Theo Fairfax."

"You do?" It was on the tip of his tongue to ask why, but he wasn't entirely sure he'd be comfortable with her answer. "Why?"

"Not sure. Oh, you can definitely use some loosening up, which I've decided might just be my number one goal for as long as you're here. But yeah. I can see some promise in you."

He wasn't entirely sure what to think. Not about Sydney Calvert and, so far, not about Hawai'i. But he supposed he owed it to himself—and his job—to work on reaching a conclusion.

While he wasn't one to rock the boat at work, he also wasn't one to shine a spotlight on himself. Standing out in his job performance was one thing, but he'd always been content to sit back and let others sop up the attention and compliments. He'd learned early on that other people—his sister, for example—not only welcomed the spotlight, but also thrived in it.

Sydney was so easy with her words, so comfortable with him. He couldn't imagine ever being so...open with anyone, let alone a perfect stranger. "I'm here to work," was all he could think to say.

"How about eat? You do that, don't you?"

"Occasionally."

"Good. We do plenty of that around here, that's for sure."

"Hori mentioned something about a luau?"

"See? You're catching on to island time already. Nalani hosts them pretty frequently, but we have a baby luau next Wednesday on the beach. That's *baby* as in for a baby's first birthday, not because it's small. Because it won't be," she added at his raised brows. "The whole town should be there, actually. The pig will go in the imu at sunrise, then the party will start about five in the evening. And, because I'm sure your inquisitive mind will want to investigate, we do pretty traditional fare. Good timing on your part. You'll get the full package, both local and tourist."

"Ah, I'll probably be—"

"Working?" Sydney snorted. "Yeah, think again. No one works when there's a luau in Nalani." She pinned him with a stare. "No one. Be sure to include that in your report."

"Actually, I meant I'll be home by then."

"Oh? Short trip?"

Very. "My return flight leaves that afternoon."

"Well, that's too bad." And her frown seemed to indicate she truly believed it. "You've never had a full island experience without an authentic luau."

He'd get by. He and the beach were not a good mix. He could feel the hives start just thinking about stepping this far out of his comfort zone. He'd only been to the beach a handful of times in his life, and each visit had been more disastrous than the last. He should have accepted that as fact after the first time, when he'd been knocked tail over teakettle by a surprise tide. To this day, if his feet didn't touch the bottom of a swimming pool, he had to stave off a panic attack.

All of that definitely boded well for spending a week or more where there was no escaping the ocean. Or its tide. Or the bazillion grains of sand just itching to get into his shoes.

"You hungry?" Sydney asked. "I was thinking we could stop off for something to eat—"

"I ate on the plane." He was also anxious for some peace and quiet. "And it was a long flight. I'd prefer to settle in." He had a lot of plan adjustment to do, and the latest financial reports from GVI were waiting in his inbox.

"Oh, sure, yeah, of course." She nodded despite her surprise. "I guess I'm used to people being kind of excited to be here. You aren't, are you? Not even a little bit."

He couldn't help feeling the way he did. But he found he didn't like being a disappointment to this woman. "Perhaps the excitement is simply delayed."

"Maybe." But she didn't sound convinced. "All right, then, Theo Abacus. A quiet night it is."

## CHAPTER THREE

HE WAS DEFINITELY a business-before-pleasure kind of man. That's what Sydney told herself as she drove home after dropping Mr. Theo Fairfax off at the vacation hut.

He'd exceeded her stereotypical expectations—a bit on the nerdy side, more than a little uncertain and dug in on his aversion to anything related to relaxation. On the other hand, he was super cute in that geeky, cautious kind of way. She'd also found him disarming and—probably without meaning to be—charming. All that said, it hadn't taken more than a passing glance at him standing outside the airport terminal to instantly identify him as her targeted pickup. She snort-laughed to herself. *So to speak.*

It had been a while since someone—okay, since a man—had made her smile. Or made her *want* to smile. There was something special about viewing the island through a newcomer's eyes that reinvigorated her. It had always been one of her favorite bits about working around the islands growing up. She could pinpoint a newbie with the briefest of looks, usually from the overwhelmed and affectionate gleam in their eyes.

But, Theo Fairfax, with his determined-not-to-have-any-fun agenda, ignited something more than an unexpected zing of attraction. She saw a challenge that needed winning.

He was as buttoned down as anyone she'd ever encountered, from his blue blazer and the top teeny white button of his suffocating shirt all the way down to his polished loafers that, if he wasn't careful, would be sand-scuffed the second he made it down the stone path to the hut. She didn't encounter his type very often. Pilots, Coast Guard active duty, bartenders? Those were more her speed, given her job back in South Carolina. Maybe that's what had captured her attention—how different he was from other men she dealt with.

Or maybe…

"Or maybe he's just a super-cute geek who

needs some loosening up." Pushing people out of their comfort zone was one of her biggest talents. She had the distinct feeling that nudging Theo Fairfax could be rewarding in any number of ways. Even just the thought was making her stomach jump in an odd, intriguing way. He'd withstood the afternoon deluge in pretty good spirits. That boded well for his stay.

Of course, it shouldn't have been necessary. Sydney would have brought the passenger van rather than the Jeep if Daphne hadn't taken it this morning for a last-minute botanical tour, but then that was before anyone knew Theo Fairfax was even coming.

It hadn't been her intention to get caught in the afternoon storm, but...the islands were filled with predictable surprises that, well, if he was evaluating Ohana Odysseys as an investment opportunity, should be included in any report.

Newcomers often found themselves face-to-face with the unexpected that rarely made it into any of the tourist brochures. The islands were notorious for hiding their secrets until just the right time, and then...

That was when people saw the magic of

this place. She couldn't wait for Theo Fairfax's illumination.

Sydney grinned and chuckled to herself as she hopped out of her car and hurried up the porch steps to the back door of the house she'd grown up in. Mr. Fairfax would probably be shocked to learn how much he'd brightened her day.

She toed off her sneakers, kicked them to the side of the porch and pulled open the door. Routine dictated she'd toss her keys into the abalone shell on the table by the front door and grab a bottle of water out of fridge in the recently remodeled kitchen.

Gone were the pale yellow walls and breezy white curtains of her upbringing. The sea foam green paint Remy had chosen brought the outside in and couched the entire home in the welcoming tones of the ocean. The new bamboo floor, which covered both the first and second levels, didn't give her bare feet the occasional splinters the original floor had. Had she more culinary talent than warming leftovers in the microwave or displaying potluck items, she was certain the high-end marble countertops and richly stained cabinetry would serve her perfectly.

The bones of her past were here, the memories and the feel. Even after all this time, she could smell the faint hint of tobacco her father had smoked in the carved pipe that had belonged to her grandfather. Sydney drew in a deep breath and closed her eyes. And there, just above the tobacco, the jasmine perfume her mother had obsessively purchased from one of the stores in town.

The house had just undergone a face-lift that, at the time, had been intended to offer Remy and Tehani a place to have their own family. It was that thought that dimmed the smile on Sydney's lips as the reality of her evening set in.

She hadn't been lying when she'd told Theo it would be tomorrow before she could provide him with any of the record-keeping files. She figured hedging her bets—and assuming her courage would fail her when it came to retrieving them—was the best course of action.

But now she had to wonder if just getting it over with was the better path to take. It was time to push through that last emotional barrier of grief and see what was on the other side.

She'd been postponing entering Remy's office ever since coming back for the funeral; she'd been dreading it for even longer. Part of her wished Tehani was here, but despite having dated for the past five years, her brother and his girlfriend had opted not to live together until after they were married. *Old-fashioned*, Sydney had teased them both. But utterly and completely romantic.

Sydney often found herself wondering if that decision was something Tehani regretted. Or maybe it was better that they hadn't, considering Remy's passing. Tehani's two-bedroom bungalow on the other end of Nalani probably served as a kind of refuge from her heartache. At least, Sydney hoped that was the case.

Now, as Sydney climbed the hand-carved spiral staircase to the second floor, a cold sweat broke out on her face and neck. Standing at the door to her brother's office made her head go light. Across the hall, the door to Sydney's bedroom stood open. Her unmade bed was a jumble and tumble of bright-colored sheets and equally colorful walls, and it beckoned, promising solace.

But she resisted temptation. She'd been hiding long enough.

It was time to move forward.

The creaks and groans of the two-story home she'd grown up in—chased her brother around in, had an idyllic childhood in—were both familiar and haunting. Homes had their own memories, and this one-time farmhouse located just beyond the main stretch of Nalani had no qualms about sharing. Every breeze that blew through the wraparound double-story porch was a breath from the past.

Sydney wasn't one to stifle her emotions, especially not ones that continued to surge to the surface. Embracing the thoughts of her parents, her brother, was the only way to push through to the next phase of her life. And it was that thought, her determination to get her feet back on the path she'd made for herself, that made her finally twist the knob and push open the door.

It only took a few barefooted steps inside before her lips curved into a fond smile. Remy had made this space his own over the years. His devotion to starting Ohana Odysseys, a business he conceived of in part to honor the parents they'd lost shortly after her high school graduation, was everywhere. From the framed photos on the wall and bookshelves to the pile of discarded business logos he'd spent hours designing.

*Organized chaos*, he'd called it when she'd called him out on the stacks and piles of paperwork and files. But this place now, with a pen tossed haphazardly on a printed-out schedule for the upcoming summer season, sat frozen in time.

The sheer gossamer curtains hanging over the shuttered plantation-style windows displayed a thin coat of dust that pretty much ordered her to do a load of laundry. On the other side of those windows, peeking in between the thick-trunked banyan and coconut trees, the ocean roared its nightly tide-promising roar that echoed down the beach. This house had seen and felt a lot of loss, but still it stood. Strong against the storm of life.

She stood only two floors above the utter peace and perfection offered by nature. How often had she come across her parents simply standing one floor below in the kitchen, arms wrapped around each other as they looked out into the ocean that, from the moment they'd met, had been their dream location.

Sydney swallowed hard. She was the only one left. And while she could still feel the presence of the family she'd adored, the home served as a painful reminder that she was now, for all intents and purposes, alone.

Well...maybe not completely alone. She had Tehani and Mano and so many others here in Nalani, but...

She sighed. *But.*

"All right. Enough futzing around. Get on with it, already." Sydney's bare feet slapped against the hardwood floor as she circled around to the desk in front of two large windows. She could hear the late-afternoon breeze kicking up as the outside light began to fade. Twilight in the islands was, as far as she was concerned, the most beautiful time of day—a time of day she purposely tried to enjoy and embrace since she'd been back. A big glass of wine and her grandfather's old rocking chair on the back porch was pretty much all she needed for the perfect ending to a day.

Now the old leather chair squeaked as she sat down and spun around to face the flat-screen monitor of her brother's old desktop. "Not so old as I remember." She clicked on the power button and waited for the machine to wake up. The faint whining of the electric fan kept her company as she began sorting through the paperwork and notes.

She glanced up when the screen lit up and found herself looking at a collection of small-framed photos lining the back of the desk. Her heart clutched at the images of her brother—all tanned skin, bright blue eyes and sun-bleached curly hair.

One was of the two of them just after he'd placed second in a local surfing competition. One was of them and their parents at Sydney's high school graduation. Remy and Mano at Christmas, decked out in Nalani-made leis; and more than a few of Remy and Tehani, radiating the perfect joy the couple evoked since the moment they'd met.

Tears burned the back of Sydney's eyes. That joy was nowhere to be found in Tehani's eyes any longer. A love like that? It didn't happen very often—or, in Sydney's case of thirty years, at all. She'd been surrounded by it, though. First, her parents, then Remy and Tehani. It was just going to have to be enough to live vicariously through those memories.

An odd buzzing in her stomach had her touching a hand to her shirt even as a shimmering image of Theo Fairfax passed through her mind. She chuckled to herself once again, noting how often she laughed at the thought of him. Being around him today had lightened her in a way she hadn't anticipated— or realized she'd needed. Her hand on the mouse, she searched for the spreadsheet program and database her brother used, clicking on the various icons along the bottom of the screen.

His email popped up as if it had only been hours, rather than weeks since it had been accessed. Knowing her brother was one of those "zero messages in his inbox" kind of people, finding five emails sitting unsent in his draft folder struck her as odd.

She clicked on the folder, then frowned when she saw one addressed to herself. Her hand trembled and tightened around the mouse as she clicked on the attached video file.

"Hey, sis." Remy's face filled the screen. Sydney sat back with a gasp, touched a hand to her heart. Remy glanced around, frowned and then looked back at the camera on top of his monitor. "It's about two in the morning out here, and I couldn't sleep," he continued. "Not a surprise, right? My brain's just spinning with..." He sighed, shook his head and raised a glass. "It's like I'm video drunk dialing you or something—but I promise, this is just water. Bear with me." He scrubbed a hand down his face. "Sorry it's been so long since we talked. I've missed a few of your calls, I know. I've just been...busy." He glanced down, his blue eyes flashing with something Sydney could only identify as uncertainty. "There's something I need to talk to you about. Something I haven't even told Tehani yet. But I need to. I need to... But that's not why I'm..."

"Remy," Sydney whispered as she reached out and brushed her fingers against Remy's image. He looked confused. Uncertain. So not like the self-assured big brother she knew.

"I've been thinking about Mom and Dad a lot these days." His voice sounded almost wistful. "I miss them so much. Maybe more now than... I've had an idea for a while, and now seems as good a time to implement it as any. We never know how much time we have, right?" He was trying to make a joke, Sydney thought, even without any humor flashing across his face. "Ohana is doing amazing, Syd. Better than I could have ever imagined. I've even had buyout offers from a few resorts and hotels, if you can believe it."

She did believe it. Not only because of the cute, quirky accounting evaluator in their guest hut down the beach, but also because her brother had built his travel business into one with a stellar reputation for customer experiences and satisfaction.

"All this interest has made me realize we could probably expand even sooner than planned," Remy continued. "Like, years sooner, but I can't keep doing this all on my own. Even if we didn't expand, I'm going to need more help. More than Tehani can offer. I need my family with me, Syd. I need you and Daphne, and Keane and Silas. Mano, too, but that's going to be more complicated since he's running the Hibiscus. I know this is a big ask, Syd. I know you've got your plans for the flight school and you're almost there with your funding, but… I want you to come home and give me the chance to convince you this is where you belong. Here, with me and Tehani. Life is so short, sis. Family is really the only certain thing we all have, and you all are mine." His smile wasn't quite as bright now, but it was oddly more intense.

"I've put together a new business plan that can open Ohana Odysseys up, make it even better than it is now and bring in even more revenue for Nalani. But I don't want just anyone involved and overseeing it. It has to be you and the others. Not outsiders who won't care about the people we help. Geez." He shook his head. "I sound like I'm babbling, throwing all this out there at you. I don't think I can do this without you. Yours is the last message I'm recording, so maybe I'm just tired. I'm going to send this and the others first thing in the morning after I get some sleep. In case there's something I've forgotten. Promise me you'll come home long enough to hear me out? I'm doing this with my face on your screen because it'll be harder for you to say no. So don't say no, okay, Sis? Just… Just get your butt on a plane and come home. I need you. Nalani needs you. Is that enough guilt?" The glint was back—the glint of challenge she hadn't realized she was missing. "I expect a response by this time tomorrow—and don't even pretend to ignore this message, because I know if you aren't in the sky, you've got your nose in your phone. Look up once in a while, Syd, okay? It's a pretty gorgeous world out there." He seemed to gaze off for a moment. "I think I'm going to go enjoy it for a while. Love you, Syd. See you soon." He reached up and turned off the camera.

Sydney drew in a shaky breath, and before she gave it a second thought, she hit Play and watched the entire message again. The second time, she didn't attempt to stop the tears.

Only after she sat in silence once more did she realize why he'd never hit Send. He'd gone to bed that night and died in his sleep. His heart had just…stopped.

*We never know how much time we have, right?*

He had a plan for Ohana? Beyond that which she'd already uncovered in his files? What plan? Feeling somewhat panicked, she clicked through to the password-protected area of his system, looking for something that would give her a hint as to what her brother had been thinking. Nothing. Which led her to a frantic search of his desk. The sound of riffling papers and sighs of frustration echoed in the empty room.

Finally, in the right-hand drawer—where he'd kept their father's hand-carved box filled with mementos and family treasures—she found it.

The folder wasn't very thick; there were only a few notes inside. But it was the main piece of torn paper with a date written across the top—the year Remy and his friends had graduated from college—that caught her eye. She scanned the information: Keane Harper's name, with a rudimentary wave sketched next to it. Daphne's name inside a crooked flower. And beside Silas Garwood's name, a little stick figure baby and a home. Then there was Mano, who looked more like a caricature, with exaggerated arm tattoos and a playful, almost-evil grin.

The giant arrow pointing at the date didn't give her all the answers she wanted, but maybe Tehani would know what this was about. Or maybe…

She looked back at the screen, and the four email drafts were there, waiting to be sent.

"Or maybe I should just do what he planned to do and see what happens?" She hovered over the files, heart hammering in her chest. She'd told Tehani she was evaluating all her options. That had only been half-true. Her options were to either sell to Golden Vistas or stay and run it herself.

But maybe Remy had just shown her another option. What if…?

She opened each email but resisted the temptation to watch the videos. It didn't matter that Remy wasn't here to approve or disapprove—those videos weren't for her. Not yet, at least. The quick note Remy had added to the email itself would have to suffice. It was what he'd wanted them to read. He hadn't been given the time to see his plans through, which meant it was up to Sydney.

Her brother needed her. One last time. To do what he hadn't been able to. Embracing her time back in Nalani meant accepting and reading the signs placed in front of her. And this was one giant, blinking sign.

Before she talked herself out of it, and because she'd have found it unnerving to receive an email from someone who had died herself, she clicked the mouse and sent each to her own account before forwarding on with a quick note. "No telling what'll come out of this," she whispered as she got to her feet and pocketed the jump drive with the financial info on it. She didn't feel any regret. "Whatever comes, at least Remy's messages will get through."

Feeling the walls of the past closing in on her, she headed back down the spiral staircase into the kitchen and, after grabbing her keys, went out the front door and back into town.

# CHAPTER FOUR

"I THINK SYDNEY CALVERT needs to rethink her definition of *hut*." Theo wasn't one to avoid talking to himself. He'd had numerous entertaining conversations throughout his life that more often than not resulted in solutions to problems he'd puzzled over for weeks. He frequently offered himself out-of-the-box solutions his silent thoughts refused to provide. Sometimes, a man just needed to hear himself talk.

On the chaotic drive to what would be his residence for the next few days, he'd imagined the "hut" Sydney described to be a rickety shack on the outskirts of Nalani, with no electricity or running water. That assumption was quickly dismissed when he realized this small town was by no means out of step with the rest of the world. Yes, the roads were narrow, and the bicycles outnumbered vehicles at least three to one. But Nalani was as typical as any other neighborhood, only with a tropical bend.

He wasn't an effusive person—descriptors tended to be short and sweet for him—but he had to admit, as he carried his bags down the winding sand-strewn path to the well-presented bungalow, he could imagine the travel brochures Golden Vistas might create with just this hidden spot as inspiration. He actually took an extra beat to appreciate the large wraparound porch located mere steps up from the beach.

He imagined anyone—not him—with affection for sand, water and, no doubt, the occasional aquatic creature could very well regard this as paradise.

Painted a beautiful glistening white, surely to reflect the sun, the house looked as if it had been plucked off a postcard, with thick, twisty vines of an array of brightly colored flowers and healthy perfumed flora. As picturesque as the exterior was, he found the yellow walls and modern decor more charming and far more practical than expected. From what he could tell, every amenity had been addressed, right down to the USB ports, filtered-water canister on the counter and stack of beach towels placed neatly on the shelves near the front door.

A solitary bedroom beyond the sitting room, with crisp white sheets and a sea green blanket folded over the bottom of the mattress, promised comfort. The ceiling fan fit the tropical feel perfectly, with large palm leaf–shaped blades made of polished wood. Matching bamboo-inspired nightstands displayed seashell-accented lamps while the tall, narrow dresser was more than large enough to hold multiple suitcases worth of clothing. As it was, the contents of his garment bag took up a fraction of the hangers in the closet.

The bathroom, while small, was modern enough to leave him nodding in approval thanks to the rainfall showerhead and fluffy towels in the small cabinet behind the door. A neat arrangement of locally produced shampoo, soap and skin-care products sat on a small bamboo tray in the corner of the sink.

Every detail had been paid attention to.

"If their books are as fastidious as this house is, the acquisition's a no-brainer."

He supposed his surprise was a result of his misconceptions about small-town island life. He'd have to make certain those judgments stopped now. "Charming," he murmured as he left the bathroom and retreated to the main area of the cottage. An open-concept plan for seating, dining and cooking were combined into a practical, pleasant space that offered coziness at a glance. The sofa was piled with quilted pillows in hues of blues and greens. The intricately stitched quilt draped over the back displayed a white background with a bright blue floral pattern that stretched the entire piece.

Theo lifted the bottom corner to read the label that had been hand-sewn onto the back. "Hand-stitched 'ulu leaves kapa kuiki by Poehina Ahina." A quick search on his phone informed him that the 'ulu leaves were a representation of the balance and symmetry of nature and that quilt-making like this was a long-held tradition in the region. "They often take more than two years to make?" He shook his head, marveling at the precise detail showcased on the fabric. This and other hand-crafted fabric items could be found locally at The Hawaiian Snuggler. *Good cross-promotion*, he thought as he made a quick return to the bathroom to confirm that the bath products were courtesy of Fresh Mojo, another local shop.

Clearly, an evaluation of the local businesses was going to have to be spotlighted in his report for GVI. The supporting economy would be a factor in the decisions the company made for potential investments moving forward. It wasn't just Ohana Odysseys they'd be investing in but the entire town. And now, after seeing just the barest hint of said town, he could envision Nalani as the saving force GVI needed to reinvent itself straight into success.

While he was in the bathroom, he availed himself of the shower, hung his storm-damp clothes up to dry, and changed into a clean and dry pair of chinos and a yellow polo shirt. The sneakers, a concession to being uncertain what to expect upon his arrival, felt stiff and tight when he laced them on.

He liked to cook, so the galley-style kitchen was another pleasant surprise. The fact that there was a plain old coffee maker and not a pod machine lifted his already buoyant spirits, as did the two packages of freshly ground coffee he found in the cabinet just above. He indulged his addiction by popping open one of the bags and taking a deep whiff of the aromatic local roast. *Ahhh.* Now *that* was paradise.

There were a few pantry items in other cabinets, along with plates and utensils, and enough cookware to give him options.

He'd seen a number of farmers' carts when Sydney had driven him through town that offered a wide selection of locally grown produce. The square table situated beneath one of two large windows draped with light green fabric would make for an excellent workspace, which he arranged with quick efficiency. He was ready to get to work.

All that was missing was the initial financial information for the company he was in charge of evaluating.

The small flat-screen TV was a surprise, as was the DVD player and a wide selection of movies that was no doubt an attempt to appeal across the board. The rather old-fashioned offering was offset by the laminated listing of streaming services also available. If this was a rental Ohana Odysseys used to supplement their business, Theo had to admit, this had been a very wise investment. Judging by Remy Calvert's decisions, Theo would say Sydney's brother had been a smart businessman with excellent taste and a good head on his shoulders. Practical. Ambitious. Clever.

*Had* been. Theo flinched. He still didn't know what to say about that. He needed to come up with something, as the topic was sure to arise again—but try as he might, anything he came up with sounded trite, rehearsed and, even worse, detached.

Condolences like "I'm sorry for your loss" felt so empty and platitude-like, especially when he was here to work. But even now he felt compelled to express something akin to understanding, though he didn't have a frame of reference himself. Other than losing his grandfather when he was six, Theo hadn't experienced significant loss. But that didn't mean he couldn't empathize with its potential occurrence.

On impulse, he checked his cell, noted the decent reception and dialed his sister's number—then felt an odd disappointment when she didn't answer.

"Hey, Beth. It's me. Just wanted to let you know I landed safe and sound. And also tell you that, once again, you were right. Hawai'i definitely holds some appeal." He winced and ducked his head. That didn't sound quite right. "Anyway, I was just thinking about you and Mom and Dad." Thinking how lucky he was to still have his family solidly in place. "My accommodations are quite spectacular. I'll take pictures and send them your way. I have the strangest desire to take a walk on the beach, if you can believe that." Not quite true. The very idea made his feet itch. "Anyway, I'll talk to you later." He hesitated. "Love you. Bye."

*Eeesh.* He must be tired if he was eking out emotions all over the place. No doubt Beth was going to hear that message and think something was seriously off or he'd undergone a personality transplant while on his trip. He mentally planned for a call back sometime in the near future.

He pulled open the front door and stepped outside. The evening breeze was a warm surge that blew over him. The waterline had seemed closer at first, and he'd wondered upon his arrival if high tide was something to be concerned about. He saw now that the distance to the shore was greater than first estimated, but he found the lapping of the waves tumbling up and over the sand to be oddly comforting.

He might not need his white noise machine to sleep after all.

Theo took a deep breath and let it out slowly as he gripped his hands around the smooth, white railing. A small table and chair had been placed in the corner of the porch. It might be nice, setting his laptop up out here occasionally to get some fresh air. Out from under the sun. Which reminded him…

He headed back inside and dug through his travel bag for the 80+ sunscreen he'd bought on his way home from work yesterday. Probably too late to be much good today, but he should leave it out as a reminder.

As someone who wasn't particularly outdoorsy—his idea of "roughing it" was going into a grocery store rather than opting for home delivery—he anticipated spending a good portion of his time right here in the so-called hut.

His stomach rumbled. He checked his watch. It was after five. The meager snack of fruit and cheese he'd had on the plane had clearly not been enough to sustain him. Maybe he should head into town and find one of those carts. Perhaps he'd pick up a burger or some of that chicken at the shack they'd passed on their way in.

He made sure he had his wallet, collected his cell phone and grabbed the solitary hut key Sydney had given him. A few seconds later he was locking the front door and making his way down the paving stone path to the road.

No sooner had he rounded the first curve, he spotted Sydney heading up the hill. She was wearing the same bright shirt and shorts, and her hair was still as loose and free as it had been on the drive into town. The breeze was still teasing it up and off her shoulders. The only difference was, obviously, she didn't have the Jeep, and her hands were filled with a couple of colorful reusable bags.

"I took a chance thinking you might be hungry," she called out before she reached him and hoisted the bags in front of her.

"You thought right." He found himself smiling and stopped walking. He wasn't used to someone thinking of him outside of an office or conference room. He really wasn't used to being in the company of such a beautiful woman. He'd thought her striking when they were in the Jeep, but now? Seeing her in her element, her lightly tanned skin glistening in the setting sun, she was a sight to behold. Unfamiliar nerves jangled in his belly, and he resisted the urge to clear his throat. "You saved me a walk."

"Considering the shoes you're wearing, I saved your feet, too," she said, with that grin he was coming to appreciate more and more. "You don't even own a pair of sandals or flip-flops, do you?"

"I do not." It took every ounce of concentration not to wince at the idea of bare feet. They made shoes, socks and slippers for a reason.

She eyed him, that teasing glint in her bright blue eyes sparking something inside him. "I give you a week, maybe ten days before you surrender and buy a pair down at Luanda's."

"I don't plan to be here that long." As beautiful as this place was, he was already anxious to get back to his life, his routine and his third-story one-bedroom apartment that was barely big enough to house both him and a goldfish. Not that he had a fish. Comforts aside, Nalani wasn't home. "What's in the bags?"

"I picked up the fixings for saimin. It's an island favorite. It's pretty easy to fix. Grabbing two was just as easy as one."

"Saimin?" He frowned. "I don't think I've heard—"

"It's the island version of ramen," she explained. "Soup."

"Oh." He shrugged and nodded. He hadn't considered whether he was in a soup-slurping kind of mood or not. "That sounds great, actually. Why don't you join me?" The request was out before his brain caught up. Clearly, he'd surprised her as well, as her eyebrows shot up and she smiled.

"Yeah, I'd like that. Thanks."

"Great. Let me take those." He held out his hands.

"I've got it, thanks." She stopped in front of him, inclined her head. "I have to confess, I was feeling a little guilty. I'd planned on bringing the accounting files with me from Remy's office."

"You didn't find them?"

"I got...distracted." The tone in her voice told him she was distracted still. "I'll get them to you soon, though. Promise."

As anxious as he was to start his examination, it didn't feel right to push. "All right. Like I said, I've got plenty of other things to do in the meantime."

"Such a shame. We need to get you on island time, *brah*." She nudged him with her hip as she passed.

*Brah?* Strange. For some reason the idea of Sydney thinking of him like a brother did not make him particularly happy. *Ridiculous*, he told himself as he followed her. He was here to work, not flirt with the subject of his company's potential buyout. *Focus on the job.*

She reached the front porch before he did, then shot him an amused look when she found the door locked. "Mainlander," she teased.

"Habit." He chuckled and pulled the key out of his pocket. His hands shook a little, and he realized she actually made him nervous. Another unexpected twist. A fascinating one. "The idea of not locking a door—"

"Takes some getting used to, I know."

"Please." He pushed open the door. "After you."

"Thanks." She made a beeline straight for the kitchen and began unloading the bags. "Since the last time I was back in Nalani, one of the local markets started offering meal kits where everything's prepped—you just have to cook or assemble it."

"I do a version of that back home." He quickly arranged the packages of fresh wheat-and-egg noodles alongside the green onion, nori and thinly sliced pork. "Just add in delivery. What's this?" He held up a compressed package of swirled pink and white.

"*Kamaboko.* Fish cake. I thought maybe you'd prefer that over Spam." Her smile was getting wider. "For now, at least."

He laughed again. "Not sure why you're determined to turn me into an islander, but you're right. I draw the line at Spam."

"Well, get over it. Around here, it's a food group. And I hope you're good with unexpected company. Word's already gotten around about your arrival, so you're going to be inundated with questions and food, which will most definitely include some of Konane's Spam musubi."

"I'm not even going to ask." He'd wait and be surprised, but anything involving processed tinned meat was not on the top of his to-eat list. "I didn't have a lot of time to research the islands," he told her as she folded up the bags and hung them on the knob of the still-open front door. "But I did read about these Portuguese doughnut things?"

"Malasadas." She let out a sigh that sounded part relieved, part wistful as she lifted a small pink pastry box and set it down in front of him. "I got some for dessert. And enough for breakfast, if you're so inclined, although you can't beat the ones fresh off Manu's cart at sunrise."

"Thanks." He could feel his blood sugar spiking already. "Speaking of breakfast, do I have you to thank for the supply of coffee?"

"You do, actually." She opened a drawer and pulled out a knife and cutting board. "I brought some of my private stash. Not that it's hard to get around here. In fact, I'm happy to take you over to Kona on the west side of the island if you want to see how it's harvested and processed."

"Now that's something I might just take you up on."

"I thought it might." Her grin was back. "You strike me as an examine-the-process kind of guy."

He was, but when she said it, he didn't sound quite so boring. They worked well in the kitchen together as she instructed him on heating up the aromatic broth.

"How about we eat outside?" she urged once she placed a sliced-open soft-boiled egg into his already full bowl of broth, noodles and various garnishes. She grabbed forks and deep porcelain soup spoons out of the drawer, but also two paper-wrapped sets of chopsticks that were included in the food package. "The cloudburst this afternoon cleared out the sky. It's shaping up to be a great afterglow."

"A great what?"

"Those few minutes just after the sun goes down, but night hasn't quite grabbed hold. There's this...glow in the sky." She shook her head, sighed. "Words will never do it justice. You'll just have to wait and see."

"Oh. Yeah. Sure."

"What's wrong? Don't believe me?"

"I'll take your word for it. But actually, I just realized I need to stock up on bug spray." He couldn't pack any since he had done all carry-on luggage.

"That same market where I got dinner should have what you need—but keep in mind, we have our own pest control out this way." Her smile was part knowing, part secretive as she walked ahead of him to the small round table in the corner of the porch.

It didn't take him more than a glance out over the tumbling waves to know his guest— or was she his hostess?—was psychic when it came to predicting the setting sun's brilliance. The play of colors splashing across the sky brought even him to a stop and left him wondering if there was such a thing as a disappointing sunset in these parts. Not that he'd paid much attention previously to compare them…

He returned to the kitchen to get them each a bottle of water from the fridge. "You've made me feel quite welcome, Sydney," he said when he rejoined her. "Thank you."

"You're welcome. It's what we do in Nalani," she told him and knocked her bottle against his in a mock toast. "There's a reason Remy named his company Ohana. It means *family*, and that's what we are here."

"I should have said earlier," he said as he sat across from her and clicked apart his chopsticks. "I'm sorry about your brother." He breathed a sigh of relief. That hadn't been so difficult after all.

"Thanks." She flashed a quick, sad smile before focusing on her soup. "You would have liked each other, I think. He'd have enjoyed pushing you out of your comfort zone."

He ducked his head, looked at his soup. "I understand it was sudden?"

"Very. He died in his sleep. Although I've since learned he'd been having heart issues. He hadn't shared that with anyone."

"He probably didn't want to worry you."

"Yeah, well, I can understand him not telling me. There wasn't much I could have done all the way out in South Carolina *except* worry. But Tehani and Mano are right here, and they didn't know about it, either."

"Tehani and Mano." He'd seen mention of both names in the initial file GVI had opened on the possible acquisition.

"Iokepa. Tehani and my brother were together for a number of years before he died." She swirled and lifted noodles up out of her bowl, then let them sink back into the richly flavored broth. "And her brother, Mano, was Remy's best friend going back to grade school. Remy and I grew up in Nalani."

"No wonder you seem to belong here."

"Not so sure about that." She shrugged. "I haven't lived here for a long time. Nalani was always Remy's place, you know? It's where he always belonged."

"But not you?"

"Suffice it to say, I'm not easily convinced."

Theo found that hard to believe, given the peaceful expression on her face whenever she looked out over the tide. He couldn't imagine her belonging anywhere else. He set his utensils down. "Some people find it difficult to find where they belong." Or to accept it once they found it.

"Or sometimes, you belong to too many places, and it's hard to decide. How about you?" She expertly plucked up a piece of pork and popped it into her mouth.

"Me?"

"Yeah. Golden Vistas is headquartered in San Francisco, right? How long have you lived there?"

"In San Francisco? About fifteen years."

"So it's home."

"It is." Maybe it was the sunset, maybe it was the quiet or maybe it was the woman sitting across from him that had him feeling unusually open. "My parents moved us around a lot when we were growing up. Six months here, eight months there. My dad had what my mom called *restless feet*. Looking back, I see it as he was easily bored. Always looking for the next challenge, the next mountain to climb."

"Has he stopped looking for those mountains?"

"Not last I heard." He could laugh about it now, kind of, but there was still a tinge of discomfort and—if he allowed himself to dwell on it—resentment when he thought about his upbringing. "Once I started college in San Francisco, I made it pretty clear my wandering days were over. They invested in a mobile home and pretty much go where the wind blows. I believe they're currently making their way across Alaska."

She leaned her chin in her hand. "And you stayed put."

"When you spend most of your childhood longing for something, it's difficult to let go of once you get it." College had been the first time he'd realized those uneasy, barbed wire knots in his stomach didn't actually belong there. "So yeah, I stayed put. Stability makes me feel…" He struggled for a moment, then surrendered. "Stable. Same city for more than fifteen years. Same apartment for the past twelve. But I've only been at Golden Vistas for two years, so there's a bit of the unexpected for you." His lips twitched. "I suppose I've just admitted to being the most boring man on the planet."

"You sound like a man who has what he wants." Now she shrugged. "If you're happy, there's nothing wrong with it. How about your sister? Beth, isn't it? Did she inherit your parents' wanderlust?"

Theo chuckled and scooped up more of the tasty soup. "To an extent. She traveled around for a long time before she landed in Seattle. She owns a bookstore up there with her wife and two stepsons. I've already called her. I had to talk to someone about this place."

"Word of mouth is our best means of advertisement. And one of the highest compliments you could pay Remy," Sydney confirmed. "He casts a long shadow here. I think when I was younger, I wanted to spread my wings beyond that shadow. He was the star at everything he tried: academics, sports, business. The only thing I ever did better than him was fly."

"So you're a pilot back in South Carolina, right? Commercial airline?"

"Nothing so, as you'd put it, *stable*," she told him. "I work for a few companies, including medical transports, private transportation—and I'm on call to assist with air rescues. I also teach part-time at a flying school. Once I get back, I'm going to be opening my own flying school."

"You love it that much?" His insides curdled at the thought of soaring through the air. Or, more likely, plummeting through it.

"The air is where I belong."

He could hear the affection and longing in her voice, even now as they sat alongside the ocean tide and watched the sky paint its farewell to the day. "It usually takes me weeks to work up the courage to step foot on an aircraft." It probably wouldn't do his ego any good to admit to needing occasional pharmaceutical assistance. One reason he'd been perfectly fine holding down the office when his supervisor took on the travel.

"That's because you haven't been up in

the air with me." She pointed her chopsticks at him. "I'm aces with nervous fliers. I took a psych class in college that examined various phobias and fears. A lot of experts believe that fear of flying stems from an inherent discomfort with not being in control. You have to trust everything and everyone around you. Control is the last thing you have as a passenger."

He folded his arms on the table. "Is that your way of calling me a control freak?"

"You tell me, Mr. Bug Spray Man." Her gaze flittered down to the table, sparked to life and then her smile widened. "Remember that island pest control I was telling you about earlier?" She pointed down and to his left. "He would be Exhibit A."

"He who?" Theo glanced down and jumped back so fast his chair skidded against the plank porch boards. The small green lizard that had somehow made it onto the table planted its tiny webbed toes onto the edge of his bowl and peeked over into Theo's dinner. "What the heck is that?"

Two bulging eyes shifted from side to side as the lizard, no more than five inches long, dipped his head and grasped a solitary noodle in its triangular mouth.

Sydney laughed but didn't make any move to shoo the creature away. "He's a cute one. See the gold sparkle on his back? He's a gold dust day gecko. They're harmless and pretty friendly, obviously. Aw. He likes the soup!" She plucked a few soggy green onions out of her own bowl and placed them on the table near the lizard. "How about you make a full meal out of it, little guy? They're omnivores," she told a still-gaping Theo. "He's harmless."

Theo wasn't so sure. The thing was chomping down pretty determinedly on the noodle. "He's eating my dinner."

"Brave little thing. Usually, they scamper away as soon as they realize they've been spotted. Here you go." She scooted an onion closer. The lizard dropped off the edge of Theo's bowl and turned to Sydney's offering. The bright blue rings around his eyes added more than a touch of character. Still...

"I think I'm full," Theo said and pushed his bowl away.

"With all the wildlife on the islands, trust

me, a lizard eating out of your bowl is only the start of your adventures."

All the more reason to stay close to his hut. If she was trying to ease his mind, it wasn't working. "Anything in particular I should be on the lookout for?"

She grinned in that infectious way she had that made his own lips twitch. "I think I'd rather you be surprised. Let's just say, the animals around here evoke as much curiosity and entertainment value as most of the people. As for your roommate—"

"He's not moving in." Theo eyed the lizard, who glanced at Theo as if he wanted in on the conversation. "You're not," he warned, and he could have sworn the gecko smirked.

"You should keep him around. They eat mosquitoes and other bugs, and they're less toxic than spray. Tons of kids around Nalani keep them as pets."

"I'm not big on sharing," Theo announced. "You can ask my sister."

She laughed. "I bet she has all kinds of fun stories about you." The gecko munched on one of the three large slices of green onion before it turned around and pinned his gaze on Theo's abandoned bowl. "It's funny—I would have pegged you as an only child."

"She's six years older."

"Ah, okay. That makes sense. You each had a good amount of time being the sole focus of the household." Sydney nodded. "Remy was only three years older than me. Every time I turned around, there he was."

Despite the fondness he heard, he couldn't ignore the grief in her voice. "I'm sorry. I didn't mean to—"

"There's no need to apologize. I don't mind talking about him." She plastered on what he was fairly certain was a forced smile. "I miss him so much it physically hurts. And confession time—I found some videos he recorded on his computer when I got home that threw me for a bit of a loop. Didn't make me anxious to spend a lot of time with my thoughts, you know?"

So she brought him dinner? It wasn't only the soup that warmed his insides. "I'm glad you thought to come over."

"Me, too. It's one thing to lose a sibling…" She stirred her noodles as if she'd forgotten how to eat. "It's another to think of what Tehani's been going through. The future they'd been planning together... Breaks a whole different part of my heart, you know?"

Theo didn't have a clue where to swing the conversation from here. Which was probably why he forced himself to take another mouthful of noodles. The good news was, it didn't taste any different after his pseudo-reptilian dining companion had had his fill. "Tehani works at Ohana Odysseys, too, doesn't she?"

"Yes, thank goodness." Relief and gratitude slipped in and over her grief. "I'd be lost without her." She laughed at her own joke. "That's how she and Remy met, when he advertised for a receptionist and office organizer. So if you have any questions about how the business runs and statistical information on our clientele..." Sydney trailed off.

"What's wrong?"

"I was going to say she's who you should go to with any questions you might have, but that's probably not a great idea now that I think about it."

"Why not?"

"She doesn't want me to sell." She hesitated. "She hasn't had much time to think about it, though. I didn't really tell her I was considering your company's offer."

"I was under the impression you were the solitary owner."

"I am." She cringed, moved her chopsticks around in the broth. "But she and my brother were partners in most every way. She doesn't believe he'd have even entertained the idea of selling."

Number crunching and analysis were two tools to use to push her into agreeing to sell, but neither came close to being strong enough to best family. "Not even for the right price?"

"Not everyone has a price." She frowned, ducked her chin. "But I suppose that's not something you believe, considering why you're here."

"I'm just here to make an honest evaluation on the business as an investment." But she was right. In his experience, most people were willing to accept a big check if it meant taking them up to the next financial level or opening a door to a new business opportunity. "I imagine Tehani's attachment to the business is an emotional one, not necessarily a practical or even logical one."

Sydney sat back, narrowed her blue eyes as if reevaluating him. "You're right that her attachment stems from emotion, but don't be so quick to dismiss the logic behind that. Ohana Odysseys is an important part of Nalani. Not only economically but spiritually."

"You're going to have to explain that to me." Businesses were black and red. Successful or a failure. Worthy of investment or not. The balance sheets always told the story for him. Throwing anything else like emotion or spirituality into the mix didn't come close to computing.

"Tehani may have reminded me that selling to a company like yours could erode what's so special about Ohana and about Nalani. She's afraid selling will sever the *mana pono* we all have to this place."

"*Mana...*"

"*Mana pono.* It's the soul connection native

Hawaiians have to the islands." She pushed her bowl toward the center of the table and earned a determined, if not expectant, look from their little green visitor. "Can I ask you a question?"

"Sure." Considering he had about a thousand of his own, it seemed only fair.

"I can't really think of a way to ask without sounding rude, but how did we even get on Golden Vistas' radar? Why did they send you? You in particular," she clarified. "I'm sure there were others who could have filled in for your boss, but as far as I can tell, you're not exactly—"

"Informed?" He couldn't exactly argue the point. "I'm not, or I wasn't. I've been working on catching up. I hope I'm here because they value my opinion. And my opinion will be entering into things."

"Of course." She hesitated. "If they weren't looking for honest feedback and interpretation, they wouldn't have had to send anyone. I could have just submitted a financial report through email."

Considering that was one of the questions he'd had when he was given this assignment, again, he couldn't argue. "I don't suppose I have an answer to that." But it was, now that he thought about it, a good question. "I have a somewhat no-nonsense reputation in the company. I look at the bottom line and present my recommendations accordingly." He stopped short of saying he'd been told the board of directors was expecting an agreement to be made that would preclude the official offer of a buyout.

"Meaning whatever your official recommendation is they'll go with it."

"Meaning they'll accept whatever I tell them as factually based and true. Assisting in closing this deal could be good for my career, but other than that, I don't have any ulterior motives. If I think this is a good investment for my company, I'll tell them so. If I don't, I'll tell them that as well. To be honest, I can already see where Golden Vistas could benefit from buying Ohana Odysseys and vice versa, but that's only surface at this point."

"The only surprise you're probably going to find in those accounting reports is that

Remy's been more successful than his projections estimated."

"And yet here we are, deciding whether you're going to sell your brother's business—your business—to my employers."

"Discussing." Her eyes darkened. "No one has *decided* anything for certain. Yet."

He might not be the greatest people reader in the world, but he could feel something off with her. "Do you want to sell?"

"My gut reaction? Yes. I could easily finance my flying school with my portion of the sale. But there's more to take into consideration." She sighed. "Tehani is right. There are a lot of determining factors to this entire proposal. I can't just go with what I want to do."

"Why not?" Now it was Theo who frowned. "Your brother left you the business. Not Tehani. And not the town. Obviously, that means he trusted you'd do the right thing."

"Yeah, Remy's *right thing* and my *right thing* are at opposite ends of the spectrum. If he'd had his way, I would have come back months—heck, even years—ago to help him run it. I just…" She took a deep breath and held out a finger to their tabletop visitor. The lizard moved closer and seemed to bump his nose purposely against her fingertip. "I just think it's important for you to see all areas this decision affects. Not just me and what I might want but the town and the people who live here. Ohana Odysseys affects every single person's lives, not just mine. That requires consideration."

"Fair enough." He pushed his soup aside again. She was right. Knowing everything he could about this place would only make his report well-rounded and effective. If he could close this deal, his future could very well be secured for decades. That stability he'd chased for most of his life was in his reach to lock down permanently. Or at least for the foreseeable future. "Educate me."

"It'll take more than one dinner conversation to do that."

"Then start with one dinner conversation, and we'll continue tomorrow." The idea of spending additional time with Sydney held a surprising appeal. Normally, he'd be just fine on his own, keeping to himself and crunching his numbers. But Sydney Calvert had him considering much more evocative ways to spend his time.

"If Golden Vistas is serious about making an impact here, they need to get some things straight first off."

"Go ahead." He tapped a finger against his temple. "I'll store it all up for later."

"All right." She didn't look completely convinced of his sincerity. "Let's get the basics out of the way." She proceeded to explain the makeup of the island, from the flora and fauna to those who lived here, and she spoke with a passion he'd never forget.

"Ohana is the foundation of this community, and anyone who wishes to belong here *does*."

"It's that simple?"

"Yes." The glint in her eye left no room for doubt. "It is."

"Then I appreciate your honesty on all these subjects." Theo nodded and made a mental note to do additional research for his report. The misconceptions she'd already debunked were adding up. "I certainly wouldn't want to say or even think the wrong thing while I'm here in regards to the people or the island and how it's thought of." And he definitely didn't want Golden Vistas to do so, either. Part of his job was to give them all the information they needed for a successful transaction. Being ignorant—or worse, misinformed—as to the realities of the history and perceptions of the islands would be a recipe for disaster. "So growing up, you and Remy were never made to feel as if you didn't belong."

"Far from it," Sydney confirmed as she finished her dinner. "If I'd had any doubt about that, it would have been erased after he died. It's been made very clear everyone here feels as if they've lost someone important. I think it made it a little easier—coming home, going through the paddle-out, knowing everyone here was grieving him as well. Are you done with your dinner?"

"Yeah." He looked down at his still half-full bowl. "Don't think less of me, okay?"

She laughed as she stood and collected their dishes. "I'll give you a pass but only for today. Tomorrow you'll just have to adjust to his presence and learn to share."

"Excuse me?" he asked as she entered the

house. "What do you mean 'adjust to his'… Oh. Hey there, gecko." Theo pursed his lips as the lizard turned quickly and blinked those bulbous ringed eyes at him. "You, ah, planning to stick around? Should I maybe make up a bed? Or how about a hammock?"

"Wouldn't be a bad idea," Sydney teased as she came back out with a plate holding two sugar-coated fried doughnuts. "Sorry, little fella. You're out of luck on dessert."

The lizard turned one way, then the other before scampering over the edge of the table and disappearing from sight.

"At least if he's ticked, he'll take it out on you," Sydney joked. "Got any hot plans for the rest of the night?"

"Whatever they were, they've been exceeded." He picked up the small doughnut and sank his teeth into the soft dough. "Okay, that was worth the wait," he said after he swallowed. The combination of not-too-sweet coconut pudding and springy doughnut explained their well-rounded reputation. "You aren't having one?"

"I'll get my fix tomorrow morning from Manu's stand." She walked over and leaned on the railing. Bathed by the day's final sun rays, the light cast her in a glow that had him rethinking his entire life. "So, no moonlit walk on the beach for you, Mr. Number Cruncher?"

"No." There weren't many things with which he could speak with authority, but that was one of them. "I'm looking forward to a hot pot of coffee and a deeper dig into Nalani and Ohana Odysseys reputation and investment potential."

"Exciting."

"For me, yes."

"Why? Was this deal your idea?"

"No." He frowned. "No, this is just part of my job."

"But you have a vested interest in making this deal happen," she accused gently.

"It wouldn't hurt my standing in the company," he admitted. "And, all right, it could put me in line for a promotion. That means more stability."

"Does it mean you can learn to relax?" she ribbed, and he actually laughed a little.

"I don't know that I can ever learn to do that."

"Tell you what," she said. "You work on relaxing and do your deep-diving into Ohana's investment potential, and that way, when I quiz you tomorrow, you'll be prepared."

"What's tomorrow?"

"Well, I've got morning tours to oversee, but I'm pretty sure my schedule is clear for a few hours around noon. How about you meet me at the office around then, and I'll give you the walking tour of Nalani?" She angled her gaze down at his feet. "In the meantime, I strongly suggest you reconsider some sandals. You're going to get blisters walking around in the heat in those clodhoppers."

"Clod—"

She waved off his confusion. "Something my grandmother used to call heavy oversize shoes. Enjoy your malasadas," she said as she backed away and headed for the stairs, kicked off her sandals and sank ankle-deep into the sand. "I'll see you tomorrow. Night, Theo."

"Good night." He blinked and found himself transfixed as he watched her walk down to the shore and leave footprints in the tide-soaked sand before she slipped out of sight against the afterglow.

## CHAPTER FIVE

AFTER BACK-TO-BACK morning Jeep tours along the coast that took Sydney and her clients up into the mountains around Hilo and back, she pulled the vehicle into its usual spot in front of Ohana Odysseys and killed the engine. Climbing out of the car, she checked her watch.

She had a good three hours before her next excursion—Ohana Odysseys' Zip Line Adventure package, which included a complimentary dinner at the Blue Moon Grill once everyone was back on firm ground.

Nalani was on its best behavior today, with a postcard-perfect cloudless sky and the ever-present plumeria accenting the air with its summer-is-fast-approaching fragrance. Spending the evening with Theo, followed by a long walk home on the beach, had resulted in the best night's sleep she'd had in weeks. The burst of energy that accompanied her waking was not something she planned to waste.

Across the street and up the hill, she could hear the excited squeals and laughter of the school playground as it received its daily dose of juvenile high jinks. The weekend was on its way, which meant a full schedule loomed.

She dropped her head back and sighed, taking a long moment to recover from the frenetic, excited clients who had consumed more than their fair share of caffeine along the way. She'd dropped her second group— a trio of former college roommates here for a reunion—back at the Hibiscus Bay Resort just in time for the hula lessons one of the guests had challenged the others to participate in.

Silently wishing their instructor luck, Sydney embraced the quiet as she gathered up her belongings, then felt her spirits boost with the significant tip she found in the front cup holder.

That more than made up for the headache she felt knocking on the back of her skull. Hauling the cooler she used to store water and some fresh snacks out of the back of the

Jeep, she dumped the melted ice at the base of one of the enormous coconut trees before heading up the steps to the office. "We can put the O'Hurley family on the books for a surf lesson tomorrow with Kiri," she called on her way inside, only to find herself speaking to an empty room. No one behind the front counter. No one at either of the two desks beyond. "Tehani?"

Sydney left her stuff on the round table near the coffee station. Unease prickled the back of her neck. Tehani was as predictable as the sunrise, always at her desk well before Sydney was probably waking up. She also rarely left the office without putting up a Be Back Soon sign.

"Bathroom." Sydney snapped her fingers and shook her head. She headed over, knocked on the door. "T?"

"Out in a minute!"

Sydney frowned. Her friend's choked voice sounded as if maybe Tehani was on the other side of a particularly vicious hangover. Not one to judge, Sydney grabbed the cooler, wiped it out and stashed it with the others in the back storage and equipment room.

"Sorry," Tehani said when she emerged.

"Did you say something about the O'Hurleys?" She tugged at the hem of her blousy red tank and rolled her shoulders.

"I did." Sydney walked across the spacious open office. "They want to book family surf lessons with Kiri tomorrow if there's room."

"Um. Yeah." Tehani nodded and gripped the edge of the counter as she walked around to her computer. "Should be okay. Let me…" She stopped, closed her eyes and swayed before she dropped into her chair.

Sydney darted around before the chair wheeled out from under her. "What's wrong?" She touched her friend's shoulder. "You look terrible."

"You have such a way with a compliment." Tehani's smile was beyond strained, and her face looked pale and drawn. "Nothing's wrong. Just having some stomach issues. Nothing contagious," she said quickly. "Don't worry."

"I'll worry, contagious or not." She touched the back of her fingers against Tehani's forehead. "You feel a little warm."

"It's Hawai'i." Tehani pushed her arm aside. "We're all warm. It'll pass."

Yeah, she was protesting a bit too much.

"Maybe you should take the day off," Sydney suggested. "Go see Doc up at the clinic just to be sure."

"I don't need to see Doc again." She tapped on her keyboard and scooted her chair closer. "It'll resolve in a few months." Sydney stepped around so she could look at her as Tehani caught her lower lip in her teeth. She glanced up, uncertainty shining bright in her dark eyes before tears filled them. "I guess I can't keep it a secret any longer. I'm pregnant."

"Pregnant?" Sydney gasped and covered her mouth as an overwhelming combination of joy and anguish swelled inside her. "Oh, Tehani! Why didn't you tell me? How long have you known? Oh, T, this is…" *So many things*, Sydney thought. *So many, many things.*

"I found out about a week before…" She cleared her throat as she tried to keep typing. "I was trying to come up with the perfect way to tell him when he…well, when Remy died." The tears spilled over. "After that, I…" She sighed and swiped at her cheeks. "There was so much going on I couldn't think straight. Heck, I can barely think straight now. He wanted to be a father so badly, Syd."

"I know."

"It was the main reason he was finally ready to take some time off so we could get married, but…he got busy again and…" Tehani's breath shuddered. "I never got the chance to tell him. Now I never will."

Sydney walked around, bent down and wrapped her arms around her almost-sister-in-law from behind. She'd been lamenting all that Tehani had lost when Remy died, but she hadn't come close to understanding the true tragedy of it. Not until now. "You should have told me sooner," she whispered, resting her cheek on the top of Tehani's head. "Why didn't you?"

"I was going to. Yesterday, actually." She wrapped a hand around Sydney's arm and squeezed. "Then I read that email about you wanting to sell Ohana, and I chickened out. I don't want you making a different decision because of this. You need to do what's right for you."

Sydney squeezed her eyes shut as guilt crashed down over her. Intended or not, Tehani had managed to sway things for her with only a few words. "I need all the information I can get to make an informed decision," she managed around a too-tight throat. "And besides, we agreed to six months, remember? That'll be plenty of time for you to have this little one." She shifted, dropped down and pointed to Tehani's stomach. "I'm going to be an auntie. Not just an island auntie but a real one!"

"You are," Tehani laugh-cried. "I hope that's okay with you."

"Are you kidding?" Tears she'd been holding back for what felt like years surged into her throat. She couldn't speak; she could only nod. "It'll be like a part of him is still here," she finally managed. "I don't know that you could have made me any happier, T." She reached up and caught T's face between her hands. "You're going to have a baby."

Tehani nodded again, and even though she didn't say it, Sydney knew what she was thinking. That she'd be having Remy's child without him. It didn't need to be voiced. Not when both of them were feeling the loss so exquisitely.

"We need to celebrate," Sydney announced. "Oh! The luau! It'll be perfect."

"I'm not horning in on a one-year-old's celebration," Tehani insisted as Sydney pushed to her feet. "Leora gets her day. We'll do something special another time. Besides," she added with a guilty wince, "you're the only one besides Doc who knows."

"You haven't told your brother?"

"He's been so busy with the resort and helping with all of the arrangements for Remy. I didn't want to bother him. You know marriage and family and babies are a tricky subject with him."

"It's his own fault it's tricky," Sydney said. "He's the one who drove Emilia away before they could start a family of their own." She'd always liked Mano. Heck, she loved him like a second brother, but that didn't mean she didn't see his very evident flaws. Mano's determination not to turn into his and Tehani's father had triggered fallout he hadn't anticipated until it was too late.

"Funny enough, reminding him that he screwed up with his marriage always throws him straight into a mood," Tehani said. "I think because he knows I'm right. Never mind the fact he could actually fix things with Emilia if he really wanted to."

"He should want to," Sydney said. "I miss her. She was good for him." It had been three years since Mano's wife left the islands. Three years Mano had thrown himself completely into his work as operations manager and part owner of the Hibiscus Bay Resort. He was successful for sure. But was he happy?

"Yeah," Tehani whispered. "He wasn't the only one who suffered when she went back to the mainland. Anyway, once I tell him about the baby, we can celebrate. Hopefully by then, I'll stop puking my guts out every morning. And afternoon. And night."

"It sounds as if I'm interrupting."

Sydney spun around at Theo's uncertain voice. "Oh! Theo, hey." She glanced at the clock on the wall. Noon. She should not be surprised he was bang on time. He wasn't a man to defy expectations; he fulfilled them.

He was wearing those clunky sneakers of his, along with crisp beige chinos and another polo shirt, this one in hues of blue. The man looked as if he ironed himself the second he climbed out of bed.

"I can come back later." Theo took a step back. "Or we can reschedule."

"Oh, um." Sydney glanced back at Tehani, who was already getting to her feet.

"No need to do either," Tehani said as she walked around the counter and held out her hand. "Aloha, Mr. Fairfax. Welcome to Nalani. I'm Tehani Iokepa. It's nice to meet you."

"That's kind of you to say, and it's Theo, please."

"Theo. Has Sydney talked you into taking one of our tours?" She gestured him forward in that elegant, welcoming way she had.

"I haven't had a chance to create an itinerary for you just yet," Sydney said. "But I bet Tehani would love to. She specializes in creating personalized experiences for guests who want to get the most out of their visit." Sydney fluttered her lashes at him. "And you do want to get the *full* Nalani experience, don't you?"

"That depends," Theo said without missing a beat even as he angled an arched brow in her direction. "Am I more or less likely to end up on a helicopter?"

"He hates to fly," Sydney explained to

Tehani. "A chopper tour isn't on the top of his list."

"You'd be surprised how often we hear that," Tehani said. "Tell you what. Why don't you fill out this quick questionnaire I created? Think of it like a dating profile for tourist activities." She leaned over the desk and pulled up a clipboard with two pieces of paper on it and handed it to him with a pen. "This will help me immensely. I'll let Sydney be the one to convince you about the chopper." She flashed Sydney a look that had Sydney flinching. "This will also give you an idea as to how we operate Ohana Odysseys. We pride ourselves on giving our customers as unique and personalized experiences as possible."

"If you're trying to talk me out of thinking this business is a good investment, you're going about it wrong," Theo said.

"Oh, it absolutely is, but we don't need anyone's help," Tehani said easily. "How about some coffee?"

"I'm good, thanks. I've already worked halfway through my supply at the... I'm sorry. I cannot call that place a *hut*," he told

Sydney. "We'll just go with *beach cottage*, shall we?"

"Works for me," Sydney agreed, finding herself entertained.

"I was, um, I was wondering," he said with more uncertainty than she was used to hearing from him, "if you had those financial records saved for me yet?"

"Oh. Yes." Avoiding Tehani's pinpoint stare, she returned to her desk for the jump drive she'd brought from the house. "Sorry it took so long. If there's anything missing, just let me know."

"Will do." He pocketed the drive with a quick smile.

"So." She rocked back on her heels. "How did you fare with your roommate?"

"You brought someone with you?" Tehani asked.

"More like, someone found him," Sydney teased as the tension in the room faded. "Little gecko joined us for dinner last night."

"Haven't seen him since," Theo said. "You offended him when you denied him dessert," he added. "I'll just get to this, shall I?" He wandered off to the circular table in the back corner. The open window provided a beautiful early-afternoon breeze as the sun climbed its way to its zenith for the day.

"You two had dinner?" Tehani circled around and shot Sydney an accusing look. "Cozy."

"The three of us did," Sydney corrected. "And don't read anything into it. I didn't want him to starve on his first night in town. Stop it," she ordered under her breath.

"Stop what?" Tehani's eyes went too-innocent wide.

"You know what. I haven't committed to anything as far as selling Ohana, I promise." Why did she have the feeling she was going to be uttering this statement frequently for the next few weeks?

"Doesn't mean he isn't cute," Tehani observed. "And you're—"

"Not interested." But even as she said it, she knew she was lying. And *cute* seemed wholly inadequate to describe a man who reminded her of those smoldering, unassuming heroes in waiting on the verge of breaking into superstardom. Handsome features framed behind wire-rimmed glasses. What she assumed was thick, slightly wavy dark brown hair he kept perfectly trimmed. To be fair to Tehani's observation, Theo Fairfax was one of the most interesting men she'd met in a long time. Granted, most of the guys she dealt with possessed egos the size of small aircrafts. Theo was different. A fish out of water doing his best to swim despite being woefully unprepared for the dangers of the deep.

But he was also curious, which she found appealing and promising. The idea of challenging him opened up possibilities that could lighten both her heart and mood with considerable ease.

"You're daydreaming," Tehani sang quietly as she tap-tap-tapped on the keyboard again. "I bet I know about who."

Sydney was, by no means, a gambling kind of woman. "How about we focus on booking some new tours? Let's start with the O'Hurleys and those surf lessons tomorrow."

"I'M REALLY SORRY I interrupted you and Tehani," Theo said a while later as he and Sydney made their way into town. The walking paths along the road were wide enough to feel safe and shaded, with a long line of trees that sheltered them from the growing heat. The air, despite a constant breeze, felt as thick today as it had yesterday. Muggy. Funny, he'd never really understood exactly what that word meant before he'd arrived in Hawai'i.

"No apology necessary." Sydney's hands were shoved into the front pocket of her cut-offs.

The oversize tank top she wore was bright yellow and emblazoned with one of the Ohana Odysseys' hibiscus logos. Once again, beneath the wide straps, he caught sight of the thin ties of an orange bikini top, yet it dawned on him he'd yet to see her in the water. Maybe swimsuits were simply a precaution around here? Did one ever spontaneously swim?

Sydney half sighed, half laughed. "Right now I don't care if it's inappropriate to say anything—I'm too darned excited. Tehani's pregnant. I'm going to be an aunt!"

He'd gotten used to her smile, even found himself craving it, but this was the first time the action lit up her entire face. "Your brother's baby." Something inside him shifted and softened. "That's nice to hear."

"Mmm." She nodded and sniffed back

tears as she waved to a young man wheeling past on his bike that contained a front basket full of bright ripe mangoes and bananas. "I had to share with someone, so tag, you're it."

"Happy to oblige." Theo wouldn't wipe that joy off her face in exchange for hitting the mega-millions lottery. Not that he ever played. The prospect of the tax issues alone would give him nightmares. "I'd ask if you like babies, but I don't think your answer matters."

"Not with this baby, it won't," she assured him as she turned around and walked backward. "Do *you* like babies?"

Well, he'd walked right into that one, hadn't he? "I haven't spent a whole lot of time around them, but when I have it's been an adventure. Jack and Jace were four when Beth and Carmen got married, so our side of the family missed the baby stage. I'm not averse to the idea."

She chuckled and shook her head. "Your nephews sound like they should have their own TV show."

"They could definitely qualify as fictional

inspiration. Are you going to tell me where we're headed?"

"Why? You have someplace to be?"

"No. I just like to know where I'm going."

"The impulsivity gene completely missed your DNA, didn't it?" she teased. "In answer to your question, everywhere."

"Oh, good." It was impossible not to fall into her good mood. "You've narrowed it down."

She glanced at her watch and pivoted again. "Make that as much of everywhere as we can hit before three since I've got an afternoon zip-lining group. I've got an extra seat in the van." She looked up at him with fake expectancy. "You want to come?"

"Along for the ride? Sure." He shook his head. "But catapulting my way through nature on a rope is not on my list of ever-want-to-do activities."

"I'm beginning to think excitement and adventure is missing from your genetic gene pool as well."

"Think that all you want." His lips curved into a smile as they stopped to let a middle-aged couple make their way out of the small storefront called Seas & Breeze. "It's absolutely the case. What's this place?"

"Seas & Breeze? Dessert."

"Before lunch?" he asked as she reached for the brass door handle.

"Perish the thought," she chided. "If you did your homework last night, then you'll soon understand the pit stop. Oh, hang on." She let go of the door and buzzed past Theo toward a pair of figures making their way out of the shaded path to the beach. "Aloha, Benji. Aren't you looking dapper today? Is that a new shirt? Snazzy!"

Theo followed, amused, not only by the old man's ear-wide grin but also by the rather high-pitched squeal that erupted from Benji's pet.

The stooped man stopped beside a weathered bench, his neon yellow shirt practically stunning Theo as he joined them. At first glance, Theo thought Benji's shirt pattern was flowers, but he soon saw that it was a mishmash of tropical cartoon birds wearing various hats and other accessories.

Polished military lapel pins dotted the worn sun visor on Benji's head, calling attention to his thinning, almost-nonexistent gray hair. His shoulder-forward walk—make that *shuffle*—almost had Theo diving forward to catch him before he tipped over. Benji's knobby, thin legs looked like two bent tooth-picks sticking out of worn sneakers.

Though all that faded into the background when Theo's gaze landed on the man's pet: a lumbering pot-bellied, dark-spotted pig at the end of a long tattered rope. A pig clad in a matching colorful shirt—sharp collar, tiny white buttons and all.

"Theo Fairfax, this is Benji Tatupu. Benji, Theo's here visiting for a few days."

"Ah, malihini." Benji attempted a kind of wink in Sydney's direction. "Aloha."

Since he'd spent significant time on the internet after dinner last night, Theo had picked up a bit of the language. "Aloha. And yes," he said with a slight nod of his head, "I am most definitely a newcomer." He'd be lying if the impressed surprise in Sydney's gaze didn't give him a bit of a zing.

"Keeping eyes on this girl, are you? Good, good. About time." Benji smiled wryly at Sydney. "Can't believe no one has snatched her up yet."

"That's because I'm waiting on you," Sydney teased.

Benji cackled, and before Theo could shake the befuddlement over a shirt-wearing pig loose, Sydney dropped down and grabbed hold of the pig's face, earning a melodious string of grunts in response. "Hey there, Kahlua. How's my favorite porcine town mascot today? You had a good morning?"

Kahlua squealed, grunted and nodded his head as if providing an answer.

"Tehani told me about your new golf cart," Sydney said in a tone that confirmed what Theo thought about the older man. He definitely wasn't steady on his feet. "Coming up on the heat of the day. Why aren't you driving that beauty around town, Benji?"

"I've been walking up and down Pulelehua Road every day for more than forty years, keiki." Benji's craggy voice carried more affection than annoyance.

"That's why your neighbors chipped in and got you the cart," Sydney said easily as she gave the pig a firm pat on either side of its substantial haunches. "We like seeing you in town, and it's a long walk from your house. What happened? Is something wrong with the cart?"

"Maybe. Don't know." Benji heaved a heavy sigh. "It might have died a few days ago."

Sydney didn't miss a beat. "Did you remember to plug it in the last time you got home with it?"

"Might have forgotten to do that." Benji's wrinkled face scrunched, and he tightened his hold on Kahlua's rope. "I'm never sure what goes where with that thing. Plugs and cords and doohickeys. I don't have time to deal with all that nonsense when I've got two good feet capable of taking me where I want to go."

"Then I guess you don't want me to stop by and get you back up and running." She sighed. "That's okay. I'll just have to give Tehani my leftover macaroni salad." Sydney glanced over her shoulder and grinned at Theo.

"Your special macaroni salad?" It wasn't just Benji who shifted to attention; Kahlua let out an approving squeal that shot right through Theo's ears.

"My mom's recipe," Sydney confirmed. "Same one she made for every luau. And your birthday," she added. "Did you want some?"

Benji looked down and shuffled his feet. "Suppose it wouldn't be bad to have someone hook up that cart and get it running again."

Theo couldn't help but smile. They all knew she'd played the old man perfectly.

"I'll stop by tomorrow morning on my way into the office," she assured him as she rose.

"Best make it after eight," Benji said. "Kahlua's got her training session at sunrise. If we don't get it done early in the day, she's done for later on."

"After eight it is." She stepped back as Benji and Kahlua walked past.

"Tell me something," Theo said as Benji and Kahlua wobbled their way down the sidewalk. "Is it at all possible I saw that pig on the beach this morning, riding a surfboard?"

"You were on the beach?" There was no mistaking the mocking surprise on her face.

He bit the inside of his cheek. "I was on the front porch."

"Right." She clicked her tongue. "Silly

me. Yes, it is entirely possible. Kahlua's in training. Benji's determined she's going to be part of the surfside Christmas pageant this year. This comes after last year, when Kahlua mastered the skateboard," she continued. "The year before that, it was roller skates. You ever see a pig wearing roller skates?"

"No." He felt safe assuming most people hadn't.

"There's video on YouTube. Kahlua has his own channel and fan base. There are T-shirts, ball caps, beer cozies. Local businesses even hire him to make personal appearances at their events. You know, ribbon cuttings, dedications... But he has a really hard time holding on to those giant scissors—"

"Okay, now you're teasing me." It took him long enough to realize it, and his cheeks went hot.

"Yes, I am." She linked her arm through his and held on tight. Behind them, the roll of the ocean provided its comforting white noise even as the warm air breezed by them. "You really need to loosen up, Abacus, or the only thing you'll be going home with is a sunburn."

He shook his head, grateful for the sun beating down to excuse his flushed cheeks. "I can't believe I bought into that."

"Some of it was true, like Benji teaching Kahlua to surf. Back in the day, Benji was quite the champion on these waves. Before my time, of course. And Kahlua is the town's mascot, so he turns up all over the place. Except at luaus. Kahlua does not do luaus."

"Of course not," Theo agreed with a solemn nod, reveling in the casual way she'd grabbed hold of him. "That would be ridiculous. What about Benji?"

"Benji loves luaus. He even brings his ukulele."

Noticing she'd pronounced it "ook-uh-lele," he knocked off another long-held misnomer. "I meant, what's his story? That is what this afternoon's excursion is all about, isn't it? Showing me the people potentially affected by Golden Vistas' buyout?"

"I'm that transparent?"

"Yes." But he wasn't offended. If anything, it was simply confirmation this woman had a heart far too big to be contained in such a feminine frame. She wore it on her sleeve and in those beautiful blue eyes of hers. "Even after such a short acquaintance, I feel comfortable saying you're quite predictable in that area."

"You aren't upset?"

"At your attempt at emotional manipulation? Of course not. It's your job, isn't it? To act as a representative for this town. For GVI, at least." He stopped short of mentioning that he couldn't be upset when it meant spending time with her. That seemed a bit too…forward.

She was, in a word, *entrancing*. Being around her pushed nearly every other thought out of his very organized mind.

He couldn't recall the last time he'd gone this long without thinking or worrying about work. But now that he did think about it, he had to admit that work required him to make the best-possible argument for buying out Ohana Odysseys.

So far, he could see both sides of this business deal easily. GVI could most certainly use an above board, positive addition to their profit line, but until Theo had evidence to the contrary, near as he could tell, Ohana didn't need GVI. Sydney might. But her brother's business? Not so much. Then again, he hadn't exactly witnessed anything business related yet. Maybe he was wrong in his assumptions. All the more reason to continue along with Sydney's plans for him.

Doubt, emotion, connectedness—none of it could enter into his evaluation. It was a numbers game, plain and simple.

"Should I take your resulting silence to mean you're contemplating the information I've provided so far?" Sydney asked.

"More like, I'm weighing my options before I turn the tables on you."

"How about I continue with my plans and aim to get you strapped into a harness?"

His brow furrowed. "Excuse me?"

"Zip-lining, you dolt." She lightly smacked him on the arm. "Honestly."

One thing was for certain: he could easily spend all day listening to Sydney Calvert laughing. "I can assure you, that will never happen. Are you going to tell me about Benji?"

"What would you like to know? He's eighty-seven, and his lineage goes back…"

"He's kanaka." He smiled in pride. "I did some extra homework last night."

"Yes, you did," Sydney said. "And yes, Benji is native Hawaiian. His mother was the first female mayor of Nalani, before Benji was in his mid-seventies, I think. He's responsible for the Hibsicus Bay Resort being built here. In a way, it's his legacy."

"Sounds like a man with more than a few stories."

"The elementary schools and high schools bring him in at least once a year to talk to the students about how Nalani has changed and why it's important to not only be aware of our past but to embrace it moving forward. Up until a few years ago, he headed up an annual field trip to Pearl Harbor and the Arizona. I've often thought of Benji as Nalani's heart walking around town."

Theo could understand that, especially as he witnessed people calling out and waving to Benji and Kahlua as they made their way down the street. "Benji's right. History is important," Theo said quietly. "It doesn't just tell us where we've been but also guides us where we're going."

Sydney nodded. "Exactly. Which is what I'm determined your visit is going to be about. I want you to get a real feel for Nalani. Right down to your soul. Take this area of town, where the beach and the businesses kind of merge? We call this *pukapuka*. Meeting place. In about two and a half hours, straight down that hill—" she pointed a little off to their right "—all two-hundred and four students in school will come streaming down like baby hatchling sea turtles heading for the tide. Most will head for the beach—"

"Shocking."

She arched a brow at him. "And what were your after-school activities? Chess club?"

He chuckled. She really did have him pegged. "For your information, I was my high school's chess champion for three years running."

"Shocking." She grinned. "Okay, so beach—check. Yes, most of them will head there, and others will spread out and hit the snack shops. You think this town looks alive now, just wait a little while. We won't be able to get a foot in the door of this store. Don't worry. We don't have to hit the beach. Yet," she teased as she indicated the store they'd almost walked into. "I wanted to start at Seas & Breeze because it's one of the oldest businesses in Nalani. They've been selling shaved ice and house-made ice cream here since before my parents arrived on the islands." There was no mistaking the pride in her voice. "And right up there, behind that thick grove of coconut trees—that's the Hibiscus Bay Resort."

Ah. Now that was a business he was very familiar with. "That's the resort Tehani's brother runs." He'd seen frequent mention of it in the files he'd been given access to. Five floors of rooms catering to a maximum of two hundred guests at a time. The hotel was on his list of places to explore in the coming days.

"Mano's the managing partner. If you look just a little bit off to the right, that bright white steeple?" Her hand raised higher. "That church was one of the first buildings built in this area. The resort uses it for their weddings, and it's become very popular for destination celebrations. The granddaughter of the artist who made the stained glass windows has her own shop on the other end of town." She indicated the main thoroughfare, currently teeming with buzzy little rental cars and the jingle of bicycle bells. The bike lanes on either side of the narrow two-lane street were just as wide and twice as occupied as the road itself. Nalani, while small, was hopping and bustling but not overly crowded in a tourists-can't-move kind of way.

"You want a souped-up coffee smoothie in the morning? Jolt. Two blocks down and around the corner. It's run by the great-grandchildren of the first mayor of Nalani."

"You weren't kidding about the history tour, were you?" She was proving her point. Everything—and every*one*, it seemed—was connected.

"As you predicted, I'm making a point." She didn't give any indication of stopping. "Going on, the main sundry and gift shop at the far end of Pulelehua—"

"That's this main road, right?"

"Yes. It's the Hawaiian word for *butterfly.* Always growing and transforming. There's a small grove that is teeming with various species. I'll show you that later, if you want. For your shopping needs, Luanda's is our local version of an ABC Store."

"Okay, *that* I know. Those are convenience shops that are all over the islands." Shops that sold everything from T-shirts, swimsuits and sunglasses; to touristy gifts like every kind of macadamia nut imaginable, island-produced sea salt and bags of island coffee.

"Is that code for 'I don't need to go on'?"

"You can if you want, but I get your point. You're showing me there's more to this town than a tour business, resort and a profit margin."

"Every one of these businesses has a story. The people who own and run them have stories, and those stories are directly tied to traditions and heritage. Nalani isn't a place where some big-box store comes in and makes a killing. The locals have built everything you see. When the Blue Moon Bar & Grill burned down six years ago, there wasn't any question about it getting rebuilt. The entire town took it on and, until it was ready to open again, other restaurants opened their kitchens so they could keep cooking take-away meals for their customers. We've got three different food trucks now that toddle around because of that. And as a result, we've got a food-delivery network, something that keeps our elder folks fed and checked on." She faced him, tilted her head as if weighing him up. "I need for Golden Vistas to see all of this, Theo. I can trust you, can't I? To make certain they do? If I'm even going to consider accepting their offer, I need to know all of this, these people, matter. That they'll continue to matter if I decide to move on."

He didn't like the uneasy sensation rolling through his stomach. A feeling that had him skirting the edge of truth. "I have no trouble promising I will put it all into my report and recommendation. They'll know what they're investing in. That this isn't just about buying one business—it's about investing in a community. Is that enough?"

"I guess we'll see, won't we?"

Yes, they would. "One thing I'm definitely going to warn them about is the heat." He tucked a finger into the collar of his shirt. "How do you-all deal with this every day?"

"This what? The weather?" She raised her arms and lifted her face to the sun. "This is glorious. And for the record, today is cool when compared to what it'll be in a few weeks. You're an AC junkie, aren't you, Abacus?"

Her teasing nickname was growing on him. "I do prefer not to sweat excessively."

"Lunch should take care of that." She stopped, pulled him to a stop when he started to head back to the street. "I was going to suggest Off the Hook. They specialize in personalized poke bowls. You know what it is?"

"I've eaten my weight in sushi over the years." *Well, what do you know?* He'd surprised her again. This was getting fun. "Off the Hook definitely sounds up my alley."

"Chances are, your lunch was swimming in the ocean just a few hours ago. But first, I've got a quick history lesson for you. Here we go." She tugged him back to the door of Seas & Breeze, a brightly painted seascape of an interior that boasted familiar glass cases filled with colorful bins of custom local ice creams and shaved ice flavors, plus tiki-style bamboo tables and chairs, most of which were filled with eager customers.

"Sydney, aloha!" A thirty-something woman, whose head barely rose above the line of the glass cases, popped up on her toes, a dripping ice-cream scoop clutched like a torch in one hand. "I thought you'd sworn us off for at least five pounds."

"Aloha, Ema! Just dropped by to share some of our history with my new friend.

Unless you've got a batch of lehua-honey ice cream hidden somewhere."

"Freshly made this morning with hibiscus honey," the woman confirmed.

"Awesome," Sydney said. "Plan on a return visit after lunch," she told Theo. "Here's what I wanted you to see." Still clutching his arm, she led him to the far wall, where the chairs and tables were away from the wall covered with dozens of framed photographs—some in bold, contemporary color; others in time-stopping black and white.

While none of the faces were familiar to him—faces that represented decades of Nalani residents, families, and business owners—their expressions were indicative of pride and affection and lives well lived. *This is important to her*, he thought as he pulled free of her hold and slowly, carefully examined each and every image.

Children's birthday parties, holiday celebrations, a ribbon-cutting ceremony—minus any pigs—for a remodeled Seas & Breeze from fifteen years before. There was a certificate from the mayor and another from the governor, honoring Nalani for its dedication to the protection and promotion of the islands. He found himself drawn closer to a photo from the national surfing championship of 1967, where a very familiar—albeit it young—Benji Tatupu stood proudly beside his board with his hand over his heart. He could almost, if he let himself, hear the sounds of days gone past in this one display of town history.

"You've made your point, Sydney." Every one of these images, thanks to his eidetic memory and Sydney's determination to show them off, would go with him from here. He might not understand or be comfortable with the island's way of life, but he could certainly accept that this, and other small towns like it, deserved to be paid attention to and heard moving forward. "Thank you. For sharing this with me."

"Well, the plan is to share a lot more, if you're up for it." She was standing behind him, arms folded over her chest as she rocked back on her heels. "I'm sure Tehani will have your excursion itinerary set up by the time we get back—but for right now, it might be best if we got lunch. Otherwise, I'm going to dive face-first into a vat of honey ice cream. Aloha, Ema," she called out as she led him through the shop door.

## CHAPTER SIX

"OKAY, NO ONE can feel bad with a big cone of shave ice in their hand," Sydney chided Theo post-lunch as they exited Seas & Breeze for the second time that day, only this visit was punctuated by an early crowd of students clamoring for an afterschool treat.

As promised, after a fresh poke bowl and another trip down Nalani's memory lane thanks to Off the Hook's entryway, they'd taken a quick detour around Hibiscus Bay Resort before hitting the creamery again for dessert. Dessert Sydney was currently scarfing down so she wouldn't be late getting back to Ohana Odysseys.

"What's wrong?"

"Nothing. That's the problem." Theo bit a tooth-freezing chunk out of his sweetened coconut milk-soaked ice. "Up until now I was convinced San Francisco had the best sushi I'd ever eaten. Thanks for blowing that theory out of the water. I think Nalani's ruined me for it now."

"Always happy and willing to destroy preconceptions and opinions." She slurped up the dripping sweet, floral cream before it flowed over the back of her hand. "Sorry to be in a rush, but I've got that group at three—"

"I'm going to decline your earlier offer to join you," he said.

"Boy, this day is just full of surprises. Although I think I should warn you, I'm going to get you on that zip line at least once before you go home." She frowned at the odd pang in her chest. She'd enjoyed spending time with Theo Fairfax today. More than she'd hoped to. Far more than she'd expected.

The man had a great—if not subdued—sense of humor, which, as far as she was concerned, placed him in the top-five percentile of eligible and appealing men. He was easy to be around, be with; and while he was superintelligent and quick to pick up on things, he didn't lord it over anyone. The fact that he appeared genuinely curious about Nalani only added to his likability quotient.

Not that she needed that quotient to be

high. Theo Fairfax had his life on the mainland, and she had hers. Or at least, she would in a few months. There wasn't anything about their lives that meshed.

Theo had only been here a little more than a day, and already she had trouble imagining walking down Pulelehua Road without him by her side. Well. She took a big bite of her ice cream and cringed from the sinus pain that sliced through her head. She had to get that out of her mind immediately, didn't she?

She and Theo Fairfax were as polar opposite as two people could get. The very idea they could be anything other than friends...

"What do you think?"

"Huh?" Sydney blinked against the sun before shifting her focus back to Theo. "I'm sorry. I guess my mind wandered."

"I bet I can guess where."

"Yeah?" She choked and covered her mouth when she coughed. "You think?"

"Out there." He inclined his head to the ocean peeking out between the thick tree trunks lining the road back up the hill to Ohana. "I've been wondering why you've worn a swimsuit every time I've seen you, but I've yet to see you go near the water. Are bathing suits just a precaution around here?"

Funny. She'd never thought about her automatic routine in the morning. Putting a bikini on under her clothes wasn't just her habit; it made sense. "Well, my appointed duties these days involve a man with a severe aversion to aquatic activities," she teased. "The water, the beach—they aren't your thing, either?"

"No. But they're yours."

"They were Remy's." For the first time in weeks, speaking her brother's name didn't bring that sharp pain of grief. "I do okay with the water, and you're right—I'm itching to dive in and probably will by the end of today. I belong up there." She speared her ice-cream cone into the sky. "I've never been able to find the words to describe the utter peace and fulfillment being in the sky brings me." It was so much easier to show than it was to tell.

"I find it hard to believe you're more comfortable anywhere else than how you are."

"Well, believe it." But even to herself, she sounded a bit overenthusiastic. "Back in South

Carolina, every once in a while I head out to Kiawah Island in the Outer Banks. I can't tell you how many times I've extended a flight just so I can buzz the shoreline and try to graze the tide as it's coming in off the ocean." It was as close to home as she could get out there. "As anxious as I feel about getting back into the water, that's nothing compared to the desperation I feel to climb into the cockpit and take off."

"I'd almost pay to see that."

She eyed him before taking another bite out of her cone. The floral tinted honey danced on her tongue. "You don't have to pay to see it, you know. You want to come up with me? Just say the word."

As expected, he did not say the word.

He turned and faced her. "I have to admit, hearing you describe what flying means to you makes me curious."

"Curiosity is a good thing."

"Yes, it is," he agreed. "It's an excellent thing to embrace at times."

"Feel free to embrace it anytime." The pressure of anticipation pressed in on her, and her excitement clicked in. "I can show you as much of the island as a tank of gas will allow."

"Funny. It's not flying I'm currently contemplating embracing," he said as if reasoning out a particularly troublesome equation. "Although rational thought would require accepting that your tours would be a big part of what GVI would be investing in."

"Ah, the logical rationale has never sounded so sweet." She patted a hand against her heart. "Bet you didn't have this on your bucket list."

"I don't have a bucket list," Theo said as they resumed their walk.

"I'm sorry?" She tapped the side of her ear as if she'd lost her hearing. "I've never met anyone without a bucket list."

"There's nothing I've wanted to do that I haven't done." He shrugged. "Although I suppose, now that I think about it, there's never really been anything I've wanted to do that required particular planning."

"Oh, Abacus." She shook her head and laughed to herself. "You've never stepped out of your comfort zone, have you?"

"It's called a *comfort zone* for a reason." He tipped his paper cone upside down and emptied it into his mouth before dumping it into a recycling receptacle on the side of the street.

"See, you say things like this and my brain just…" She flicked out one hand's fingers as if they'd exploded. "Isn't there anything that gets your pulse racing? Something exciting and unexpected that you just want to, I don't know, grab hold and not let go of?"

"Now that you mention it, one thing does come to mind."

As she passed him, he reached out and caught her arm and spun her back into him. Her mouth dropped open as he looked down at her, those amazing, sexy, dark eyes of his assessing her. Eyes that shifted to amusement as he lowered his head and kissed her.

It was, Sydney thought as the icy sweetness of his lips captured hers, a bit of a surprise. To be kissed in a way that made her wonder if she'd ever been kissed before. To feel the surprising and spine-tingling realization rocketing through her that a man like him could kiss like this. Softly, thoroughly, purposefully, as if every single millisecond was nicely calculated and planned out.

She melted faster than the ice cream dripping down her arm. His hands moved around to the base of her spine, gently pressed there, and she moaned into his mouth as he angled his head, taking all that she offered before ending the kiss. He pressed his lips together and, without thinking, she mirrored his action, tasting the sweet coconut of his dessert blend with hers.

"Interesting." He inclined his head, pressed a quick kiss to the tip of her nose. "I have to admit, I'm now convinced there's something to be said for impulsivity after all. So." He stepped back but caught her when she stumbled to keep her balance. "We both need to go back to work. Have fun zip-lining, Sydney."

"Yeah," she finally said, but he was already out of earshot. She turned, blinking at his back, then smiled to herself when he glanced over his shoulder and waved.

SUNDAY MORNING BLOOMED bright and warm as Theo emerged from the bedroom and headed straight for the coffee. With sunlight streaming through the slats of the shutters, he came up short and froze a few steps from the counter. He stared, only half-surprised at the sight of the familiar glittery green lizard poking his head up on the other side of the partially filled fruit bowl.

"All right, my little green friend," he said after a long moment. "You and I are going to have to get the rules of the house settled."

The lizard blinked and angled his head up when Theo clicked on the light. But he didn't move or scamper away. If anything, he seemed to increase his attention on the person who could fulfill the desire no doubt circling inside his teeny-tiny brain. "You hungry?"

One firm eye blink.

"I can't believe I'm talking to a lizard." He shook his head as the sound of his cell phone vibrating caught his attention. "Hold that thought." Theo returned to the bedroom and, after seeing the name on the screen, answered. "Hey, Beth."

His sister's voice carried across the ocean. "Hey, yourself. I left a few messages but figured I'd try again. How's the business trip?"

"Good. It's good, actually." Words clearly

weren't his forte this morning. After spending yesterday with Ohana's horticulture expert, Daphne Mercer, hiking his way through a bamboo forest, he found he was missing the distracting presence of one Sydney Calvert. It unsettled him, the way she kept popping into his thoughts and, in an effort to get himself back on professional track, he resisted the temptation to stop by Ohana Odysseys' office to ask Sydney to dinner before he headed back to the cottage—alone. Now, regretting his reasoned decision—and the two beers he'd allowed himself before turning in early—he headed back into the kitchen and, seeing his guest had maneuvered around to the front of the fruit bowl and had one skinny little foot planted on top of a ripe mango, surrendered to one of the tiniest forces on the planet. "Hang on. I need to feed my guest. Going to put you on speaker." He tapped the speaker icon, set the phone down and retrieved a mango pitter from the drawer.

"A guest?" Beth's voice raised a good two octaves. "Good heavens, Theo, don't let me interrupt—"

"Not that kind of guest." But there she was again, Sydney Calvert, bursting straight into his mind. "This is the four-legged kind of visitor who has taken to visiting me at various times. Haven't you, little guy?"

He lined the pitter over the mango and pushed down. He could smell the fresh, ripe fruit the second the flesh was exposed. So could the lizard, who inched just a bit closer and raised his nose. "Hang on there, Noodles." Theo cut a few tiny pieces and set them on the far side of the counter, drawing the lizard away from any sharp implements and, more importantly, the coffee machine.

"You named a dog Noodles?" Beth asked.

"Of course not," Theo said as he filled the filter with the last of the ground coffee and then the pot with water. "Noodles is a gold-speckled gecko with a penchant for saimin and, I'm guessing, ramen. He came with the rental," he explained. "I say he's about five inches long. Eyes are almost as big as his head and… Well, hang on." He wiped his hands, picked up his phone, took a quick picture and sent it.

"Aw," Beth sighed. "How cute is he? Question—who are you, and what have you done with my brother? You despise reptiles."

As if he'd comprehended the accusation, Noodles swung around and, with half a chunk of mango hanging out of his mouth, gave Theo an accusing look of utter disbelief.

Theo couldn't help it. He laughed. "I may have been cured of that particular aversion. But that doesn't mean I'm ready to embrace Ellery." Theo practically shuddered at the thought of his nephew's two-year-old gopher snake. "Chew your food, Noodles."

"You're beginning to worry me, little brother," Beth said. "But I actually feel safe in asking how you like Hawai'i."

"I like it a lot, actually." Except for the sand, which, despite him not venturing onto the beach, still got everywhere. And the sun, which had deposited a good second-degree burn on the back of his neck and forearms. And the heat… He was never going to get used to the temperature or the humidity, was he? And don't get him started on the sore muscles and backside he had after a ninety-minute valley trek on horseback.

His day of fun and frolic with two of Sydney's tour guides had proved to be far more adventurous—and painful—than he was capable of enjoying. At least, not without Sydney. Despite his personal issues and failings, he had to admit, Ohana Odysseys definitely provided an excellent day of activities for him that had, in actuality, exceeded his expectations. "You and Carmen should come out here to Nalani on your next vacation. I think the boys would like it."

"Bringing the boys would not make it a vacation," Beth said. "And I think it'll be a while before we're traveling. That's one of the reasons I'm calling. The in vitro took. Carmen's pregnant."

"Beth." He abandoned his sentry duty at the coffee machine and returned to the phone. "Congratulations! That's great news."

"It really is," Beth gushed. "We only had enough money for one shot, but it looks like it took. Baby's due mid-September."

"I'll make plans to fly up shortly thereafter."

"You will?"

"Certainly, I will." He didn't quite understand the shock in her voice. "I know how much you two have been wanting to have another baby. And I was recently reminded I don't have much experience with them." It was time he fixed that.

"Okay, now I'm convinced you've been replaced by a pod-person. How on earth would you be reminded... Oh." Her voice lightened, and he swore he heard his sister giggle. "Oh, you've met someone, haven't you? Someone of the two-legged, two—"

"I'm capable of being reminded of things without it being romantically triggered," Theo told her. "But okay, yeah. The woman who owns the business I'm evaluating—"

"He's evaluating a woman's business!" His sister's muffled shout told him she was sharing the conversation with her wife. "No, seriously, that's what he said! Hang on, I'll put him on speaker. Carmen's on with you and Noodles."

"The woman's name is Noodles?" The second disbelieving female voice carried more of an elegant lilt than his sister's. "Hi there, Theo."

"Hi, Carmen. And no, the lizard is named

Noodles." At least, he was now. "The woman's name is Sydney Calvert. She owns a local tour company and works as a pilot."

"Wow. A pilot? As in, planes and helicopters?"

"Those are what pilots fly, yes." Theo shook his head at his sister's question. "She's just been showing me around the island. Making sure I know everything the town has to offer GVI."

"Uh-huh." Carmen's skeptical comment had him wishing he'd kept his mouth shut. "How pretty is she?"

*Stunning. Gorgeous. Amazing.* "She's not bad."

Carmen and Beth giggled. "That's what you called Priscilla Underton back in high school," Beth reminded him. "Didn't she end up as a supermodel?"

"For a while," Theo admitted, thinking back to his former classmate on the cover of one of the hottest swimsuit issues in the magazine world. Sydney could easily make that same cover. Heck, she *should* make a cover. Funny how he believed that so completely, considering he had yet to see her in just her bikini. Funny how he was determined to change that. "Carmen, you feeling okay?"

"I'm feeling great, thank you," his sister-in-law assured him. "Makes me think it's a girl since I was sick for months with the boys."

"He's going to come up when the baby's born," Beth said as if this was a grand pronouncement from on high.

"He is? You are?"

"Maybe before," Theo said. Maybe it was the Nalani influence, but he had a strong desire to reconnect with his family. "If you can put up with me. We'll figure out a time once I'm back home and on the other side of this trip."

"Maybe you'll bring Sydney with you?" Beth asked.

"I doubt it," he said. "She's locked in here for a while, and after that, she's heading back to South Carolina. She's opening a flight school back there."

"Oh. That's too bad. For you," Beth said quickly. "Not for her. She sounds amazing."

"Yeah," Theo said without hesitation. "She kind of is. Okay, I've got grocery shopping to do today, and I want to get it done before the heat hits. Anything else you need to tell me?"

"Nope. I think I've got all the information I need, thanks," Beth said, in a way that made Theo roll his eyes. "You enjoy the rest of your trip to paradise, Theo. We'll talk when you get back. Bye."

"Bye, Theo!"

Theo clicked off just as the coffeepot finished filling. He poured himself a mug and watched Noodles gobble down his last piece of mango before scampering down the side of the cabinets and, after Theo walked over and opened the sliding door to the side of the patio, disappeared outside.

Despite his continued aversion to the muggy mornings, Theo wandered onto the porch and sipped his coffee while the morning beachgoers drifted past. He waved to a few familiar faces who, after only a few days on the island, felt almost like friends. Of course, Sydney had been very careful not to let word of what he was really doing here leak out. He understood why. It was a close-knit community that was partially financially reliant on the business Ohana Odysseys brought in. Hearing she was considering selling could cause a panic or worse—fear. Theo didn't want that any more than Sydney did.

He was about to go back into the house when a gray-haired woman popped up around the corner, her wide dark eyes peering at him as if he were caught under a magnifying glass. He hadn't seen her before. He would have remembered the almost-wild hair and worn, oversize orange-and-gold-flowered dress that hung all the way to her bare feet.

"Hello." He smiled, walked over and noticed her eyes narrowed in suspicion. "Can I help you with something?"

"I heard you went up to Pau-ole Falls yesterday," the woman said. "You come back alone?"

"Ah." Theo frowned. "I was on a tour with some other visitors. Daphne took us—"

She ducked down, looked under the house. "Sometimes the *menehune* hitch a ride back. They're tricky. Sneaky." She tilted her head up. "They like fooling with people. Especially—"

"Especially malihini?" Theo finished.

She grinned, the light in her eyes sparking. "You're smart, aren't you?"

"By some standards," Theo said. "Would you like some coffee?"

"No, thank you." She stood up, straightened her dress. "I need to keep up my search. If they get a hold, they're hard to get back to the falls."

"It was nice to meet you," he called out after her, earning a distracted wave in response.

"Sydney was right," a male voice echoed around the corner of the porch before a man stepped into sight. "You have a natural way with people. Mano Iokepa." He walked forward, hand outstretched. As Theo shook it, he noticed the extensive tattoo work on both the larger man's arms. He shared the same dark, glistening skin as his sister, Tehani, as well as the same eyes and shiny dark hair. "I see you met Haki, our local *menehune* hunter."

"Is that what she is?" Theo stepped to the side so he could keep an eye on the older woman as she made her way down the beach.

"Is that an official Nalani job? Hunting trickster creatures that live in the forest?"

"It is hers," Mano said. "She's been looking for the little buggers for as long as I can remember. Anything goes wrong in Nalani, they're her first suspects."

"Are they, um, real?"

"The *menehune*?" Mano didn't blink. "It's never been proven that they aren't, and I'm not about to question the possibility. I'm headed into town for breakfast. Care to join?"

"Ah, sure." Why did Theo get the idea this was more than a casual invitation? "Or if you have something you need to ask me, you could just ask."

Tension Theo hadn't realized was on Mano's face now eased. "Straightforward. I like that. Okay, I want to talk to you about Golden Vistas' interest in Ohana Odysseys."

Theo nodded. "Thought as much. I'm happy to tell you what I can but on one condition."

"What's that?"

"You show me where I can get the best *loco moco* in Nalani."

"Yeah? You a fan?"

"More like, curious," Theo admitted. "Sydney mentioned it's a must-try while I'm here." And he was definitely ticking off a lot of those boxes.

"All right, man. You want it, you got it."

"Great." At Mano's nod, Theo toasted him with his mug. "Give me a few minutes."

"You've got to be kidding me," Sydney groaned as she sagged over her desk and closed her eyes. "Both tours canceled? Seriously?" She kept her pathetic whining low so Kiri and Daphne wouldn't overhear. The two were organizing the supply room before their own classes and tours resumed for the day.

"On the bright side, it's not because of us," Tehani said quietly. "Heat stroke took out one group, and the other, well…" She sat on the edge of Sydney's desk. "Let's just say they tapped out on Shalvi's local brew about half a keg in. Word around town is the lot of them had to be poured into Hori's cab just to make it three blocks."

"Still—"

"Be grateful they didn't go up in the air

with you this morning," Tehani advised. "Otherwise, you'd have a right mess on your hands."

Sydney held up one finger. "Point to you, T."

"And yet another silver lining, neither protested paying the last-minute twenty percent cancellation fee, and your schedule just opened up for the day."

"Mmm." Sydney squeezed her eyes shut. She didn't want her schedule open. She wanted—no, she *needed*—to be busy. Otherwise, she was going to spend entirely too much time dwelling on that kiss sexy brainiac Theo Fairfax had planted on her two days ago.

Two days. How was she still thinking about that kiss two blooming days later? She raised her head, rested her chin in her hand. "Nothing else on the books for me to help with?"

"Nope." Tehani sounded entirely too cheerful. "The sunrise fishing tour is already back. Kiri's got a large class coming up in about a half hour—right, Kiri?"

"Fifteen newbies." Kiri poked his head out of the supply-room door.

"I can help," Sydney offered.

"Ah, no, thanks," Kiri said and disappeared back inside. "I've got it!"

Sydney pouted. "That wasn't discouraging at all."

"You haven't been in the water in weeks," Tehani reminded her. "You get back on the board, you show him you're up to riding those waves again and he'll—"

Sydney laughed. "No, he won't. Kiri's standards are way too high for me to meet."

"True," Tehani agreed.

"Hey, Daph?" Sydney called out. "What about you?"

Daphne, long red hair tied back in a braid down her back, clasped a collection bucket in one hand. "What about me, what?"

"You have anything I can assist with?"

"Oh." Daphne straightened to her full five-foot-ten-inch height. "Oh, well, I suppose—"

"She's got an overnight tour up to Pahoa. Botanical students from UH Hilo," Tehani said. "Eight of them. Do you really want to spend the day playing Pick the Plants with flower nerds?"

"Hey!" Daphne scowled for a moment,

then shrugged. "Okay, fair. But we can be fun."

"Playing 'What's the Latin Name for That Leaf?' does not constitute fun," Tehani said. "Trust me on this," she whispered to a laughing Sydney.

"You have your fun, I have mine," Daphne pushed her glasses higher up her nose. "Your loss."

"It's really not," Tehani assured Sydney. "If you want, I can call up to the resort and see if they have any guests at the hotel who want a discount chopper tour? Or, better yet, go out yourself. Nothing stopping you from taking some you-time."

"Nah." Sydney sighed. "That's not financially responsible." Better they end up ahead for the day than in the red because she needed to get some air around her. That said, she'd been craving time in the sky. So much so, she'd woken up two hours earlier than necessary and gotten the bird ready to go. Not that she'd slept that well before then. Mr. Numbers Man, Theo Fairfax, was proving to be quite the slumbering distraction. What was wrong with her? The man was… Never mind what the man was. The man lived a completely different life from what she did, in a completely different city. And the last thing she needed to add to her already complicated life was an impulsive fling that she had no doubt would leave her wanting more.

"I'll take this as a sign and get some surfing time in." Sydney shoved herself to her feet and, after touching Tehani's arm as she passed, squeezed her way into the supply room to retrieve one of the boards Kiri had set aside. "I'll go catch some waves."

"Yeah?" Kiri's eyes went wide. "You sure you remember how?"

"Watch it," Sydney warned, jokingly, as she smoothed her hand over the purple-striped fiberglass board. "Respect your employer."

"And my elder," Kiri added at Sydney's warning smirk. "Kidding. Just kidding." Kiri, laughing, held up both hands in surrender. "You're not there. Yet."

"Getting there, though," Tehani said as Sydney hefted the board under one arm, making her way to the door. "I don't have Theo booked for anything today."

"No?" Sydney found herself both relieved and disappointed she wouldn't see him hanging around the office today. She liked watching him attempt to adjust to Tehani's whiplash tour plans for him.

"I think I wore him out yesterday. A rain forest hike with Daphne, then Kiri and Wyatt gave him a tour of the catamaran. And no, before you ask, they did not go out. Apparently, Theo got seasick while they were still docked."

"Of course he did." *Poor guy*, Sydney thought. "He really didn't do well in the elements at all, did he?"

"The horseback riding in the valley probably did him in. But I bet he's feeling better this morning. Maybe you can drop by the hut and—"

"And what?" Sydney stopped at the door.

"I don't know. Maybe show him your board?"

Sydney rolled her eyes. "Don't you have a breakfast to throw up?"

"Way ahead of you. Hours ahead of you."

Tehani waved her off. "Go take the day off. If anything comes up, I'll call, but we've got a full schedule already handled."

"Yeah, okay." Hours alone on the waves. Yeah, that should be just what her overactive imagination needed. She made her way down the stairs and headed into town, her flip-flops flapping against the cement.

While Hawai'i was partially known for its laid-back lifestyle and focus on the surrounding beauty and wonders of nature, there was something special about Sundays. Hovering in between the frantic activity-laden Saturdays and lamented Mondays when work shifted up the priority list, Sundays offered a promising respite from schedules, obligations and stress.

It was a blessing, Sydney reminded herself as she waved to passersby and shop owners washing their storefront windows, a true blessing to have a reliable staff who liked their jobs and a business that, at this point—at least, thanks to Tehani—ran itself. Or ran well enough to afford her the luxury of not only a walk down to the beach but also time in the water.

"Morning, Maru!" She detoured toward the makeshift portable market stand. The old woman was sitting in an old wooden rocking chair that had been painted in bright, crooked, colorful flowers that matched the bright pink hibiscus flowers nestled in her white hair. "Testing out a new location this morning, Auntie?"

"Gonna storm today." Maru turned her sun-kissed, wrinkled face to the sky. "Figured better to be safe than sorry."

"Storm? You sure?" Sydney tilted her head up. Through the leaves of the gently swaying palms, she saw only a clear blue sky. A sky that even now continued to call to her. "I don't know about that."

"I do." Maru pushed back and rocked faster, casting an approving look at the young woman behind the stand with her. "Lani, be careful not to squish—"

"The haupia malasadas. Pick them up gently, I know, Tutu."

Sydney could hear the restrained irritation in the teenager's voice, but it wasn't reflected on her pretty round face when she shot Maru an affectionate smile. Lani waggled her gloved fingers before turning back to the growing line of customers that would have the stand selling out of the various flavored doughnuts in no time. With almost a dozen varieties ranging from classic cinnamon-sugar to the latest tropical combination of mango-passion fruit custard, Maru continued to expand her malasada vision with every new summer season.

"Saw your Theo a few minutes ago, heading to the Hut-Hut." Maru indicated toward one of the local hole-in-the-wall eateries down on the beach.

"He's not *my* Theo," Sydney protested, only to be on the receiving end of a disbelieving look from both grandmother and granddaughter.

"Not what I've heard," Maru chided, her gnarled fingers gripping the arms of her chair. "But what do I know? I'm just an old woman."

"You know a lot, Auntie," Sydney assured her even as she inwardly cringed. "Just maybe not everything." *Eesh*. The last thing she needed was for word to get around that she and Theo were an item. It would make selling Ohana Odysseys—if she *did* sell—seem a bit…off. She needed everything to be above-board from here on. She certainly didn't want anyone to think she'd been charmed into selling. That wouldn't be good for anyone involved.

"Lani, give one of those to Sydney—"

"Oh, no." Sydney backed up, tempted to hoist her surfboard in front of her for protection. "I've eaten my body weight in those since I've been back. Maybe tomorrow," she added at Maru's frown. "Mahalo." She touched a hand to her heart and gave them both a quick wave before turning toward the path where, a few days before, she and Theo had encountered Benji and Kahlua. Instead of stopping by the bench this time, she dipped under the shade of the threes before stepping into the sunshine of the morning.

The morning air was filled with contradictory sensations. There was the chill of the morning battling against the rising sun's emerging rays, but there was also the promise of warmth pressing in from behind, kissing the breeze before the humidity took hold. While she wasn't one to argue with Maru, she didn't see a cloud in the sky, which would be necessary for the punch-packing rain the old woman had predicted.

Beachgoers were currently limited to some of the locals; the tourists were probably still noshing on breakfast back at the resort or sleeping in. Longing for the second cup of coffee she'd denied herself earlier, Sydney staked her board in the sand and kicked off her flip-flops before she shimmied out of her jeans shorts and pulled her sage green tank over her head. She lifted her face to the warmth, pulled her hair free of the ponytail she'd knotted this morning and shook her head back. The deep breath she took calmed nerves she'd been fighting against for what seemed like ages.

Still lamenting being stuck on the ground, she pushed her bare feet deeper into the warming sand. Tehani was right: she should have just taken the chopper and flown. She owned the machine; she should be able to use it as much as she wanted, but she also needed to be responsible. The chopper was a business asset, one she could get away with using for search-and-rescues, but personal meditation? That didn't make much sense.

Especially when her company was being financially evaluated. She'd have to think on that more.

Nearby, the back patio of Hawaiian Hut-Hut was teeming with breakfast customers who carried their trays laden with food into the semi-protected overhang that jutted out onto the beach. If she let herself, she could smell the familiar aromas of frying hamburger patties and eggs. The takeout-only restaurant was as close to fast food as they got in Nalani. Thinking of the menu that served everything from loco moco to various musubis to leftover malasadas from Maru's cart, she realized she needed to get into the water before she abandoned the idea altogether in favor of upping her caloric intake.

She bent down and strapped the board's leash around her right ankle before she pulled it out of the sand and headed to the water. The second her feet hit the tide, the knots inside of her loosened. Well, if she couldn't get into the air, this was definitely the next-best thing.

She waded out, pushing through the water until she got waist high; then, pulling the board in front of her and lowering it onto the surface, she waited for the next wave and got on.

"Have to admit," Mano said as he polished off the last of his sushi rice topped with brown gravy, "I think their loco moco's gotten better since I last ate here."

"Uh-huh." Breakfast forgotten, Theo found himself utterly transfixed by the sight in front of him. A sight he'd been wishing to see for the better part of his visit. A sight that had not, in any way, disappointed. Seeing Sydney stepping into the water as if she belonged there—in a turquoise bikini that hadn't come close to equaling his dreams—exceeded each and every thought he'd ever had.

How did she do that? Just paddle out, arms stretched and reaching and pulling her deeper and farther into the ocean's tide? Unfamiliar anxiety and excitement coiled in his stomach as she dipped down over one wave, only to turn, shift and somehow plant her feet firmly on her board before she held out her arms as if ready to take flight.

Out of the corner of his eye, Theo saw Mano turn in his chair. But Theo didn't remain in his when Sydney's board was caught from behind, pushed up in a way that sent her toppling face-first right into the water.

"Easy there," Mano said with a chuckle. "She's fine. Woman can swim like a fish. Don't worry."

"She can?" Theo remained on his feet, hands gripping the railing of the crowded back patio until he saw her surface, shake her hair back and grab her board to try again. "She didn't give that impression."

"There isn't an element on these islands the Calvert siblings couldn't conquer." Mano wiped his mouth and tossed his napkin into his empty cardboard container. Sitting back, he clasped his hand around the oversize paper cup containing enough coffee to supply a small army. "She'll need time to get her fins back in place, but she'll always surface."

Theo sat back down and looked at his nearly finished breakfast. "That meal should not have been that good." It didn't make any sense to him. Sushi rice, a hamburger patty topped with a thick, flavorful brown gravy and a runny fried egg. But it made sense to his palate, that was for sure. He also didn't anticipate being hungry for at least a week. "Have I eased your mind about Golden Vistas?" Theo couldn't help it.

He shifted his chair around so he could keep an eye on Sydney. This time she stayed up long enough to get to the shore, only to jump off, grab her board and head out once more.

"Honestly?" Mano tapped his other hand on the top of the tiled table. "Not really. When Tehani told me about the offer to buy Ohana Odysseys, I did a little digging. Not particularly impressed with what I've found."

"Oh?" Taken by surprise, Theo did his best to focus on the conversation. Mano's comment felt a bit like a knife swipe. Not harsh enough to cause permanent damage, but deep enough to draw blood. "What's bothering you?"

"From what I could tell, most of the businesses they've bought up no longer exist. They gobbled them up, broke them up and left the debris to the wind. And I'm not only referring to the businesses. I'm also thinking about the small towns they inhabited." Mano pinned him with a stare. "That's not exactly faith inducing."

"That all happened years ago," Theo explained. "Before I started working there, actually. I've been assured they've learned from their past mistakes."

"And now they're going to do things differently," Mano said, with more than a hint of skepticism in his voice.

"Well, they're going to do things *better*, at least." Theo didn't know how to ease the man's mind about the possible buyout, but he did know he couldn't afford to alienate Mano Iokepa, either. "There's an entirely new team leading this up," he explained. "They want to expand, to rebuild their brand, and they believe Ohana Odysseys is a good start. They made the offer because they believe in what Remy built." In what Sydney continued to maintain.

"Did they, now?" Mano smirked and drank some of his coffee. "Or did they see an opportunity to make inroads in a smaller bit of the islands after not being able to gain a foothold on O'ahu or Maui?"

"I'm sorry?" Theo blinked. "What foothold?"

Mano arched a brow. "I had the feeling you're a keep-your-head-down kind of man, Theo. I hope this is you proving that to be true. Granted, I haven't known you for more than a minute, but Sydney's attention toward you warrants acceptance that you are, at your core, a decent man."

"I like to think so." Especially where Sydney was concerned.

"Then I think you should know, Ohana Odysseys isn't the first business in Nalani GVI has offered to buy out."

Theo stared and tried in vain to ignore the sinking sensation in his stomach. "It's not?"

"It is not." Mano shifted in his chair, rested his substantial arms on the table and lowered his voice. "It's not widely known, since residents would not be happy to hear we're being targeted for a buyout." He paused, as if choosing his words carefully. "Eighteen months ago they made a substantial offer to me and my business partners. And by *sub-*

*stantial*, I mean it took a convening of the board of directors to reject the offer."

Theo frowned. He hadn't come across any such offer. How was that even possible when he had complete access to GVI's accounts?

Because accounts were solid ins and outs—payouts and income. If a deal hadn't been struck, then there would be no reason for him to have seen anything.

"You didn't sell, obviously," Theo said.

"We did not. And as long as I'm a managing partner, we will not. I didn't start parking cars at Hibiscus Bay at sixteen and work my way up to partner only to sell out to a mainland company that is clueless about the importance of this place and what it means to the people who live here. So if you're here to get your claws into Ohana in the hopes—"

"That's not what I'm doing." Theo snapped out the words so fast and hard his jaw ached. It wasn't, was it? Or was this what happened when you kept your head down at work? When you just did your job and didn't pay attention to the gossip and rumors swirling around the watercooler? Had he missed something? And if so, what? "I know what

I'm doing here and what my plans are. I'm not here to coerce or manipulate, Mano. I'm here to report my honest findings and opinions."

"Okay." Mano nodded, then nodded again. "Okay, I'll take you at your word and accept that. Unless you give me reason to doubt you."

"I sure don't want to do that."

"Good. Now. About Sydney."

Suddenly wishing he had something stronger to drink than coffee, he finished his. "What about her?"

"She's family, brah. Mine and Tehani's. With Remy gone, it's my responsibility to make sure no one hurts her. You feel me?"

"I understand you, if that's what you mean. I don't have any intention of hurting her," Theo insisted even as he told himself it didn't matter what Mano Iokepa thought of him. Except…

Except that it did. There was something quite unsettling about anyone in Nalani thinking less of him. Thinking he was here for any other reason than to fulfill an assignment he hadn't wanted in the first place.

Theo frowned as that surge of uncertainty swelled inside him once more. He'd come out here to do a simple job. A quick job. Now he was thinking constantly about a woman he shouldn't want, worrying about a business that wasn't his, and fighting the urge to protect a town and its residents that he had no place in. How and when did his life suddenly get so…complicated?

"I was going to ask you for a tour of Hibiscus Bay, just to add that bit of information to my report for GVI. Maybe that's not such a good idea now."

"Happy to give you a tour," Mano assured him. "Just know going in that there is no amount of money that will ever convince me to sell. I've paid my dues working my way to the top, and I've lost a lot because of it. No way am I going to give in and let it all go for a check."

Theo nodded. "Understood. And I will make that clear in my report." A report that suddenly had taken a detour he wasn't expecting. "I'm glad we had this conversation."

"You are? You don't look it," Mano said with a sly grin.

"Well, in case you don't own a mirror, you come off as a bit intimidating, Mano."

"You should see me in a suit and tie. Speaking of which, I need to get to work." He stood up and gathered up his trash.

"On a Sunday?"

"Every day, but on Sundays I move my office to a table by the pool for a few hours for employees to come and discuss problems or present solutions to issues we need to work on. Everyone at Hibiscus Bay has a voice."

"That comes from your time as a valet driver?"

"Partly. But it's more from when my father was a gardener who worked on the grounds. It's important, I believe, to see situations from every angle. Our staff can come to me about anything and, if I can, I address it. Or find someone who can."

"In that case, I completely understand why GVI would want to buy your resort," Theo said. "That's an admirable way to run a business."

"Thank you." Mano nodded. "I believe it is. If I don't see you before, I'm sure I'll see you at the luau on Wednesday evening."

"Ah, the birthday-party thing." Theo nodded. "I'm afraid I'll be headed home by then."

"Uh-huh. We'll see." Mano jerked his chin toward the beach. "She's out of the water now. In case you were stalling."

Theo grinned. "Was I that obvious?"

"You were. *Are.* Be careful with her, Theo. I'm not sure she can stand to have her heart broken again so soon."

Theo watched Mano carry his trash to the receptacle, then quietly tip the busboys cleaning off the vacated tables. *Admirable for sure*, Theo thought as he gathered up his own things and made his way toward the entrance to the beach.

Sydney's friend had given him a lot to think about. Too much, no doubt. He was already starting to think about where to look for past business proposals that he could easily access. He didn't doubt Mano's claim that GVI had made an offer to buy the Hibiscus Bay Resort. But it was nagging at him that this was the first he was hearing about it. Especially considering his evaluation assignment.

He'd timed it just right, reaching the tree-lined path to the beach just as Sydney made her way toward him. She'd put her shorts and tank top back on, but both were now soaked thanks to the bikini she wore underneath. Her hair hung in long, wet ropes down her back, but it was the smile on her face and the light in her eyes that stopped him dead in his tracks and left him wondering if there was even another woman on Earth.

He knew the instant she spotted him. Her eyes flitted away for a moment and dimmed, as if she wanted to avoid seeing him, and for an instant, he kicked himself for kissing her the last time he'd seen her. But only for an instant.

He could count the defining moments in his life on one hand and still have fingers left over. One was when he'd decided to enroll full-time in college and see it through to graduation. Two was his decision to stay in San Francisco after college, and three was when he'd signed the lease on his apartment a few weeks later. It had taken him years to get to moment number four: kissing Sydney Calvert.

But while she might regret his impulsive action, he never would. Especially if it turned out he'd never have a chance to do it again.

As she approached, that hesitancy vanished from her face, making him wonder if perhaps he'd imagined it.

"Well, look at you." She stopped right in front of him, planted the base of her board on the ground and kicked out a hip. "I never would have imagined I'd see this."

"See what? Me?"

"No, this." She reached up and flicked a finger against the buttons on his polo shirt. "They're unbuttoned."

"Oh." He laughed, shoved his hands into his pockets and ducked his head. "Yeah, well, it's more comfortable being able to breathe in the heat, right?"

"Uh-huh. I see you got a sunburn, too. Forgot your sunscreen yesterday?"

"Not at first. Just forgot to reapply it."

"We're no sooner going to get you acclimated then it'll be time for you to go home," she said. Droplets of water dotted her face and chest, trickled down below the fabric of her low-cut tank and disappeared. "Hope you took a long soak in the shower after that horseback trail yesterday."

"I did indeed take that advice to heart." Probably the only reason he could walk today, now that he thought about it. "So." He cleared his throat, searching his suddenly empty brain for something clever to say or ask.

"So." Her smile widened. "Howzit?"

"How's what?"

"Everything. Where are you coming from?"

"The Hut-Hut. I tried their loco moco."

"Yeah? What did you think?"

"I think if I lived here, I'd probably be about a hundred pounds heavier," he said. "I met Mano. Had a long talk with him about… things."

"What things?"

"All kinds of things. You came up. More than once. I was watching you. Out there." He pointed uselessly to the ocean behind her. "On your board."

"Oh, yeah?" She cringed. "Not one of my better days, but it felt good being back in the water. Not as good as being up there, of course."

"Yeah, I thought you had a couple of helicopter tours booked for today."

"Did. They canceled. Which means I have to wait until Tuesday for another shot." She sighed. "So goes life."

It was impossible not to see the disappointment in her eyes. "Are you looking for replacement bookings?"

"Tehani said she'd call around, but that rarely comes through." She shrugged.

"Oh." For the second time that he could remember, his mouth shot out far ahead of his brain. "Well, you could take me up. You know. If you wanted to."

She spluttered and coughed. "You? You want me to take *you* flying? You know that happens in the sky, right?"

"I do, yes." He ducked his head again and hoped his heart wouldn't explode out of his chest. "I just… Well, you said you put people at ease up there and you like challenges. Chances are pretty good I'll be a horrible passenger, but…"

"But what?"

He hoped his smile came off as genuine as he felt. "You seem sad not to be flying today. I've got an expense account, and you're considered a viable investment from what I can tell." Seemed as good a reason as any to confront one of his biggest fears.

"You really mean it? You want me to take you flying?"

"Yeah." Because he couldn't think of anything else that could bring that light back into her eyes. "Yeah, I do."

"All right, then." And there it was. Like a lighthouse beacon beaming into the darkest storm, an absolute glow came over her. "Okay, um, meet me at the landing pad in about an hour. I need to go home and change and get a few things together." She started to walk away, then turned and came back. Before he knew what was happening, she grabbed hold of his arm, reached up on her tiptoes and brushed her mouth against his. "Thank you."

"For what?"

"For trusting me. And for getting me back where I belong." She raised her chin and her gaze. "Up there. I'll see you in a bit, yeah?

Oh, this is going to be so much fun." She kissed him again and hurried off, leaving him standing there, gaping. Smiling.

It only took a few minutes before he felt his chest tighten and the air constrict in his throat. He'd just volunteered himself for a helicopter tour. A tour. In a helicopter. Which was essentially a giant glass bubble with wiper blades holding it up. "Oh, man." He pressed a hand against his stomach and headed up the road back to his cottage. "Oh, man, you have really got it bad, don't you?"

*Yes*, he thought as he walked very, very slowly up the hill.

He really did.

## *CHAPTER SEVEN*

SYDNEY WASN'T ENTIRELY sure what surprised her more: the fact that sixty minutes to the second later, Theo stepped onto the landing pad or that he'd shown up at all. Given his initial reticence regarding the very mention of getting into a helicopter, she would have laid solid odds on the latter being true, yet here he was, with shadows of doubt and trepidation on his handsome face.

"Let me guess," he said as he approached, casting wary eyes on her vehicle as she closed the cargo door where she'd stashed some last-minute snacks for a stop she planned to make. "You weren't entirely sure I was going to come."

She smiled, scrunched her nose. "It may have crossed my mind."

"You changed your clothes." He glanced down at his khakis and polo shirt, then inclined his head as he reached a hand out. "And tied down your hair."

"Yeah, well, I don't fly in flip-flops." She waggled one of her sneaker-clad feet in front of her and ran a suddenly nervous hand down her loosely twisted braid. "And the fewer distractions I have up there, the better." She sobered at his wince. "How about we get those nerves under control before we take off?"

"Not entirely sure that's possible."

"We'll see. We're all gassed up and ready to go, but to satisfy that scientifically leaning mind of yours—"

"I've watched some videos," he said as she pulled open the pilot-side cockpit door. "There was this one on YouTube, how to fly a helicopter in six minutes."

"Six minutes, huh?" She rolled her eyes. "And here I wasted thousands of hours earning my license. All right, then. Let's see what you learned." Sydney stepped back and pointed. "What's that?"

"Ah. That's the collective, and it's operated with the left hand. It controls height and moves the pitch of the blades."

"Huh." Sydney gave him an impressed

nod. "All right. How about this?" She indicated the main controller situated in the center of the pilot's seat.

"The cyclic. It'll tilt the craft forward and back. It's what you use to keep the nose of the helicopter where you're going."

She laughed. "Okay, so maybe YouTube wasn't a bad idea after all. What about the foot pedals?"

"There's two of them." He moved closer, peered in as if actually interested, which was what she was hoping for. "They work as anti-torque and maintain resistance against the blades. Without them, the chopper would just spin and spin. They're what keep the vehicle steady."

"All of it together requires a bit of a light touch. I've been flying since I was seven years old, Theo. I made my first solo flight when I was sixteen. I won't say I've never had issues up there, but I know what I'm doing."

"I believe you."

"Uh-huh. I can see that. Okay, how about some stats to help ease your mind?"

"What kind of stats?"

"Helicopter crashes, aircraft crashes in

general, are anomalies. For example, did you know there has to be at least seven catastrophic failures on a plane for it to go down?"

"If you're meaning to help—"

"I'm not saying accidents don't happen," Sydney said calmly. "I'm just saying they're rare. The odds of anything happening to us—"

"Never tell me the odds," Theo said, cutting her off. "That'll only give me something to obsess over. What about turbulence?"

"What about it?"

"It can get pretty bad, especially in a smaller craft."

"Okay, just a reminder—you going up was your idea."

"And you said you could put my mind at ease before I climbed on board."

Yeah, she'd walked right into that one, hadn't she? "Okay, you're a smart man. I have no doubt you've done your own research—"

"I have. There was this—"

"Video?"

"Yeah." He grinned, some of the trepidation leaving his face. "Scientifically, I understand that turbulence is the atmosphere essentially adjusting itself around aircraft."

"Right. And it's always there. Pilots learn early on how to work around it, fly around it or maintain the aircraft going through it. But let's look at it this way." She slipped her fingers through his and drew him around the front of the chopper. "I haven't updated my will yet, so nothing's going to happen to us today. There is one important warning I need to give you, however." She tugged open his door and motioned for him to step up into his seat.

"What's that?"

"From here on? I call the shots. You're in my space now. Understood?"

"Aye-aye, Captain." He gave her an awkward salute that had to be one of the cutest things she'd ever seen.

"We aren't in the Navy," she teased. "Hook your belt. I'll get you settled with your headphones in a sec." She closed him in and did a quick double-check of the cargo holds containing the typical emergency equipment: first aid kit, fire extinguishers, a few lengths of sturdy rope, flares and a knife. One of the things she'd learned working Search and Rescue back in South Carolina was to keep an extra stash of emergency rations just to be safe. While she didn't anticipate the need for a thermal blanket, she had a couple of those as well. Island terrain was far different from the southern east coast, but it didn't hurt to be prepared for any eventuality. Always the sign of a good pilot, something her first flight instructor had taught her back before she'd even turned double digits.

Despite having had her door open for a while, the heat of the midday sun was pulsating inside the cockpit as she climbed in.

"You okay?"

"So far." Theo was casting his eyes about as if that could change at any moment. "Just focusing on not being a control freak and reminding myself you know what you're doing. You really did this as a little kid?"

"I really did." She hooked her belt and reached up for one of the pairs of headphones hanging up and a little behind them. "These are noise-canceling phones. We'll be able to talk to one another." She tapped the small microphone protruding from one of the ears. "You feel sick, there's a barf bag in the front compartment right by your feet."

"That is the line I will not cross," he said.

"Good to know." She laughed. "Okay," she shouted as she pulled her own headphones on and clicked the connection button on the roof control panel. "Just need a few minutes to warm this baby up." She clicked the ignition switch.

Overhead, the high-pitched whirring began. The all-too familiar sound brought her instant comfort and had her settling back in her seat, her left hand resting comfortably on the collective lever, her right gently grasping what looked like an oversize palm-fitting joystick. Her feet on the pedals, she double-checked her monitors and readouts, made sure there were no warning lights flashing and that all systems were green to go.

Out of the corner of her eye, she could see Theo reach down on either side of his bucket seat to grasp the handholds, but his dead-eyed stare straight ahead told her he wasn't going to let his fears defeat him. And that, she thought as she gently pulled back on the cyclic and eased the skids off the ground, was something to admire.

There was something magical about that first liftoff of the day, a reminder of what was possible as she took flight. It shouldn't be—possible. Humans were meant to be on the ground; it had been imagination and determination that took them to the skies. She took it slow, not wanting to jar him into panic as she raised the bird up and off the platform, banking away slightly to the right so they could take the coastal route up toward Hilo before venturing deeper into the island.

"How're you doing?" Her voice slightly echoed back in her own ears.

"Okay, actually." But he didn't loosen his grip on the small bars on either side of his seat. "How high—never mind." He shook his head. "Don't want to know. How long can we fly?"

"Before the gas runs out? Quite a few hours. Plus, I have a reserve tank in case we need it, but we won't," she assured him when he finally looked at her. Seeing him sitting there, in her chopper, with those oversize muzzled earphones on his head and glasses on his face, she couldn't remember seeing a more appealing sight.

Unless it was the absolute beauty of the majestic island stretching out in front of them.

"Keep your eye on the horizon if you start feeling wiggly," she told him. "But if you can manage, enjoy the coastline for a while. Have to give you that full bird's-eye view for your report."

"It's…" He leaned forward and, to her surprise, released his hold and rested light fingertips on the dash in front of him. "It's amazing."

Her smile widened as she pulled up a bit on the collective and increased their height. "The higher we go, the better the view." She'd only been up a few times since moving back here, but every time was like the first. The breaking water over the endless stretch of sand, the dots of surfers and swimmers immersing themselves in the clear blue Pacific. "I'm going to take you all the way around. The volcano activity is stunning to see from above. I bet you've never seen an actual lava flow, have you?"

He actually laughed. "Ah, no. I definitely have not."

"You won't soon forget it. Once you get

a bit more acclimated, we'll take some dips and dives for a closer look."

"As long as you don't mean scuba dives, I'm in." He cast her a side-eyed glance. "And don't take that as a challenge. You got me in a helicopter. Nothing will ever make me strap a tank on my back and take that giant leap."

"We'll see," she sang, mostly to herself. "We'll see."

THEO WOULD NEVER have believed he'd feel remotely safe bopping around in the air in what was tantamount to a metal-and-glass cylinder. Okay, Sydney and Ohana Odysseys' helicopter was a little bit more than that, but the premise remained. He one hundred percent understood the appeal to such an excursion and, in his mathematically inclined mind, found the tour company's value soar.

After buzzing around the Big Island for about two hours, getting his spatial relations straight had taken a bit of time. Sydney was a phenomenal tour guide, pointing out various hubs, neighborhoods and smaller towns encompassing one of Hawai'i's eight islands, of which most people could only name five or six.

She hadn't been kidding about the lava flow. Statistically, the Big Island boasted the best and biggest opportunity to see a volcano in action, something he'd never imagined witnessing in person. It hadn't taken more than a few seconds of watching that molten lava spilling into the shoreline to lose himself in the power of nature. Being witness to what was tantamount to island expansion shifted a good portion of cynicism out of his psyche. The experience left him feeling grateful and like far more of an expert when it came to evaluating exactly what Ohana Odysseys had to offer its clients as well as a company looking to acquire them.

That so much time had passed surprised him, but he was getting used to seeing treetops rather than trunks and rooftops rather than patios and porches. With Hilo and Nalani on the eastern side of the island and Kona on the west, the forested area between—area that included countless walking and hiking trails, waterfalls and out-of-the way spaces—provided that confirmation of untouched beauty the islands had always boasted of.

Even in the confines of the chopper, he could see the hints of birds and brilliant arrays of flora rustling below, something he'd gained a new appreciation for thanks to yesterday's botanical hike with Daphne. While he wasn't in any rush to get off the chopper, he did feel an odd desire to dive deeper into those areas of wonder and unexplored beauty. And that, he thought with a bemused smile, was one of the magical things about the islands.

The longer he was here, the more he saw, the more he experienced and embraced—however reluctantly—the deeper Hawai'i sank into his soul. That would be something he'd carry home and keep close. Forever.

*Home.* Theo's brow knitted. Something he needed to remember. This wasn't home. This place, these people were his job. But if he'd been a different man...

"How much longer?" He glanced over at Sydney, who reached up and twisted one of the knobs on their headphones. "What's wrong?"

"Nothing with us," she assured him as she

flipped a switch. "Hang on. Yeah, local air, this is Ohana One with Ohana Odysseys out of Nalani. I'm circling Honua'Ula and seeing some storm activity banking out in the distance to the east. Please confirm—" She frowned, then nodded. "Understood. Copy that. Setting down now. Appreciate the info. Out." She clicked back onto his frequency. "All right. Our tour is going to last a little longer than expected. We need to take a bit of a detour."

"What's going on? You look ticked."

"Just at myself for not listening to Maru this morning." She winced and, as the sunlight dimmed behind heavy gray clouds, she pulled off her sunglasses and banked the chopper to the right. "She said there was a storm coming, and I dismissed it."

"Isn't that what you told me the day I got here? That the weather turns on a dime?"

"I did say something to that effect," she confirmed with a grim smirk. "Just goes to show I get tunnel vision when I can get up in the sky. Okay, keep your eyes open, and let's look for a good place to land this thing." She indicated with her chin for him to look outside his window.

"What am I looking for?"

"A place big enough to set her down and take off again. Not a lot of trees, if possible. Oh."

"Oh what?"

"I just thought of a place. It'll take us a few minutes to get there, but it should work. Hang on."

*Hang on to what?* he wanted to ask as her feet moved and she pushed forward on the cyclic.

Raindrops spattered against the windows as a gust of wind kicked up and jostled the chopper hard enough to make him grab hold of the handles on his seat. "That storm's coming on fast."

"Yeah, Mother Nature doesn't mess around. And I don't mess around with her." She leaned forward, her knuckles whitening as her grip on the cyclic tightened.

Whatever noise the headphones were supposed to keep banked, they weren't working at peak capacity. He could feel the storm pummeling the exterior.

"Glad you were prepared for an adventure today," Sydney said on a laugh. "'Cause it ain't over yet. It's gonna get bumpy for a bit."

"How far away are we going?" *And this*, he thought, *is where trust comes in*. Just looking at her and the concentration on her face, not an ounce of panic shimmering, some of the knots tightening in his chest loosened.

"A few miles east. There aren't a lot of mountain ranges on the Big Island, but there are some. Remy and his college friends hiked out to one for a few days around their college graduation. It was one of his favorite places to go when he got stressed out." She banked left, dipped down and left Theo's stomach a good thirty feet overhead. "Plus, the mountains should give us some protection from the storm."

The skids barely missed the treetops as they sped forward, keeping just ahead of the storm breaking behind them. He had questions—like how was this storm different from the one he'd experienced the day he'd arrived? How long would it last? And what would they find when they got—

"There it is." Her relieved murmur echoed in his ears. "Just like he talked about. And it's perfect to land." She reached up, flipped another few switches, then lowered her left hand and the collective lever.

*It's odd*, he thought as they dropped into the trees, *to descend so effortlessly and completely into the nature we were exploring only moments ago.* With the wind picking up huge branches, bent and swayed, the chopper itself shimmied against the forces of the sudden storm. It wasn't until he felt the skids touch down and she turned the engine and blades off that he got a blurry look at their surroundings.

"If this wasn't planned, it should have been," he said as he pulled off his headphones.

Sydney offered an absent nod, then flipped a power switch, scanned to a different frequency. "Nene, this is Ohana One. You around, Nene?"

Over the cockpit speaker, static competed against the storm.

"Nene?" Theo asked.

"Nickname, I'm pretty sure," Sydney said. "It's the state bird. Nene, repeat, this is Ohana One."

"Howzit, Sydney?" The crackly female

voice on the other end earned a relieved laugh from Sydney. "You out in this crazy?"

"Afraid so," Sydney said. "Cell reception out here is nonexistent. Can you get a message to Tehani? Let her know we're okay and we're holed up at Remy's mauka for the storm to pass? Might wait until morning to head back."

*Morning?* Theo contained his surprise but couldn't quite manage to hide his smile. A night alone with Sydney Calvert? Seemed this storm was turning into a bit of island luck for him.

"Will do, Syd. You take care, ya? Check in in the a.m."

"Copy that. Over and out." She clicked off and sighed. "At least now Tehani won't worry."

Theo nodded, a bit transfixed by the sight around him. It was as if Sydney had plucked a dedicated patch of perfect isolation out of the already overwhelming beauty of the islands. Between the trunks of the trees surrounding the grove where they landed, he could see the hints of a small lake and paths twisting in and around each other.

"I've got rain gear in the hold," Sydney said. "Give me a second—"

"I might not be able to pilot this thing, but I'm capable of gathering items from a cargo hold." He didn't come across as *that* incapable and inept, did he? "And we aren't in the air anymore. Now we're a team."

"Right. Sorry." She tucked a loose strand of blond hair behind her ear. "I'm in tour guide mode, I suppose."

"Hey." Before she shoved open her door, he reached over, caught her hand. "You were great up there. Seeing you fly…" He didn't have the words to convey the admiration, the wonder, the pride he felt in watching her in her absolute element. It was as close to a vision as he'd ever imagined seeing. "I'm glad I got to witness it firsthand."

"I'm glad you trusted me enough to give it a shot," she said with a small smile. She looked down at their hands, then back to his face. "We'll have to hole up at least until the storm passes. I know the accommodations aren't exactly your—"

"I'll be fine," he said instantly. "I'm with you."

Her smile widened, and a little color popped

out on her cheeks as she leaned forward and looked out as the rain and wind surged. "Let's hope that holds. You ready?"

"As I'll ever be," he assured her and let her hand go.

"Great. I'll come around to you. Let's go."

"As far as ambience is concerned, it isn't too bad." Theo's observation did a good job of battering down Sydney's sudden doubts.

The idea of retreating to Remy's mauka, her brother's mountain, had come to mind instantly when she'd wondered where to go. They'd been too far out to make it back to Nalani. Even if she hadn't assured Theo she wasn't one to take chances, given the unpredictability of storms these days, it simply wasn't worth taking a chance with.

"I could have made a run to Kona," she lamented as she crouched beside him just inside the large entrance to a cave. After they'd deposited their belongings inside, he'd retreated and gathered up a bunch of rocks that he was currently arranging in a small circle. "Maybe I should have."

"And rob me of a true island experience?" Theo scoffed. "This is going to be an excellent addition to my report to GVI. Who needs mattresses or electricity?"

She glanced over to the portable emergency generator she kept stashed in the chopper, one of the first things she'd grabbed out of the cargo cabinet.

Theo laughed. "Okay, who needs light bulbs. Look, Sydney, we've got water and food, we've got blankets and plenty of things to talk about to stay occupied. We need to call out, there's a satellite phone in that thing, right?" He pointed to the generator sitting beside a case of bottled water and a battery with solar backup lantern. "Just look at this as an extreme way to keep me away from work and focused on what I'm here to evaluate—your island."

A bit taken aback by his ability to adapt, Sydney rose when he did but remained where she was as he went back outside and scooped up a bunch of dried twigs and leaves. While the storm was proving to be a doozy, it hadn't pushed its way through the thick forest of trees butted up against the mountain and encircling a small lake at the base of a waterfall. Even now she could hear the flowing water competing against the rain and wind that had yet to show any signs of slowing down. The cave felt a bit dank and musty, but she could also smell the rain filtering in from the blustery air.

"Have to admit," Sydney said as he dropped the natural debris on the ground near her before he crouched to arrange it all into an oddly neat pile, "I didn't peg you as the Boy Scout type." She reached up, pulled off his rain-spattered glasses and wiped them off. When she placed them back on his face, he grinned and set her insides to flipping like a school of dolphins on spring break.

"Far from it. I told you how I grew up. I know better than most how to get along without modern-day conveniences. Heck, this is like old home week for me. I'm betting there are some matches in that emergency bag over there?" He indicated the oversize duffel bag across the way.

"Sure." She circled around, unzipped the bag and pulled out what he needed. As he started a fire, hopefully one large enough to help their clothes dry faster, she shifted the oversize paper bag closer. "Glad I thought to bring some snacks along."

"Oh, yeah?" Theo's smile went even wider, and she wondered when he'd gone from cute to drop-dead gorgeous. "What do we have?"

"I'm sure you'll appreciate some more than others."

"Spam." He shook his head. "You brought Spam, didn't you?"

"Hey, Spam musubi is an island delicacy. Plus, it's nice and filling."

"You couldn't have packed some of your mom's macaroni salad you were bragging about the other day?"

"No." Sydney ducked her head. "No, I gave the last of that to Benji. But I've got some jerky and some fruit, dried and fresh. And some of these." She pulled out two single-serving boxes of chocolate-covered macadamia nuts. "I grabbed them at Luanda's just for you."

"Dessert first?" he teased.

"Maybe." Unease and grief, two sensations she'd become acquainted with long ago, surged and twisted around one another. "I think I left something back at the chopper." She pushed up and turned away from him. "Be back in a few minutes."

She didn't wait for him to respond or follow. She couldn't, not with the tears threatening to rise up and flow out of her control. When she stepped outside, she didn't feel the stinging rain or the harsh wind whipping around her. She didn't hear the whistle the storm made as it thundered over and through the island.

But she could hear—and feel—the chest-aching pounding of her heart as she stumbled toward the lake yards clear of the cave. She looked up, up at the trio of mountains clinging to one another on the other side of the falls offering a trickling of water that would soon swell to a roar of runoff.

She grabbed hold of a tree trunk with one hand, gripped the bark in her fingers until she felt tiny shards slip beneath her nails. Remy's mountains. The mountains that had served as his refuge. And now hers.

She bowed her head, squeezed her eyes shut and tried to push the sadness down.

"Sydney."

She waited for the anger, the irritation of Theo's intrusion, to strike, but it didn't. If anything, his presence seemed to open the floodgates of emotion and left her knees trembling.

"What is it?" he asked. "Remy?"

He was behind her now, and his hand came to rest on her shoulder. She couldn't stop herself. She reached up and grabbed his hand, squeezed so hard her own fingers went numb.

"Partly. The, um, storm." She tried to stand taller, to swipe the tears away, but they continued to fall. "It just brings back a lot of stuff I'd rather not think about."

"Like your mom."

She sighed. "How did you—"

"I mentioned her macaroni salad. There was…something in your eyes. It dawned on me after you left that you told me about Remy but not your parents. They're gone, aren't they?"

"Mmm-hmm." She couldn't push out any more between her tightly pressed lips. "They died eight years ago. Plane crash on Moloka'i. In a storm a lot like this one." She looked up. "It came out of nowhere. The pilot was new, the plane was old and they were just gone." The words felt like cuts on her tongue. "Search and Rescue found them. It took two days and it was too late, of course. So I guess it was really search and recovery."

"Is that why you joined SAR?" His question wasn't one she hadn't asked herself a million times.

"I was aiming in that direction before their passing, but it probably solidified my decision. The flying now, believe it or not, tempers the hurt." Unfortunately, SAR wouldn't have been in time to help her parents. The accident report confirmed everyone on board had died instantly. There hadn't been anyone to rescue. But it had been an SAR chopper that located the site. "Now Remy's gone, too." She took a slow, deep breath. "I guess everything kind of hit me at once. Like I needed the reminder that I'm all alone now." Contrary to her words, she clung to his hand and found such comfort in his touch that the pain very nearly vanished.

"From what I've seen, that's not remotely true, Sydney." He pulled her around to face him. The trees protected them from most of the rain and wind, but the roar of the storm continued as tiny escapist droplets of water cascaded down. "I don't know if you noticed, but I am a realist with cynical tendencies."

"You don't say," she said before trying to laugh, but the sound froze in her throat when he tilted her chin up. She couldn't help but look into those amazing fathomless eyes behind his glasses.

"I don't think I've ever met anyone so wholly connected to a place. You make everyone you meet smile, Sydney. They—Nalani—love you."

"I'm nothing special, Theo. They love everyone. Even you."

"I think I'm still hovering low on their like-a-meter at this point," Theo teased. She could feel the strength of his words, feel the conviction in his touch as he held on to her, drew her closer. "I'm sorry about your parents. It must be difficult, being here in Nalani now that they're gone."

"You'd think." And maybe that was another reason she'd been reluctant to come home for any length of time. "To be honest, I think I've found it a bit of a comfort." Her lips tipped as the memories swirled. "And it helps that so many people in Nalani loved and miss them, too. Besides, I can still feel them, their presence. They loved the islands with everything they had. And every once in a while, when I'm very still and I listen closely, I can hear their laughter in the wind. Or feel their love in the afternoon sun." She shook her head. "Sounds silly, I'm sure, especially to someone like you who reserves judgment for actual evidence, but—"

"There's nothing silly about missing the people you love, Sydney. Don't ever apologize for it."

She'd reached the point where looking at him without wanting to kiss him was impossible. She wanted to, so badly. So very, very badly. She wanted to fall back into his arms and make everything other than the two of them fade into the distance. It wouldn't take much. A small step forward. But right now that one step felt like a mile-long trek. One she wasn't remotely prepared to embark on.

She'd fallen into that vacation-in-paradise trap and knew she'd already tipped significantly into something more than friendship with him. But she couldn't let herself fall any further. He wasn't staying. And neither was she, she reminded herself. They each had their lives to get on with. Him back in San Francisco and her in South Carolina…

Two utterly different lives where the other didn't particularly fit. Wouldn't ever fit.

No matter how much she might wish otherwise.

She dropped her forehead onto his chest, tried not to notice how he smelled of the sea and rain and promise. How was it possible that this man—this unassuming, left-brained, logical-minded man—had somehow slipped into the heart that, until this moment, she realized she'd purposely kept locked down? No one had ever felt like serious-relationship material. No one had ever made her think about the future or forever or even the little things like taking a sunset walk along the beach she'd learned to swim and surf at.

It didn't make any sense. More importantly, she couldn't allow it to.

"Would it make you feel better," he murmured as he rubbed her back and pressed a kiss to the top of her head, "if I said I'd try the Spam?"

She couldn't help it. She laughed. And when she did, she lifted her head and gazed up at his face. "It might."

"I was afraid you'd say that." But there

was no displeasure on his face as he spoke. Only kindness, understanding and affection.

"You really are one of a kind, aren't you, Theo Fairfax?"

"So I've been told. But I've committed to it now. The Spam."

"Yes," she whispered with a nod. "Yes, you have." And because she could no longer resist, she reached up on her tiptoes and pressed her lips against his. "Maybe sudden storms have their silver linings after all," she murmured against his lips, then slid her hand down his arm and slipped her fingers between his. "Let's get out of the rain."

## CHAPTER EIGHT

THEO WASN'T ENTIRELY sure what woke him up—but one moment he was cozily dreaming about snuggling with Sydney by a fire he'd made with his own two hands and the next he was sitting up in a chilly cave, all alone.

After the storm had lulled them to sleep last night, the near silence this morning made his ears hurt. He sat up, one hand clenched against the thermal blanket they'd put on the ground to share. Searching for his glasses, he found them on a rocky outcropping by his head and pushed them on.

His stomach rumbled as he made his way to the entrance of the cave, attempting in vain to brush the wrinkles out of his shirt and pants. They'd made a significant dent in the food she'd packed. Enough so that what was left would barely take the edge off for either of them.

He could hear water rushing, but nothing like when they'd landed. Beneath the countless tall trees, he could feel the newness the storm had brought, a cleansing of sorts as he made his way through the winding path that took him away from both the cave and chopper and toward the lake.

He found Sydney's pile of clothes—her jeans, sneakers and T-shirt, even the band that had tied her hair down, tossed in a heap on a grassy bank, as if she'd simply stepped out of them and walked on.

The lake stretched a good hundred yards out, and across the way and up at least thirty feet, the narrow waterfall cascaded down in its post-storm glory, catching against the morning sun and casting tiny ghostly rainbows against the steam. He stood there, scanning the surface of the lake, hand shielding his eyes from the morning sun, searching for her. His head knew she could take care of herself and that she was fine. But his heart?

He began to think his heart might just be wherever Sydney was.

Finally, a flash of color above him caught

his attention, and he stepped back, mouth falling open.

"Sydney!"

She stood there, at the top of the falls, wearing a bikini the same startling blue as her eyes. She waved and then, to his utter horror, she took one step forward and dropped straight into the lake. She barely made a splash upon entry.

He cursed and was tugging off his shoes and shirt faster than he could think. His pants went next, leaving him wearing only a pair of boxer shorts with tiny calculators on them. He'd no sooner tossed his glasses down and dived in than he saw her surface just beyond the pluming of the falls.

Theo reached out one arm, then the other, anxious to catch her. He stopped at the sight of her slicking her hair back and grinning over at him. He treaded water, and the relief that she was all right was instantly banked by the sheer beauty of her as she made her way over. "You scared the life out of me," he said as she swam up, the most glorious smile breaking across her face.

"Sorry." She swiped a hand down her nose.

"Didn't mean to. I knew it was deep enough to dive, and the idea was too tempting to ignore." She circled him and he followed, slowing spinning as she swam lazily around him. "There's a nice path up the back of that hill, if you want to try it."

"I think I've reached my adventure and danger quota for the time being," he admitted. It had been so easy yesterday, last night, to gently urge her into opening up. Talking about her parents. Her rationale behind her career choice. And Remy. The more she'd talked about her brother, the more he regretted having never met him.

But he felt as if he knew Sydney's brother more now. And he understood what a huge loss his death had been not only to his family but to Nalani as a whole.

"You can swim."

"What? Yes, of course I can swim," Theo insisted.

"I guess I just assumed, given your adverse reaction to the catamaran and your determination not to go anywhere near sand—"

"An impossible feat," he cut in. He felt as if he were caught in some kind of dream, watching this stunning, glorious mermaid hydraulically stalk him in what had to be the most luxuriously relaxing lake he'd ever encountered. "And for the record, boats and I don't get along very well."

"I have to say, seeing you in the water is a wonderful surprise," she added before she ducked under the surface, then came back up into the circle of his arms. "Hello."

"Hi." Instinct pulled at him as effectively as he pulled her in. He felt their legs tangle in the depths of the water; her arms encircled his neck, and his hand skimmed the bare skin of her back. "Nice way to start the day," he said, barely recognizing his own voice.

"I agree." She brushed her lips against his. "I don't think there's anyone else I'd rather be stranded with than you, Theo Fairfax."

"Yeah? Want to do it again?" He kissed the tip of her nose and reveled in the smile that lit up her eyes.

"Maybe. Before you leave."

"Yeah." Before he left. It wasn't a thought that brought any particular kind of happiness or relief. Rather, it felt more like a circling tide pool determined to suck him back into his safe, predictable life. A life that would, in no way, involve or include Sydney. "Yeah, maybe before I leave."

She pushed away from him to stretch out and float on her back, looking up at the now-cloudless sky. "I suppose we should head back soon."

"You have a tour today?"

She mesmerized him, moving in the water the way she did. "Not until much later."

"Then I guess we can swim awhile longer, yeah?"

"Yeah?" She popped back up, surprise on her face. "You want to play hooky a little longer?"

He was due to send in a preliminary report by the end of the day, but the day was just getting started. "I think I do." Especially if he got to do so with her.

"If you're hungry, there's some Spam musubi left in the cooler," she teased.

"If that's your way of trying to say I told you so—"

"No," she warned. "This is." She dove down, came up in front of him again. "Told you you'd like it."

"Yeah, well, I probably won't put it on my list for a last meal." But he wouldn't turn his nose up at it again.

"I will take what I can get," she assured him. "I wonder." She caught her lower lip in her teeth and sent his thoughts scurrying.

"Wonder what?"

"How competitive are you?"

"Not too."

"Want to race to the falls? Winner chooses where to eat for lunch."

"Does the loser get to make suggestions?"

She laughed. "Maybe. Depends on who loses."

He still had his heart set on trying that huli-huli chicken. "All right. First one to the falls wins. On your mark? Get set?"

"Go!"

"How in the world—" Sydney demanded of Theo a few hours later as they made their way around the slowing blades of the chopper and to the stairs of the landing pad. Every cell in her body was singing after that morning swim. He was, in every infuriating way, a perfect gentleman. A gentleman who had left her with distracting thoughts that would make getting through the rest of the day a bit more difficult. "—could you possibly have won? I grew up swimming. I'm half fish, for crying out loud!"

"I was properly motivated." Theo hefted the overstuffed duffel over his one shoulder. "And I promised Noodles some leftover huli-huli chicken."

She stopped. "Noodles?"

"The gecko."

She sputter-laughed. "You named him Noodles?"

"It seemed appropriate."

"It's completely appropriate and endearing." The main hub of Nalani awaited them in the distance, and Sydney could feel herself being pulled back into normalcy and routine. "You continue to surprise me, Theo. But Noodles won't be impressed with chicken. Now the house salad on the other hand—"

"Ah, right. Herbivore. That reminds me, I'm out of mangoes and papaya."

"Spoken like a true islander." She shook her head, once again astonished at the way this man made her laugh. She never, in a million years, would have expected it of him. "Maybe next time we go flying, I'll give you the controls for a while." There. That should keep him quiet.

"If I watch a few more videos online, I might take you up on that." He sounded so matter-of-fact she blinked. "Conquering one's fear can be done by learning to do that which scares you."

"You had to have gotten that out of a fortune cookie."

"Nope. Out of here." He tapped a finger against his temple. "So. About lunch—"

"Can we make it dinner?" she asked impulsively. "I need to check in with Tehani about my afternoon tour. Rather than feel rushed—"

"Yeah, no. Dinner would be great."

She narrowed her eyes at him as they continued on their way into town. "Why does it sound like that was your plan all along? You could have just asked me."

"I'm still boosting my self-confidence," he said. "Besides, that'll give me a chance to catch up on some work and get that initial report typed up."

"Right." Sydney chewed on the inside of her cheek. "The report. You know, I think maybe we should talk about..." She stopped dead in her tracks at the sight of Hori's sparkling white cab pulling up to a stop in front of Ohana Odysseys. The man who emerged from the back seat set her heart to jumping. "I don't believe it."

"Don't believe what?" Theo asked as she picked up speed down the hill.

It didn't take more than a glance to take in the new arrival's khaki board shorts, the loose navy blue tank and a head of hair that should have qualified him for a designer shampoo ad. Heck, he should be a poster boy for island tourists, which of course he had been once upon a time, at the height of his swimming career.

His very appearance brought a smile so wide to Sydney's face she could feel the late-morning breeze on her back teeth. Seeing him, even with all the memories he brought cascading down on her, she felt a very large open wound on her heart heal.

"Keane!" She dumped the items she'd been carrying on the ground and sprang forward. "Keane Harper, is that you?" He turned at the last second, grinned and held out his arms, just in time to catch her launching herself at him. The second his arms closed around her, the fear she hadn't let herself feel banked and settled. "You came. I can't believe you came!" She leaned her head back, beamed up at him and, as usual, marveled that the man had gotten even more handsome in the years since she'd last seen him. "You're here."

"I'm here." He pressed his forehead to hers, and their noses touched. "I wanted to come sooner. I wanted to be here for Remy."

She nodded, hating the tears that blurred her vision. "You're here now." She stepped back once he set her on her feet, but she grabbed hold of his arms and hung on. Hori unloaded a solitary carry-on from the trunk of his cab.

"Welcome home, brah," Hori said as he circled back around to the driver's side. "See ya, round, yah?"

Keane pointed a finger at him. "Bet on it."

"You got the email." Sydney couldn't stop smiling.

"I got the email." There was sadness in his sky blue eyes. A sadness she was all too familiar with. "Have to admit, kiddo, you definitely know how to get a man's attention."

"Already with the *kiddo*?" She groaned as she released her hold. "I'm only three years younger than you, you know."

"That's three years in little-sister age, which definitely makes you *kiddo*." He reached up, brushed a finger against her cheek. "Howzit?"

She shrugged as her heart squeezed. "You know."

"Yeah," he said. "I miss him, too. Hi." His attention shot directly over Sydney's shoulder. "Keane Harper. You a friend of Sydney's?"

"Oh. Geez. Theo." Sydney took a step back and did her best to ignore the sudden heat in her cheeks. "I'm so sorry. I saw you and I just—"

"Yeah, you just," Keane teased as he held out his hand. "Keane Harper. Old friend of the family."

"Very old," Sydney ribbed.

"Theo Fairfax." Theo lowered the duffel to the ground. "We just got back from Sydney flying me around the island."

"Yeah?" Keane shook his head. "You going to take me up while I'm here, kiddo?"

"Only if you stop calling me *kiddo*. Ah, Theo. Right. Dinner tonight? I'll text you with a time."

"Sure." Theo's brow furrowed and he nodded. "I can help you take all this stuff inside."

"That's okay, brah. I've got it." Keane hefted the duffel in one hand, grabbed his carry-on with the other. "Tehani inside? Did you tell her—"

"About the emails? No. You'll be a complete surprise. Oh, I can't wait to catch up!" She tempered her squealing once he was climbing the stairs. "Sorry about that," she gushed to Theo. "I haven't seen him in I don't even know how long."

"Looks like you two are close."

"Well, yeah. He went to high school with Remy. Back before Keane got all famous and successful. He's a champion swimmer. He missed out on that Wheaties box by this much." She held her thumb and forefinger an inch apart. At Theo's skeptical look, her cheeks went even hotter. "Oh. Oh, Theo, no. There's nothing—" She couldn't stop the laugh building inside her. "He's like my brother, Theo. Well, okay, yeah, he's eye-catching—" The distinctive feminine squeal erupting from Ohana Odysseys didn't seem particularly helpful. "Okay, proving my point."

"What email was he talking about?"

"Oh. That." Sydney's smile dimmed. "When I was gathering up the financial information you needed, I came across a bunch of emails Remy had drafted to some of our friends. He wanted them to come home and work with him here at Ohana." Guilt and uncertainty returned on a swell of unease. "I probably should have told you."

Theo shrugged, but there was doubt in his gaze. "It's none of my business who you communicate with."

"Who I...? Theo, this isn't a big deal." But Theo didn't move. He barely blinked. She couldn't have moved if a tidal wave had crashed over her. Well, this was a first. "Are you...jealous?"

"What?" Theo's eyes went wide. "No, of course I'm not."

"Well, good," she said, not believing him for one blip of a second. "Because you have no cause to be. He's a friend, Theo. A good friend. But that's all."

"Okay."

"Theo." Now she did move and took two deliberate steps forward to stand in front of him. "It wasn't Keane I was wishing would kiss me again in that lake. It was you." She reached up and rested her hands on his broad shoulders. "Why didn't you?"

"Why didn't I kiss you?"

"Uh-huh." She nodded in a way that she hoped would draw out an honest answer. "You could have, you know."

"I know." The doubt seemed to drop from his face. Mostly at least. "But one more kiss might not have been enough."

"Be careful, Theo Fairfax," Sydney warned and rose up to press her mouth to his. He was right. One more kiss might never be enough for her. "You're in danger of turning into a romantic. I'll text you about dinner, yah?"

"Yeah. Text me."

She didn't like the confusion in his voice, but there was nothing she could do beyond assuring him Keane was only a friend. The kind of friend she needed now more than ever. She watched him head back up the hill, veering off toward the beach and the cottage, then bent down to scoop up her belongings and headed up the stairs.

IT WAS OBVIOUS what was going on. Theo made his way back to the cottage in record time. Clearly his heart and head had decided to sever all communications and leave him flailing like a jealous, directionless nincompoop.

He froze halfway up the porch stairs. *Nincompoop?* When had that word entered his vocabulary?

But it seemed as apt a word as any, given how he was feeling. He had no reason to doubt Sydney in her declaration that Keane Harper was simply a family friend. And Theo could probably attribute that protective glint he'd seen in Keane's eyes as exactly what Sydney had said: brotherly affection.

He was being ridiculous. He didn't have the right to stake a claim on Sydney's heart in any capacity. He was a temporary visitor

to her island, to her town. One isolated evening away didn't constitute anything other
than a deeper understanding into who and
what she was.

What she was, he concluded, was an
amazing woman who left him convinced
there wasn't anyone else like her. When she
turned that smile on him—on anyone—it
transported him to a place where only the
two of them existed.

He dragged his hands through his hair.
Maybe he was jealous. Wouldn't that be...
remarkable.

Insecurity was not something Theo was
used to. He couldn't compartmentalize the
emotion. Heck, he didn't even have a compartment to put the emotion in a time-out.
But coupled with the dead-on jealousy Sydney had teased him about displaying, well...
the entire encounter had put a serious ding
in his day.

"You're being ludicrous." He pushed
through the unlocked front door, had a moment of panic when he glanced around and
noticed his laptop wasn't on the kitchen table.

Then he remembered he'd stashed it in

one of the empty drawers in the bedroom dresser just to be safe. He pulled his cell out of his back pocket, powered it up and set it on the table before scanning the dwelling. Nothing appeared out of place. Not that he'd expect an intruder to do the three dishes and dirty glasses he'd left in the sink. Something he took care of immediately.

He'd been in such a rush yesterday to get back to the helipad that he'd neglected to do all the things he usually did—like lock the front door.

Movement out of the corner of his eye told him he was not alone. "Noodles, boy, I wish you could talk right now. I could use a good pair of ears."

He glanced down as Noodles took up a spot near the soap dispenser and looked at him as if he expected Theo to continue. "You have this problem?" he asked the gecko. "You ever wonder if some other guy has the potential to move in on your...love interest?"

Theo frowned, twirling that notion in his head like a red pencil on Tax Day. He wouldn't mind if she was. Although, there could be pitfalls ahead.

Sydney Calvert's way of thinking was the complete opposite of his, and yet he'd never found anyone so utterly fascinating. The fact he'd let her talk him into getting in that helicopter spoke either to her persuasion abilities or maybe it was just his desire to please her. Either way, it hadn't turned out too badly, had it?

"Stuck at my desk, memorizing spreadsheets." That didn't feel nearly as interesting or fulfilling as it once had. "Okay, this isn't getting me anywhere." Time to take a step back and look at the situation rationally.

Keane Harper was a good friend of Sydney's. That was the reality of the situation. Theo didn't have any say in that. Not when he and Sydney were just...whatever they were. "You know what I need to do?" he told Noodles in a firm voice. "I need to get on with this assignment and see what's waiting for me on the other side." Obviously, the sooner he got back to his life, his routine, his job, normalcy would return. The longer he stayed here, the more fantastical his thoughts became. Not only about Sydney but about...everything.

Island influence, no doubt. *Work*, he told himself.

*Focus. On. Work.*

His cell phone buzzed in his back pocket. Startled, Theo dried his hands and pulled the phone free and only now noticed all the texts and emails he'd missed over the past day. Thinking his supervisor's timing couldn't get any better, he still cringed at Elise's name on the screen when he answered.

"Hi, Elise. How's the leg?"

"Broken in two places." Her normally calm voice seemed unusually stressed. "Waiting to hear if I'm going to need surgery."

"Ouch."

"The painkillers are taking care of most of it. But there is one rather large pain in my butt I need to take care of."

"Oh?"

"I take it cell reception isn't the greatest where you are—otherwise you'd have answered at least one of the calls I made to you yesterday."

"Right, ah, sorry about that. I was out of

range." It wasn't a lie. Of course it hadn't helped that he'd turned his phone off before getting into the chopper. Before everything had gotten seriously blown off course. "Cell reception can be spotty in areas."

"Definitely something to note," she murmured as if to herself. "So everything is coming along?"

"Yes, absolutely. I should have my report ready to deliver by the time I get back." He hadn't even begun to think about what he was going to write. How did he put any of what he'd experienced into words? How did he whittle it all down to numbers and facts when so much of Nalani was about heart? "I've been, ah, exploring Nalani and meeting a lot of good people. I certainly understand why GVI is interested in buying Ohana Odysseys. It's definitely a viable investment."

"Excellent. Great news, great. So she's open to an offer?"

Theo frowned at the relief in his supervisor's voice. "I still have some things to address, and I've started examining their business records for the past few years—"

"Don't get bogged down with minutiae,"

Elise said. "The business records are secondary at this point. Hearing you believe it's a good investment for us is going to go a long way to getting this deal underway."

Warning bells he'd never heard before blared in his brain. He'd told Mano he'd been assured GVI had learned from past mistakes, but...had they? "I don't think taking my word for it alone is grounds for a major investment of this type. There are some details—"

"And it's that attention to details that makes you such a valuable member of the GVI family," Elise told him. "We appreciate all the work you've done, and as far as I'm concerned, you've earned your stripes, especially if you're confident this new owner—"

"Sydney," Theo said carefully. "The new owner's name is Sydney Calvert."

"Right. Are you confident she's willing to sell?"

"I think she's open to the possibility. I'm not sure the other employees are." But even as he said it, he felt his stomach tighten. Theo had been so preoccupied with Keane Harper's arrival and its personal effect on

Sydney, he'd neglected to consider her explanation as to what had brought her and Remy's friend to Nalani in the first place.

From a financial standpoint, bringing in too many investors with a personal interest could open the door to trouble. But they'd also bring something to the business a company like GVI wouldn't: respect and devotion to the original spirit and idea of Ohana Odysseys.

"I believe Sydney said she has some other options she'd be exploring," he said cautiously. "But I believe she'd be willing to look at and consider a fair offer."

"Good, good. We've got plans for the area, and we need to move on this soon. This is good news for you, Theo. Providing you still have your eyes on moving up to the cushier offices?"

"I'm open to all forward momentum in the company," he admitted. "I'm a little surprised you know that, however."

"You were ID'd as a reliable investment back when we hired you, Theo. You're a numbers man, plain and simple. Emotion doesn't enter into anything for you, does it? No, my broken leg aside, you were definitely the right man for this evaluation. Once you're back and everything settles, we'll discuss what your next role should be with Golden Vistas."

"That's great. Thank you." He waited for the burst of accomplishment, the acceptance of finally being on his way to making his goal a reality, but the promise of a promotion didn't bring him anything other than an odd sense of worry. "I'm not sure Sydney's ready to make a final decision just yet."

"Well, we'll find out soon enough. And I feel confident she'll accept what I know to be a very generous offer. I have no doubt it won't take very many zeroes to dazzle her."

Theo opened his mouth to protest, to tell his supervisor that Sydney wasn't the kind of woman for whom any zeroes dazzled. Zeros didn't have, what had Sydney called it? *Mana pono.* "I suppose an offer would tell us where she stood with things."

"Exactly what I needed to hear."

Clearly it was, as the caution and tension he'd heard in her voice was now gone. "I'd planned to finish my financial analysis—"

"When you get to it is fine. We've got

you returning home, what? Wednesday afternoon, I understand? I'll pencil you in for a meeting for Thursday morning. Congratulations, Theo. You are officially on your way up."

"Thanks." That knot in his stomach was dipping deeper and tightening. "I appreciate the vote of confidence."

"You've earned it. See you when we're both back." She clicked off before Theo could respond.

Theo set his phone on the counter, waiting for what he'd always hoped to feel: pride in the success of a job well done. Instead...

He rubbed a hand across his suddenly sour stomach.

Instead, he couldn't shake the feeling that something wasn't quite right. Not with his promotion. And not with Elise's overwhelming relief at the news Sydney was open to selling.

Theo's attention to detail was legendary at work. He could work a spreadsheet and accounting records the way a master conductor led an orchestra. But he also found it impossible to ignore a potential hiccup or mystery that could get in the way of success.

"I'm not overthinking this, right, Noodles?" The gecko had moved closer and planted his two front feet on the edge of Theo's body. "I suppose you don't really care, do you? You're just hungry."

Noodle's head ticked to the side. Theo clicked open the door and dug out the last of the fruit he'd stashed after dinner the other night. He cut the chunks up into teeny bits, then set them on the container lid, which he pushed toward the gecko. "Guess I need to do some grocery shopping if I'm going to keep us both fed."

But even as he went in to shower and change, he couldn't shake the feeling that something was seriously off with Elise in that call. She was only a few days out from a major physical injury. Why on earth was she checking in on him regarding a deal that, at least as far as he'd been told, was months away?

Why was this bothering him so much? He had what he wanted. He'd gotten that promotion, at least a verbal promise of one. If anything, he should think about moving his return flight forward so he could move on.

But moving on meant leaving Nalani. It meant leaving Sydney, and honestly? He wasn't ready to do either.

"Just keep your nose pointed into the headwinds." Everything he'd been working for was waiting for him when he did get back. A solid and secure future. A predictable, anticipatory life straight ahead.

Seeing it through was the best way to go. Wasn't it?

# CHAPTER NINE

"Jackpot!" Tehani slapped her hand on the desk after hanging up her phone.

"Good news?" From where he was seated at the round table nearby, Keane kicked up one leg and pushed his chair onto its back legs. An iced coffee in one hand, he had a copy of the *Nalani Weekly* in the other.

"Only the best," she boasted. "Sydney?"

"I'm listening?" How could she not be? Tehani's bold declaration was unlike her almost-sister-in-law, who leaned more toward down-to-earth, practical pronouncements rather than pie-in-the-sky dreams.

"Remember that wedding party Mano told us about?" Tehani asked. "The one all but taking over Hibiscus Bay Resort in a few weeks?"

"Yeah, sure," Sydney fibbed. "I think I remember him talking about some big to-do—"

"'Big to-do.' Understatement of the decade." Tehani made her way over to the coffee station and, after a lamenting sigh of distress, chose a decaf herbal tea. "The Benoit-Harrington wedding has been all over social media for months. The TikTok of the bride choosing her gown got over a million and a half hits in less than a week."

"Yay?" Sydney looked to Keane for support, but he only shrugged and shook his head.

"Okay, so maybe the bride had a little bit of a meltdown when one of the gowns she wanted wouldn't be available in time—"

"Seems an appropriate thing to have a meltdown over," Keane observed.

Tehani rolled her eyes. "Just because you go into shock whenever anyone even mentions marriage—"

"I do not," Keane said easily. "A mild case of hives, perhaps, at the idea of being locked down and tied to one person for the rest of my life, but I wouldn't call it *shock*."

Sydney's lips quirked. Who would have thought Theo Fairfax would be more of a romantic than superstar athlete and superhot Keane Harper? "All that aside," Sydney said, marveling at how she hadn't seen Keane in more than five years and he'd slipped right back into life on Nalani as if he'd never left, "what was the call about, T?"

"Mano's assistant manager said the Benoits want to book at least five exclusive days with us for the entire wedding party the week before the wedding. They want to do everything on the menu. Catamaran dinner cruise, snorkeling adventure, horseback riding, surf lessons—"

*"Exclusive?"* Sydney frowned. "I'm not sure shutting out other customers and clients—"

"No, sorry. Back up. They want to have separate exclusive outings. Which means we can hire some more guides and teachers. And, and, here's the best part—they're willing to pay fifty percent above our rates to do it." Tehani squealed. "Isn't that great?"

Sydney did the quick calculations. "It's something," she agreed. She also couldn't help but wonder how high-maintenance this group might be, considering how much cash they were willing to throw at the potential for exclusivity.

"Part of the charm of Ohana excursions is meeting other people," Keane observed.

"You really want to start catering to exclusive groups and clients?"

"Why not?" Tehani asked. "Sydney wanted proof we can make this business work without Remy—"

"That isn't exactly what I said," Sydney said, somewhat panicked at the accusatory look from Keane. "You didn't tell her?"

"Tell me what?" Tehani's excitement faded as she faced them, steaming cup of tea in one hand. "Sydney, you promised no more secrets," she accused. "What's going on?"

"I'm sorry. This was something I…I didn't know if anything was going to come of it," Sydney admitted in the hopes of couching Tehani's disappointment. "When I was going through Remy's files, I found some emails he'd planned to send before he—before he died." She still couldn't quite push those words out without feeling as if she was losing her breath. "He wanted—"

"He wanted us to come back and buy into Ohana," Keane said when it was clear Sydney couldn't find the right words.

"'Us'?" Tehani rested her arm on the high counter above her desk. "*Us* who?"

"Keane, me and Silas," Sydney explained.

"The idea was for all of us—that included you, Tehani, and Daphne and Mano—to make this a true Ohana operation."

Tehani glanced at Keane, disappointment shining in her dark eyes. "That's why you came. Because of a business opportunity?"

"I came because that email arrived at the right time," he said easily. "And before we go any further into this discussion, I need you to know, I wanted to be here for Remy's memorial." His hesitation came with a number of shadows passing in front of his eyes. "It just wasn't…possible."

"What changed?" Tehani asked.

"Well, my employment status, for one," Keane admitted with what sounded like forced humor.

"You quit your job?" Sydney couldn't keep the shock out of her voice. As much as Keane loved competitive swimming, as much as he'd excelled in the sport, he was even better as an elite college coach. "Keane, you love coaching. Heck, didn't they just short-list you as a potential swim coach for the next Olympics?"

"Still on that list, as far as I know. I'm just taking some time to… Well… To see what my options are. When Sydney sent that video message from Remy—"

"It was a video message?"

The longing in Tehani's voice was only another reminder of Sydney's screwups. She was so used to only having herself to worry about, only herself to consult, she kept forgetting she wasn't alone on Nalani. She kept forgetting she had other people to look out for.

"Can I see it?" Tehani asked. "Would you mind?"

Keane sat forward, reached into the right pocket of his board shorts and pulled out his phone. "I don't have a problem with it. Syd?"

"I should have thought of it myself," she assured Tehani and Keane and glanced at the clock. "I've got a newlywed couple coming in for a coastal tour in a bit. I'm going to head back to the chopper and get it ready."

"Need any help?" Keane offered.

"No, thanks." It dawned on Sydney that what she needed was some time to herself. Watching Tehani slowly sink into one of the chairs across from Keane, seeing that curtain of grief drape over her face, felt like a solid swipe against her heart. "On second thought, Keane," Sydney said before she left. "Could you escort the couple up when they get here? Save me a walk back?"

"Sure, of course. Put me to work wherever you need me. That's what I'm here for," he reminded her, with a look that told Sydney they'd be having a more in-depth conversation on this subject at a later time.

Speaking of later...

Once outside, she pulled out her cell and texted Theo, suggesting they meet at six at Hula Chicken so he could get his huli-huli fix. For once, not even the thought of the open-air spit-roasted spiced chicken improved her mood. But receiving an instant thumbs-up emoji response from Theo did the trick.

She missed him. Disbelieving the idea, she shook her head. How was that possible? He should have been the last person on her mind, considering they hadn't been out of each other's company for nearly twenty-four hours. But there he was, front and center. Had her wishing he was there for her to talk to. Wanting to see that smile of his and the way his eyes lit up behind those glasses.

Apparently, it wasn't just the promise of

getting into the sky that could boost her disposition. Theo Fairfax did a darn good job of that himself.

"BEAUTIFUL, AREN'T THEY?"

Theo glanced over his shoulder at the tall, slender red-haired woman standing behind him. "Hey, Daphne." He shifted his attention away from Ohana's guide, who had led him on a surprisingly informative and entertaining waterfall trek and back to the collection of hand-stitched quilts, pillows and other cloth creations. "Yes, they are. I was just wondering if maybe they had a baby quilt? My sister and her wife just announced they're expecting." And when he'd realized a gift was in order, this was the first place he'd thought of.

"I'm sure they do. When I moved here a few years ago," she continued as she stepped closer and tapped a gentle fingertip against the store window, "I spent half my first paycheck in this store." Angling her chin up at the carved-wood sign identifying The Hawaiian Snuggler, a fond smile tipped the corners of her lips. Wearing a simple pair of denim shorts and a loose-fitting coral shirt that surprisingly didn't clash with her hair, she blended in effortlessly as a local. "One of the best investments I ever made."

"Moving here?" He asked. "Or buying out the Snuggler?"

"Both." Her smile widened. "You look a bit intimidated."

"Only at the potential selection." He'd left the cottage—and the idea of work—behind on impulse, something he wasn't entirely comfortable with. He was a man used to routines and found comfort in them. But today? Heck, the last few days, settling into expectations and predictability felt confining and—if he was honest with himself—a bit suffocating. It had nothing, he told himself, absolutely nothing to do with the niggling doubt he couldn't dismiss about GVI's business tactics where Sydney was concerned. "I don't suppose you'd be willing to lend me some advice?"

"You'd like help shopping for a baby gift?" Daphne's eyes brightened. "Isn't that something you'd like to ask Sydney to do?" The teasing lilt in her voice made Theo shove his hands into his pockets.

"Let me guess—the gossip grapevine? Rumors?"

"Rumors? Hardly." Daphne laughed. "You two left in that helicopter of hers yesterday afternoon and didn't come back until this morning. You jumped right over rumors and straight into reality. Come on." She grabbed hold of his arm and tugged him toward the open glass door. "I'll introduce you to Shani. I'm sure she'll have some suggestions for you."

The small storefront was barely wider than the front display window itself, but it was organized in such a way that made it feel larger. The subtle fragrance of summer flowers wafted through the air, carried off from the beach and through the trees.

"Howzit, Daph?" The woman sitting behind the counter looked up from the wooden hoop in her lap. The fabric draped over her was a bright white, the floral appliqué she was hand-stitching a bold blue. Her dark pixie-cut hair was tinted pink at the ends, while the tattoos winding up and down both arms and around her shoulders displayed what he now recognized as Polynesian symbols of ancestral connections.

"Doing okay, thanks. Shani, this is Theo Fairfax."

"Ah, you're the mainlander hanging around with Sydney. Aloha." Shani set her work aside and slid off the tall stool. She barely reached his shoulder as she made her way around. "It's nice to meet you. Welcome to Nalani."

"Mahalo."

Shani's eyebrow arched. "A word that can never be overused. What brings you two in?"

"My sister's expecting a baby later this fall." He glanced around the displays. On the far wall, three rows of hangers were neatly arranged with various quilts. There were also various quilted pillows, wall-hangings, book covers, and bags and purses. "There's a quilt in the cottage where I'm staying that's beautiful. I like the idea of bringing something home from the islands."

"We like that idea, too," Shani confirmed. "I tend to recommend the breadfruit pattern for first-time quilt buyers. And makers," she added. "It's meant to bring focus to a bountiful life. I have a few in stock for you to choose from. Daphne, I'm expecting a new quilt from Maylea in the next week or so. She mentioned a new purple-hibiscus pattern she's been working on."

"Then you know to set it aside for me," Daphne said. "Oh, this is lovely." She reached up and pulled a stark white background quilt with a variegated yellow pattern. "This would work well for a boy or a girl."

"It would." He looked to Shani. "Do you have that in a crib size?"

"I believe I do, actually." Shani moved between them to one of the lower rows. She sorted through the hangers and pulled one free. "What do you think?"

He accepted the hanger, held it up, and imagined it either in a crib or hanging on the wall above. "This looks like Beth to me," he said with a nod. "Yeah, I think she'll like that." He considered. "Actually, I'll take the larger one as well. For Beth and my sister-in-law," he explained. "It's never too early to shop for Christmas."

"In that case, let me show you something that just came in." Shani picked up both hangers and brought them back to the counter, then ducked into the back room.

"Sydney tells me you went to college with

Remy," he said to Daphne, who seemed to appreciate every piece offered in the store.

"I did. Came out to the islands for the first time to celebrate our graduation." She shook her head. "Something happens that first time. It's like the islands get a hold of you and don't let go."

"So you moved here."

"Remy and I remained close," Daphne said. "Well, as close as we could with me living on the mainland. When I found out he was looking for a nature guide, I couldn't say no." Something in her voice told Theo there was far more to the story, but he wasn't one to pry.

"No regrets?"

"About moving here? No. It's not everyone who finds exactly where they belong."

"And Nalani gave you that."

"It did. You have to have felt it," she said quietly. "That sudden shift inside of you, as if you've found something, some place you didn't know you needed."

Had he? Theo ducked his head, frowning. He'd just chalked all that up to anxiety and wanting to get back home to everything he was used to. Funny. He had a difficult time even picturing what his apartment looked like at the moment. "If everyone had that feeling, Nalani wouldn't be so small anymore, would it?" It was a very weak attempt at a joke. One that didn't even strike him as particularly funny. "That must mean you know Keane as well."

"Keane?" Daphne's eyes went wide. "How do you know about Keane?"

"Ah, because he's here?" Even as he said it, he wondered if he should have. "Sydney and I ran into him once we got back."

"What's this? The *kolohe* is back in Nalani?" Shani said as she emerged from the storeroom, her arms loaded with folded quilts.

"Ko-low-hay?" Theo echoed. He really needed to brush up more on the local colloquialisms.

"Roughly translated, it means *rascal*, or *wild one*." Daphne laughed. "Oh, man, Keane Harper." She shook her head, then frowned at Theo's blank look. "You've never heard of him, have you?"

"No." Not before today, he hadn't. "Sydney said he's a swimmer?"

"Uh, yeah, a swimmer." Shani chuckled. "Man was practically born with gills. He competed in the adult-surfing competitions around here as a teenager. Back in the day, he and Mano were front and center on Nalani travel brochures. He even got himself a sponsorship back when he competed. You want a mystical experience? Just watch Keane get anywhere near a wave."

"He traded in surfing for swimming in college." Daphne moved back to the counter to *ooh* and *aah* over a number of the quilts. "Look at this one. It's like…"

"Afterglow," Theo murmured, recalling his first Hawaiian sunset. The mingling and mixing of colors within the floral design against a barely blue background was a marvel to behold.

"It is," Daphne agreed. "This isn't Maylea's work, is it?"

"It's her granddaughter," Shani said with pride. "Sixteen years old, and look what she's doing already. This is her first finished quilt. To sell, anyway. Took her more than two years. Love seeing the younger ones embracing the tradition. Makes me think I can keep this place going forever," she added with a laugh.

"It's stunning." As someone without any creative talent, Theo was gaining an even bigger appreciation for people who did. "You going to get it?" he asked Daphne.

"As much as I would love it, no. I have rent to pay." She chuckled.

"You don't even know how much—"

"I've bought enough of these to suspect. But you go right ahead," Daphne cajoled and even knocked her shoulder against his arm.

If he didn't grab it now, he had the feeling he may very well regret it for the rest of his life. "I'll take it." No second thoughts. If anything, it felt like one of the best decisions he'd made in a long time. "And I'd like that hibiscus quilt in the window, unless you have another in the back? My mother will love it."

"Your mother raised a good and generous son," Shani told him. "Why don't you come back tomorrow and pick them up? I'll gift-wrap them for you, in a way that's easy for travel. Complimentary, of course."

"That would be appreciated," Theo said, glancing at his watch. "I'd just as soon rather not lug them around with me to dinner."

SYDNEY SLID INTO one of the few empty picnic tables at Hula Chicken a good ten minutes before Theo was due to arrive. As usual, the outdoor eatery was filled to its nonexistent rafters, with both local and tourist customers alike. Strings of colorful lights had been woven into an unintentional maze overhead and would soon blink to life. Beside the oversize pickup window, the beverage station was buzzing with employees filling drink orders.

Giant roasting racks held dozens of butterflied chickens spinning ever-so-evenly on the always-burning coals, sending a spicy, heavenly perfumed smoke into the air. One of the smells of her childhood—roasting chicken mingling with the fresh-tinged air of the ocean only a few steps away.

There were areas of Nalani where you could see the entire town simply by turning in a circle. Hula was one of those places. The resort and church off to her left, the main road into the center of Nalani to her right; she was bolstered by the majestic mountains in front of her with the sea at her back. *Precisely the way life is meant to be*, she told herself.

Images of a hulaing chicken—*huli*, its namesake-cooking style, literally meant *turning*—covered the green plastic tablecloths.

An eco-friendly utensil, napkin and condiment receptacle sat at the end of the table, while Makai, one of the local bands, tuned up at the far end of the patio.

"Aloha, Sydney." Vivi Ahina, whom once upon a time Sydney had babysat for, spun away from one table to face her. She was on the short and chubby side, with a round face and the kindest eyes Sydney had ever seen. Her green tank was the same color as the tablecloths but only displayed one dancing chicken on her shoulder. "Haven't seen you much since you've been back."

"Aloha." Sydney rested her chin in her hand and sighed. The last few days were closing in on her. At this point, she had to hope she could stay awake through dinner. "Been busy."

"Yah, so I hear." Vivi's dark eyebrows waggled. "Also heard you and the mainlander got stranded during the storm last night."

"The mainlander's name is Theo, and yes, we did." Sydney had to laugh. Nothing was ever a secret for long in Nalani. "He's meeting me for dinner in a few, actually. He's been dying to try the huli-huli chicken ever since he got here."

"That's because we make the best huli-huli on all the islands," Vivi said. "I'll let Dad know we've got a special order. You want the works?"

"Might as well break him in before the luau on Wednesday. You coming?"

"Who isn't?" Vivi asked and pointed back at the sign in the front window of the food shack, which announced they would be closed from four that afternoon until the next morning. "Leora is a miracle baby. Everyone around here's looking forward to celebrating her first birthday. What can I get you to drink?"

She had to work tomorrow, which meant she should be responsible and order a soda—but darn it, she'd earned a boosted-liquid bonus. "Mai tai, heavy on the pineapple skewers," she said. "Probably a beer for Theo, but I'm not sure."

"On it. Give me a wave when he's here, and we'll get you taken care of."

"Thanks, Vivi." *Time*, Sydney thought as the young woman moved off to check on her other customers, *is a very funny thing*. It could slow to a sea turtle's beach-banking pace or speed along like a porpoise beside a catamaran. It didn't seem so long ago she'd rocked Vivi to sleep before setting her in her crib. Now? Vivi was a year into college at University of Hawai'i Hilo, on her way to an engineering degree. "And yet I haven't aged a day," Sydney said to herself, then laughed.

"Not for as long as I've known you, at least." Theo's voice brought an instant smile to Sydney's face. He came up behind her and slid onto the bench across from her. "I'm not late, am I?"

"You are not." She'd bet half Ohana's income he'd never been late a day in his life. "I was just anxious to put the day behind me." She inclined her head. "You bought a new shirt." She reached across, flicked a finger against the collar. "Ukuleles with leis." She pinched her lips together to stop from smiling. "You met ChiChi, didn't you?"

"Maybe." He glanced down, plucked the fabric away from his chest. "How'd you guess?"

"Because he can spot a tourist at a hundred paces." And Theo had clearly played right into the old man's hands. "I bet he gave you the 'everyone on the islands has one of these' pitches, didn't he?"

"He might have." But instead of looking sour about it, Theo smiled at her. "It's nice and cool to wear. Temperature-wise," he added. "The pink flowers on blue might be a bit garish."

*Garish.* She sighed and shook her head. How she loved this man's way with words. "If you aren't careful, you'll end up with an actual ukulele by the time you go home."

"Already bought one," he confirmed, then broke into a laugh at her shocked expression. "You aren't the only one who can tease."

"No," she said slowly as he got more comfortable in his seat. "I guess I'm not. Thanks, Vivi." She sat back as her mai tai was delivered. "I wasn't sure what you wanted to drink," she said.

"Local beer is fine, thanks," he said, earning an impressed nod from Vivi before she left again. "I'm learning that buying local earns you quite a bit of goodwill."

"Wearing that shirt's going to get you a lot of good laughs, too," she teased. "Where else did you go?"

"Hawaiian Snuggler. Got my Christmas and baby shopping done in one fell swoop. Also got a call from my credit card company confirming I'd actually been the one to use my card," he added.

"That must have put a smile on Shani's face."

"I may have earned her 'favorite customer of the day' award. I believe Daphne held the title before me?"

"She is the undisputed champ," Sydney confirmed. The evening breeze picked up, blowing the last of the day's heat up and over the mountains.

The band began to play soft, subtle island music that brought back all the memories of her growing-up years, when her family had spent countless evenings out and about with the locals. Since she'd been back, if she wasn't at the office getting her bearings with the business, she tended to hole up in her house or head down to the beach, content with her memories and the ghosts in the house. Those memories had served their purpose and pushed her through the roughest part of the grief. Now she had something better.

She sipped the fruity, frothy, rum-kissed drink and reached across the table to slip her fingers through his. "I'm glad we're doing this."

"Me, too." He didn't break eye contact as he squeezed his hand around hers. "I missed you today."

"Yeah," she said and sipped more of her drink. "I had the same thought. Looks like we're having one of those island romances I always swore would never happen to me."

"Know a lot about those, do you?"

"Not to bring up a sore subject, but you met Keane earlier. He's kind of known for them," she added when his hand tensed. "Oh, relax, Theo. You two aren't in any kind of competition, and even if you were, you'd win with me, hands-down. Besides, he is not the settling-down kind of guy."

"Good to know."

"You'll like him when you get to know him," she said quietly, wondering if he'd realized what he'd inadvertently confessed.

"I won't be here long enough for that to happen."

"No." Now it was her hand that tightened. Always with the reality, this man. "No, I don't suppose you will be."

"But that doesn't mean we can't enjoy the time we do have."

"Right." It felt both like forever and only hours away. She couldn't explain it. Actually, she didn't really want to. But there was part of her that couldn't imagine this place without him. How had *that* happened?

"Here you go." Vivi returned with Theo's beer and a platter of side dishes that she set individually on the table, followed by a small stack of biodegradable plates and disposable utensils. "Chicken will be out in a few."

Sydney tugged her hand free from his as Theo's eyes went wide. "This looks like the entire menu."

"It is," Sydney said. "Since you won't be around for the luau." She did a quick rundown of their selections, which included macaroni salad (not nearly as good as hers); fresh steamed rice; purple sweet potatoes; fruit salad made up of guava, lilikoi and pineapple; and authentic haupia coconut-pudding squares. No sooner had they filled their plates than Vivi was back with a whole cut-up chicken, spit-roasted to perfection and glistening with goodness.

"I probably won't eat for a week after this." Sydney said.

Sydney grabbed a drumstick and, as always, bit in before she let it cool off. That familiar heat burn, along with the explosion of flavors on her tongue, felt like home in one mouthful. "The heat makes you metabolize spice faster," she said. "Be sure you save some of the fruit salad to take home to Noodles."

"Way ahead of you. All right." He stabbed a thigh and plopped it onto his plate.

"Uh-uh." She reached over and nudged the fork out of his hand. "This is food you eat with your hands. Embrace the chaos."

"Right." He shook his head, that adorable befuddled expression on his face striking an untapped chord inside her. He was such a dichotomy. Such a surprise in so many ways. She'd never been around someone who made her laugh so much. Not only with his words but at herself. Who would have thought an uptight number cruncher would have slipped as completely and sneakily into her heart? She swallowed hard and, for a moment, didn't taste a bit of her food.

She'd always wondered if she ever took

the fall if she'd even notice. But it was impossible not to notice anything about Theo Fairfax, especially the way he made her feel. Like she was the most interesting person he'd ever met. As if she was the only person he wanted to be around.

*Projecting*, she thought before finding herself on the receiving end of another one of his heart-stopping smiles. A smile that made the entire world, at least for an instant, stop in its tracks.

"What?" He swiped the back of his hand down his nose. "Am I making a mess?"

He was, with his greasy and spice-coated fingers, but it only added to his appeal. "You are indeed. Might have to take you down to the ocean to clean you off."

"Oh, no." He finished his chicken and shook his head as he sat back. "No, I draw the line there. Me and sand and water are not a good combination."

"When are you going to accept that pushing you over your lines is part of my job? I like a challenge, remember?" she boasted and reached for the bowl of lomi-lomi salmon. "And you have most definitely been that.

Save room for dessert. They make a killer coconut cream pie that is a must try."

"I'm going to have to up my running routine when I get home."

She swallowed hard. His reminder took the shine off her mood. She kept forgetting he was only here a little while longer. Before she knew it, he'd be gone and she'd be…

She'd be just fine, she told herself, as if that would make it true.

"You really like San Francisco, don't you?"

"Of course." He shrugged. "I mean, it's no Hawai'i, right?"

"No," she agreed with a slow nod. "It's not." Neither was South Carolina. Something she hadn't let herself think on for too long. She had a life, she had plans waiting for her back on the mainland. "Do you think you like it because it's where you went to school? Where you finally stayed put for a while? Or is it something else?"

"Interesting question," he said. "I think the fact it was the first place I spent more than a few months in has a lot to do with it. I'm comfortable there. It's a good place to work, and there's this feeling of being alive, being a part of something bigger than yourself." He glanced around, smirked. "You know what that's like. You have it here, in Nalani. You probably have it back in South Carolina as well. Well, you must. Otherwise you wouldn't be anxious to get back there."

She waited for internal confirmation that he was right. To silently agree with him. But…it wasn't so much that she wanted to get back to a *place* as it was her *plans*. Plans that had stagnated considerably since Remy had died.

Plans she'd barely thought about since Theo arrived on the island. The truth was, she wasn't particularly anxious to get back. Not anymore. But then that was part of the temptation of the islands, wasn't it? Who would ever want to leave paradise?

"Everything okay with Ohana?" Theo asked as his brows knitted.

"Everything's great, actually. We're in the process of booking a big wedding party for next month. Why?"

He gestured with his chin. "Tehani and Keane are headed your way, and Tehani looks, I don't know, determined?"

Sydney dropped her second piece of chicken

and looked over her shoulder, lifting her leg up and over the bench as she watched the two approaching. Dinner churned in her stomach. That wasn't Tehani's determined look.

She was angry.

"T? What's wrong?" Sydney looked beyond her friend to Keane, who gave her a warning shake of his head.

"This." She slapped a stack of papers onto the table beside what was left of their meal. "If you're going to sell Ohana, maybe you should consider a company who can get their email addresses straight."

"This is from GVI?" Sydney glanced at Theo, who didn't look as surprised as she would have liked. "Okay, hang on." She scooted back and grabbed the tub of disposable wipes to clean her hands.

Keane walked around the table and took a seat beside Theo.

Sydney scanned the email, her frown increasing by the second. "They're making an outright offer? Already? Before you've submitted your financial review?" She looked at Theo. "Did you know about this?"

"I spoke to my supervisor earlier, so I

knew it was coming. Didn't realize it was happening so soon, though."

"You told me, you *promised* me, you'd give it six months." The desperation in Tehani's voice couldn't be ignored. Not by Sydney, not by Theo and Keane, and not by the customers at the nearby tables. Or Hula Chicken's employees. "I don't care how much money they're offering you, you can't sell Ohana."

Sydney cringed at the gasps and protests she heard rumbling through the restaurant. She cast a quick look to Vivi, who looked as horrified as Tehani. "I haven't agreed to anything, T. I told you that, and it was the truth."

"Then why did they send you a contract?" Tehani demanded. "If you—"

"That's on GVI, Tehani," Theo cut her off before Sydney could find the words. "I told them that Sydney hadn't made a decision yet, and they asked if an actual offer might help." He shrugged. "I honestly didn't think it could hurt."

"Boy, were you wrong," Keane muttered.

"An offer isn't an agreement," Sydney told Tehani, and made sure her voice carried to everyone within earshot as she flipped through the pages. When she got to the purchase-price offer, however, she shivered. "They're kidding, right?"

"They put it in writing, so I'm guessing they're not," Tehani said.

"Can I see the contract?" He motioned to Keane to hand him the tub of wipes and cleaned up. Sydney passed over the papers, watched his face as he read. Only his expression didn't change. Not even when he lifted his eyes and met her gaze. "That's a lot of money."

"I don't care," Tehani said. "You can't put a price on the soul of Nalani. Don't you do this, Sydney." Angry tears burst into her eyes and coated her voice. "Don't do this to Remy."

Sydney's throat tightened. "I haven't—"

But Tehani wasn't listening. She'd already spun around and walked away.

"I'll talk to her," Keane offered, grabbing one of the sweet bread rolls off the table as he got to his feet. "She probably just needs to walk it off."

"I don't think this is a walk-it-off situation," Sydney told him. "Why didn't you tell me the offer was coming?" she asked Theo once Keane was gone.

"I assumed you knew it would be the next step in the process."

"Did you tell them I would sign?"

"No." He hesitated. "But I told them you were close to making a decision."

"Sydney." Vivi stopped beside the table. "This is a joke, right? You aren't seriously going to sell Ohana Odysseys, are you?"

How many times was she going to have to say the same thing? "I haven't made any decisions about anything, Vivi."

"What is this GVI?" she demanded.

"Golden Vistas Incorporated," Theo said, in what Sydney was certain was an effort to deflect Vivi's obvious anger. "We're a hotel and resort corporation. We've got a number of properties around California, and we're looking to expand out here to the islands. Nalani is on the top of our list."

"'Our list'? You work for them?" Vivi asked. "That's why you're here? To *evaluate* us?"

"Vivi—" Now it was Sydney's turn to deflect.

"Did we pass?" Vivi asked in a tone that left Sydney cringing.

"We must have." That wasn't just a good amount of money. It was life-changing money. Money that would allow her not only to get her flight school up and running but also give a significant amount to Tehani so she wouldn't have to worry for herself and the baby. Sydney looked to Theo. "I need to go talk to Tehani."

"Yeah. Of course. Go. I'll take care of all this," he offered.

"Sydney." Vivi reached out and caught her arm as Sydney got up to follow her friends. "You can't do this."

"I haven't done anything but entertain an offer," Sydney said, but the disappointment she saw in the young woman's eyes struck hard. Tehani was right about one thing: Ohana Odysseys was more than a few employees entertaining tourists. It was one of the lynchpins that kept Nalani solvent and its residents provided for.

"Remy trusted you." Vivi stepped back, and only then did Sydney realize what else she saw in Vivi's tight expression. Fear. And panic. "He trusted you with Nalani. He trusted you with us."

"I know."

"Do you?" Vivi accused. "I'm not so sure."

Sydney swallowed hard, ducked her head and walked away, hoping there was some way to fix this. And somehow to make everyone happy.

# CHAPTER TEN

PRINTED CONTRACT IN HAND, Theo watched a defeated Sydney head off after Tehani and Keane, guilt and confusion pressing down on him.

"I'll get you some take-home containers," Vivi said stiffly before she headed back to the food shack.

His head buzzed, as if a hive of direction-less bees had taken up residence, keeping his thoughts from finding some kind of cohesion. He knew GVI liked to move fast on opportunities, but he'd never—not in all his time with the company—known them to pounce this hard. He scanned through the contract one last time, but he stopped at the same place he had before: on the purchase price.

"It's too much." Ohana Odysseys was a great investment opportunity. There wasn't any doubt about that. But the amount GVI was offering was obscenely high. No. Not *obscenely* high. "Desperately high." The second he said it, he knew he wasn't wrong. It made sense now. He hadn't understood the big push, not until now. But seeing that dollar amount in black and white? He had a pretty good idea what was going on.

"Do you think she'll sell?" Vivi's voice carried a bit more trepidation than anger now, Theo observed as he looked up at the young woman.

"I don't know," Theo said truthfully. "Vivi, neither Sydney nor I knew the offer was coming so soon." It normally took weeks to get the contract details together. There was no way it had been drawn up in the few hours since he'd spoken to Elise. No. GVI had been ready to spring this immediately, despite Theo's insistence that Sydney wasn't a guaranteed lock. "Sydney agreed to hear their pitch, which is how I came to be here. She's been gracious enough to show me around and help me understand what Nalani is about."

"And do you see?" Vivi asked. "What we are? Who we are?"

He did. In full-blown Technicolor. "I'd like to think so."

"Then you understand why she can't sell."

*Can't?* No, he could absolutely understand why she could. The financial incentives alone would make whatever she wanted to do with her life potentially feasible.

But *should* she sell? That was an entirely different question. "I haven't known Sydney for very long," he told a stubborn-looking Vivi. "But I think I can safely say she will make the best decision for everyone involved. Give her time to mull things over, okay? Maybe neither of us should be pushing her into a corner."

She blinked at his statement, then nodded, the tension on her face easing a bit. "You may be right. It's just that she's been gone for so long I don't know if she realizes…" She shook her head. "If she didn't know that offer was coming—"

"She didn't." He didn't want anyone here in Nalani thinking Sydney was acting in any way other than in the best interest of the town. Or its people. "She'll make the right choice for all of you. I'm certain of it."

"I hope so." Vivi nodded and efficiently packaged up the leftovers and slid the containers into a reusable shopping bag branded with the restaurant's hula-chicken mascot. He paid the bill and headed out.

He'd assumed dinner with Sydney would have led to a leisurely walk through town, maybe sitting on a bench near the beach and watching the sunset. Instead, he found himself hurrying back to the cottage. While his laptop woke up, he set the contract on the table and unloaded the leftovers into the fridge after he scooped out a tiny portion of guava and pineapple into what he'd designated as Noodles's bowl.

He left the front door and windows open, welcoming the evening breeze into the house. He toed off his shoes, changed into shorts but kept his new shirt on, as it truly was the most comfortable piece of apparel he'd invested in, possibly in forever.

Checking the time, he jumped online and, after brewing himself a pot of coffee, got down to work.

A few hours later, he sat back in his chair, a new wave of dread and concern weaving through him. He shouldn't have ignored that inner voice of his. That uncertainty that had been niggling at him ever since he boarded his flight to Hawai'i vanished. His inclination to ignore watercooler gossip and not listen to all the rumors that plagued a big company may as well have been a huge pair of blinders.

It had taken dozens of spreadsheets and reports; information he as a midrange financial analyst and number cruncher didn't have easy access to. But he'd gotten access now, and what he'd found tilted his solidified future off axis.

Taking all things together—the overreaching offer GVI had made to Sydney, the urgency in his injured boss's voice when she'd called for an update, the speed with which the contract had arrived—he was left with a completely different picture than he'd had yesterday.

GVI's bid for Ohana Odysseys was absolutely a grab at getting a foothold in the islands. But not in an effort to expand and grow.

It was, at its core, a desperate last-ditch effort to remedy their past mistakes and mismanagement.

But it would be Nalani that would ultimately pay the price.

SYDNEY WASN'T ONE to appreciate the silent treatment. She hadn't as a kid, and she certainly didn't now.

That said, the next morning, at least where Tehani was concerned, Sydney would have welcomed it. Her friend's terse, clipped answers and comments to anything Sydney said left them both on edge and Sydney anxious to head out on the first of two scheduled island tours of the morning.

Chasing Tehani and Keane down the beach after her dinner with Theo had proved pointless. Her late-brother's girlfriend hadn't been in any mood to talk. Not wanting to push, she'd let Keane take the lead and walk Tehani home.

The tension wasn't going to do anyone—not Sydney, not Tehani and certainly not Ohana Odysseys—any good. No. The only way through this was for Sydney to make a decision: Did she stay here in Nalani and make a go of her brother's dreams?

Or did she go home and focus on her own?

The question was moot, at least right now. She'd promised she'd give it six months before she decided, but she couldn't shake the feeling the longer she waited, the harder it would be to walk away.

A lot could change in six months. A lot *would* change. By then, Tehani would be a mother. How could she even think about leaving?

Leaving now made the most sense. Sydney rubbed a fist against the center of her chest. Did that mean it was the right choice?

"Sydney!"

Halfway down the hill, on her way back to Ohana, she stopped and faced Theo as he jogged toward her. "I was hoping to catch you this morning, but when I stopped by the office, Tehani said you were already up in the air."

"Busy day," she said. "Have another tour this afternoon, so I don't really have time—"

"We need to talk."

Now was not the time to have *that* conversation. She resumed her path. "We probably do—"

"About the offer from GVI."

"Oh." She stopped again, frowned. "Yeah, I'd like the contract back. I'd rather not kill another tree by printing a second copy."

"I've got it back at the cottage, but that's not the—"

Sydney's phone rang. She might have ignored it were it not for the custom ringtone she'd assigned to the Search and Rescue unit. She held up a finger. "Hold that thought."

She reached into her back pocket and answered. "This is Sydney."

"Syd, Captain Brubank. We'll need eyes in the sky over Hamakua. We've got two children, ages eight and ten, who've wandered away from their campsite. Could use the air assist."

"How long have they been missing?" She pivoted and headed straight back up the hill.

"Since sometime during the night. We've had ground units searching the area, but so far no luck. Moving inland now and got teams along the exit."

"Understood. I can be in the air in less than ten."

"Roger that. Report in fifteen."

"Copy. Out." She turned to call over her shoulder to Theo, only to find him beside her. "Sorry. We've got two missing kids. Need to get in the air." She dialed her copilot, Spencer, only to get sent directly to voice mail. "Darn it. Forgot Spencer's visiting his parents in Kona for a few days."

"Who's Spencer?"

"My copilot. Second pair of eyes," she added as she picked up speed and made it back to the landing pad in record time. "I'll text you when I get back." She took the stairs two at a time and gave silent thanks she'd had the forethought to refill the chopper after the last tour. "No idea when that will be."

"You're going up alone?"

"Looks like." She wrenched open the door and jumped in, hit the engine button and set the blades to spinning. Sydney belted in and closed the door, was reaching for her headphones when the passenger door opened and Theo climbed in beside her. "What are you doing?"

"Going with you." She watched, somewhat astonished, as he settled in with the efficiency of an enthusiastic lifelong flier. "You need extra eyes. I've got four." He pointed at his glasses.

"Cute. I'm fully capable—"

"Of course you are. You're also wasting time." Theo grabbed a pair of headphones and gave her a thumb's up. "I won't be a distraction."

"Yeah," Sydney muttered to herself. "Not sure that's entirely possible." The man had been distracting her since she picked him up at the airport. "This isn't going to be a leisurely tour," she warned him as the engine geared up. "You're going to have to trust that I know what I'm doing."

"I wouldn't be here if I didn't," he said without hesitation. "Let's go."

"All right. Here." She handed Theo her cell. "Call Ohana. Tell Tehani I'm out on a rescue call and that we'll check in when we're on the way back. She might need to reschedule this afternoon's bookings."

"Roger that." He grinned as he took the phone. "Always wanted to say that."

"Hang on." She pulled up on the cyclic and raised the skids off the ground in one fluid motion. Once they were clear, she pressed down on her left foot, angled with the cyclic and headed north toward the Hilo.

There was a mindset that came with a rescue flight. A mindset that had her looking at their surroundings with a completely different eye from the one she used as a tour guide. It was so easy to miss something. She'd flown far more sea rescues than land; she also found them less complicated. Or perhaps it was what she was used to.

Something about identifying anomalies in the water felt easier to her. With the topography of the mountains, mixing with the coastal volcanic-rock formations, people were easily camouflaged, so she knew to look for signs of distress.

The anxiety and worry were there, knotted low in her belly, but she could control that almost as easily as she could the chopper. Nothing made her compartmentalize faster than knowing someone was waiting for her to find them.

She buzzed over homes and strip malls. Local businesses and streets and freeways, all the while mapping out the grid she'd fly once she was overhead of the forested area.

She could hear Theo's voice yelling over the sound of the blades that were dulled by her headphones. She glanced over when he hung up. Theo clicked the dial on the side of his headphones and activated his microphone.

"She said to fly safe," he said. "Where are we headed?"

"Hamakua. It's a forest reserve at the north end of the island. There's only two of us, so it shouldn't take us longer than fifteen, twenty minutes to get there." The fewer people on board, the faster they'd move. "They've got the exit and surrounding areas covered, so that gives us a general place to start. I'm going to approach from the west and move in."

"Grid search pattern?"

"Yeah." She had no doubt his mathematically minded brain was going to come in handy. "Keep your search area tight and look for anything out of place."

"This happen a lot? Missing campers?"

"Not so much, thank goodness," she told him. "Hikers, especially solitary ones, are more likely. I'm betting these kids got bored or curious—"

"Probably both," Theo agreed.

"Sometimes, it's a dangerous combination. They've got a ton of people looking for them, which always evens out the odds." She changed frequencies, checked in with the base unit. "Ohana One reporting in. Approaching southwest end of Hamakua. Please advise."

"Base to Ohana One. Got you on radar. No update as of yet. Proceed with search upon arrival."

"Copy. Over and out." They flew in silence for a while, and she noticed he was already in search mode. The intensity with which he focused on the ground revealing an entirely new side of him. He hadn't hesitated, jumping into the copter with her. He'd seen something that needed doing, and he'd done it. Affection and gratitude bloomed inside her, swelling to the point of dismay. Never in her life had she met anyone so prone to surprise who impressed her. A few days ago, the idea of being in this vehicle had been an impossibility, and now here he sat, in command of his emotions and fears as she was. Or so it seemed.

Time would tell.

"Theo, there's an emergency bag under your seat," she said as they approached the reserve. "Should be a pair of binoculars in there. They might help. Six eyes," she said and earned a chuckle of appreciation. "Be ready. We're going lower." And lower she went, until she could practically feel the tops of the trees brush the skids.

She heard his sharp intake of breath, but he raised the binoculars to his face. "Do we know what they're wearing?"

"Negative. I'm hoping that once they realized they were lost, they stayed put." It was what she and Remy had always been taught.

*Stay put and we'll find you*, her father had said. *I promise, we'll find you.*

"Your father sounds like he was a smart man."

"What?" She hadn't realized she'd said that part out loud. "Yeah. He trained us pretty early on. Remy wasn't exactly easy to corral."

"I'm betting he wasn't the only one." Theo kept his gaze moving, angling down and up as she kept a tight hold on her pattern. "How large an area is the reserve?"

"Ah, a little over four thousand acres."

He lowered the binoculars, his brow furrowing for a moment. "Okay, so that's almost seven square miles. Where was their campsite?"

"Good question." She hit the switch on her radio. "Ohana One to base. Requesting location of missings' campsite? Over."

"Roger, Ohana One. One point three miles in from the entrance. Over."

"Roger, Base. Out. That help?"

"The entrance is…?"

"A few miles in from the shore." A shore she could see in the far-off distance.

"We're too far out. No way two kids travel this far. Move in."

"Math to the rescue." She ditched their current area and did as he suggested. "You're thinking, what? Three, maybe four miles out from the campsite?"

"At the most. If they were wandering, it was probably in circles. I'd guesstimate a maximum of three."

She was a woman who trusted her gut, and her gut was telling her he had rationed this out with care. There was a certainty and confidence in his voice that made her trust him without hesitation. She glanced at her instrument panel, pushed forward on the cyclic and took four miles off their search. "Tell me if you see anything."

"Yep." He was scanning the ground, leaning so far over the edges of the binoculars knocked against the windshield. But he didn't flinch. He didn't quit. And neither did she. Keeping a steady hand, they hovered and shifted above the trees for what felt like hours, the silence becoming a barometer of failure.

Her arms began to pull with that familiar ache, the muscles along her back tightening as the tension mingled with the passing minutes. She glanced at her watch. More than two hours since they took off from Nalani. It would be a while before they ran out of gas, but she'd been known to fly on fumes before.

"What's that?" He pointed in front of him. "There, go back."

She repositioned the bird, waiting for his signal to stop.

"Can you go lower?"

"I can." The question was, could he? She pushed down on the collective, the lever in her left hand, and took them down.

"It's them." The wonder in his voice popped the anxiety bubble building in her chest. "One is jumping up and down, waving his arms." He looked over at her. "We found them."

"Math never fails." She radioed back in. "Ohana One to Base. Over?"

"Base here."

"Be advised, missings located." She rattled off the longitude and latitude of where they were. "Possible injuries but communicating. Over."

"Understood, Ohana One. Thanks for the assist. Out."

"Now comes the fun part." She offered Theo a quick smile at his arched brows. "We need to drop that emergency bag. Can you check it?"

He hauled up the small canvas bag and looked inside. "There's a first aid kit, a ration of snacks and a couple of bottles of water." Once he'd zipped the bag back up, he looked at her. "Drop it how?"

"You'll need to open your door."

"Right." He checked his seat belt as he stared at her. "Right. Okay." He took a deep breath. "This is what I get for wanting to help. Here I go." He pushed the lever latch down and pushed open the door, just enough to send a gust of wind into the vehicle and for him to drop the bag. She pushed the nose of the chopper down, and they watched as one of the boys retrieved the bright yellow bag. She flashed the chopper lights and earned a wave before she banked to the left and headed back toward Nalani.

"Well, that was an experience I didn't anticipate having," Theo said.

"You did great," Sydney told him. "You're a natural."

"Yeah?" He looked impressed at the idea.

"Yeah. You did exactly what I told you to

do. And that's the most important thing," she said.

"That's a great feeling, being able to help people like that. Those parents are going to be so relieved their kids are okay."

"Yeah." Sydney brought them to a higher altitude and eased back on the cyclic, anxious to take a more leisurely pace back home. Around them, the island she'd always called home opened up in front of her and pulsed in all its resplendent beauty. "Yeah, it feels pretty good."

"Must be nice, knowing you can do that work anywhere. I mean, your talents and ability aren't limited to your location."

"No," she murmured, frowning behind her sunglasses. "No, they aren't, are they?"

It was really that simple, wasn't it? The answer she'd been looking for had always been there, right in front of her, waiting for her to realize the truth.

No matter how long she'd stayed away, no matter how hard she tried to convince herself otherwise, Nalani was her town. Her home. She knew this island well enough that years later, she'd been able to fly overhead and help bring two kids home sooner than later. Her instincts about the Big Island hadn't dimmed over the years. They'd been enhanced.

She'd been brought back here for a reason. Because Remy had essentially asked her to, but it was more than that. A lot more.

"Should I call ahead and let Tehani know we're on our way back?" He glanced at the instrument panel. "What are we, fifteen minutes out?"

She shook her head. "You're getting good at this."

He beamed. "I really am, aren't I?"

He really was. Just in time for him to go home.

"IS SOMETHING WRONG?" Theo waited until after they'd gotten back to Nalani, after Sydney had refueled the copter and restocked her emergency supplies, before asking. "You got awfully quiet all of a sudden."

He'd assumed they'd stop at Ohana Odysseys' office, but she'd kept walking, something that didn't disappoint him in the least. He had a bit of an adrenaline rush still surging and he wasn't entirely sure what to do with the excess energy. Now, as they approached the tree-lined pathway to the beach—and he saw Benji and Kahlua sitting on the bench at the end of the block—he found himself feeling grateful for the opportunity his job had given him.

"Sorry." The smile she flashed him didn't come close to reaching her eyes. "Just thinking."

"About anything in particular?" He knew what he was thinking about. He wanted to take her to dinner, to erase those lines of sadness that had appeared around her eyes. He wanted to hold her hand and watch the sunset and pretend as if leaving her wasn't going to make him feel like an empty shell lying alone on the sand. He wanted as many memories firmly in place before he headed home tomorrow. "Care to share?"

"Yes." It was the way she said it, as if she'd been hoping he wouldn't ask. "You were right. Earlier. We do need to talk. About the buyout offer."

"Right." He still hadn't found the right way to tell her that he suspected the entire deal would, if not sooner than later, cost Nalani everything.

"I know the deal is important to you, Theo."

"It is. It was," he corrected quickly. "I'll get a promotion out of it for sure, but—"

"I can't do it." As soon as she said it, her spine straightened, and she seemed to grow taller. She pushed out a breath, shook her head. "I thought that would be more difficult to say, but it wasn't. I'm not selling Ohana." She inclined her head, met his gaze. "Not to GVI or anyone. It's…mine. Ours."

She took a long look around the street teeming with locals and tourists, the store-fronts welcoming people and allowing them to explore small-town island life at its most perfect. "I've spent so much time trying to define myself apart from Remy, from making a difference the way he did. I didn't think I could do that in Nalani. But that's exactly what we just did. Not only can I live in his shadow, I need it. It's a part of me. This is my home, Theo. Ohana Odysseys is my home. And that isn't for sale. At any price."

Relief he'd never expected surged through him. For an instant, he felt as if he'd been caught in a riptide, trapped between being dragged out to sea, into the unknown, and landlocked right in this spot. With her. There wasn't much he could say beyond, "I understand."

"Do you? Really?"

"Of course I do." He nodded. "My job wasn't to convince you to sell—it was just to present the facts." It hadn't stopped him from trying, though, had it? However inadvertently, he'd encouraged the idea of following her dreams back home and turning Ohana over to GVI. He'd gone so far as to remind her about what waited for her in South Carolina, that she'd already worked hard to make that part of her future a reality and yet...

And yet how could he ignore that the woman he loved was already exactly where she belonged?

"Tehani will be relieved," he told her, tamping down on the mind-numbing realization that he'd actually, in the matter of a few days, fallen head over heels for this amazing, inspiring, gorgeous woman. "All of Nalani will be."

"Yes." She nodded, and this time when she smiled, the spark was back. "It'll be a lot of hard work, and we'll have to make some adjustments, but I can do everything I wanted to right here. Not to mention I'm going to have a niece or nephew to help with in a few months. I won't be so alone anymore."

He reached out a hand, drew light fingers down the side of her face. "You've never been alone here, Sydney. Deep down, you know that. If there's one thing Nalani has taught me, it's that family isn't necessarily defined by blood. And that's the true meaning of ohana, isn't it? It's all around you." He saw it everywhere he looked.

She caught his hand. "I guess that means you'll be leaving tomorrow as planned."

"I guess so." He shrugged. "How about dinner tonight?"

"If it's all the same to you." Her lips trembled and she ducked her chin. "I think maybe I'd rather say goodbye now." She raised up on her toes and pressed her mouth to his. He caught her arm, tried to pull her closer, but she stepped out of reach. "The sooner I start to get over you, the better, Abacus."

"Sydney—"

"Goodbye, Theo."

She stepped back and, without looking at him again, turned and walked away.

# CHAPTER ELEVEN

THAT NIGHT, Sydney wandered the house and listened to the old creaks and strains of memory, found some comfort in the evening breeze buffeting against the shutters and lost herself in the white noise of the ocean that, long before dawn, she watched, curled up in her father's old rocker on the back porch.

Despite her search-and-rescue epiphany, any resolution she hoped to have with Tehani would have to wait. By the time she got back to Ohana Odysseys, she'd found Keane manning the front desk, along with the afternoon clients, as Tehani had gone home early. Keane had insisted she was fine—physically, at least—but Sydney suspected the emotional toll her indecision had taken was responsible. After the afternoon tour, which lasted longer than expected due to some surprise high winds, Sydney had texted Tehani to check in. While the response had been enough to reassure Sydney that T's issues had nothing to do with her pregnancy, she'd agreed to Sydney's request to come by the house before work. Of course, the promise of fresh passion fruit malasadas had absolutely nothing to do with it.

Now that the decision was made, Sydney kept waiting for the doubt to descend. For the second-guessing to begin. But it didn't happen. If anything, she felt an odd sense of peace knowing that she was exactly where she belonged. Her dreams were still possible—they'd just taken a bit of a detour and revision.

The money she'd saved for her flight school could be easily reallocated and invested into the business. She was going to have to find some additional office help to assist Tehani, and if she was going to put her entire heart and soul into Ohana, she'd have to invest in some additional guides and instructors. Even as the thoughts had circulated in her brain, she felt the excitement kick in. By the time she'd purged everything into one now very full notepad, the sun was on its way up, peeking over the horizon and bathing the sky in its promising, colorful ribbons of light.

Settling in one of the teak rocking chairs her father had bought for the family a number of Christmases ago, Sydney cupped her hands around her now-cool mug of coffee and reveled in the start not only of a new day but also her new life.

A new life that wouldn't include Theo Fairfax. And that—she sighed heavily and dropped her head against the back of the chair—was the only dark cloud in her otherwise sunshiny future.

What had she been thinking, letting herself fall for a mainlander on vacation? Okay, maybe not *vacation*, vacation, but...

"You're starting to sound like Haki searching for her elusive menehunes," Sydney muttered to herself. She was going to miss him. She already did. Far more than anticipated, and he hadn't even left yet. But it was better this way. They'd had one last adventure together, had ended things on a positive, memorable note. Something he could talk about, hopefully with fondness. She snorted. Who was she kidding? Theo wouldn't talk about her to anyone.

But he would hopefully think about her, although not nearly as often as she would think of him. He had a life back in San Francisco. A job he was good at. A job that, as far as she could tell, he liked. What was she supposed to do? Ask him to leave everything he knew? Everything he'd worked for? For what? An island girl at heart whose entire life was currently up in the air?

Below, on the beach, early surfers mingled and prepared to take on the challenges the morning tide would provide. Shouts and waves of welcome, and the wobbling sunrise excursion of Benji and Kahlua to the shore, brought a small smile to her face. While the visitors to Nalani slept on, the heartbeat of the town—its residents and caretakers—embraced the day with exuberance, affection and dedication.

This was her town. Her island. Her people. And now that she'd chosen to stay permanently, she had the strangest feeling she'd earned something special. "Maybe it's just a *mana pono* kickback," she told herself.

Despite the now-still morning air, her mother's collection of wind chimes, situated beneath the overhang of the back porch, jingled and clinked to life. *A sign*, Sydney thought, as she smiled in gratitude and acceptance.

She'd known the moment she came back for Remy's memorial that her life would never be the same. Since that time she'd embraced all that was offered to her and fallen in love. She glanced up at the cloud-filled sky. Somewhere up there, Remy was getting one serious kick out of this. She toasted him with what was left of her coffee. "Life doesn't get much better, does it, big brother?"

Two hours, one group text message and a very long, hot shower later, Sydney slid her third pot of fresh-brewed coffee out of the maker and returned to the back porch. "Anyone want a refill?"

"Fill it up." Keane hoisted one of her mugs from his spot on the floor of the porch, where he could look out into the water. "Forgot how rough jet lag can be."

"Any idea where Mano is?" she asked.

"Last-minute breakfast meeting," Keane said. "He said to catch him up later."

Daphne and Tehani rocked gently in their chairs, Tehani sipping her tea and Daphne nibbling at one of the malasadas Sydney had asked her to pick up from Maru on her way over.

"For the record," Kiri said while covering a huge yawn, "Remy never once called a sunrise meeting for his employees. So much for a day off."

"Yeah, well, I'm not Remy," Sydney said, purposely avoiding Tehani's gaze as she set the coffeepot down on the side table. "Since Tehani suggested we close for the day in order to get ready for the luau tonight—"

"You know T only said that because she expects you to make bucketloads of your mom's macaroni salad," Keane said.

"I figured as much." She had a grocery run on the top of her to-do list for the day. Sydney leaned her butt against the railing and crossed her arms over her chest. "I thought it fitting we have a meeting regarding where I see Ohana Odysseys going from here."

"I knew it," Kiri said sourly. "You're selling to that Golden Vistas thing, aren't you?"

Sydney took a deep breath. She should have known word would have gotten around town. Especially by now. When Tehani refused to look at her, Sydney sighed. "No, actually, I'm not."

That earned her four surprised gazes.

"Really?" Keane asked with a narrowed gaze. "Syd, that's a boatload of cash you're turning down."

"We don't need it," she said.

"What about your plans?" Daphne said. "What about your flight school and your job—"

"I've got a job here. Heck, I have an entire business. One that a lot of people rely on. And not just the ones sitting on this porch. As for the school?" She shrugged. "No reason I can't run one here, if the opportunity presents itself down the road. I've even looked into maybe becoming a part-time helicopter instructor." She had Theo to thank for that. If she could help him get over his fear of climbing into one, she could probably convince anyone. "I'm ready to give this a shot. A real shot. The last few weeks, I've been playing, I know, but that's over now. Remy passed this responsibility to me. It's time I accept it completely."

"Ha!" Keane smacked his hand down on his knee. "I knew it! Daph, you owe me twenty bucks."

"No one likes a sore winner." Daphne scowled before she grinned. "But this is one bet I'm thrilled to lose."

"Kiri, that means you're going to be given some more responsibility around Odysseys. You up for it?" Sydney asked.

"That mean you're hiring extra surf instructors?"

"She already did," Keane said. "I've got some months to kill, Syd. You want me, you've got me. Put me in the water, I'll be even happier."

"Put him on a new brochure, and we'll have surf lessons sold out through Christmas," Daphne added.

"T?" Sydney asked after the laughter died down. "How about you?"

"Do you mean it?"

Sydney didn't like the doubt she heard in Tehani's voice, but Sydney couldn't blame her. She'd been back and forth with this so many times she'd given her friend whiplash, not to mention kept her from finding solid footing where her future was concerned. A future that included Sydney's soon-to-be niece or nephew.

"I mean it, T. No joking around this time, no hedging or hesitation. This is where I'm meant to be." She offered a small, sad smile and looked down the beach to where the cottage sat on the shore. "It's where I want to be."

Tehani rocked a few more times, then, after setting her mug of tea down, pushed out of the chair and came over to Sydney. "Then I finally feel safe in saying this." She stepped forward and wrapped her arms around Sydney in a tight hug. "Welcome home, sister."

"THANKS FOR MEETING with me on short notice." Theo took a seat across from Mano and pulled the other man's attention away from the early-morning view of the ocean.

"Not a problem." Mano eyed him cautiously, an expression Theo had come to understand was the man's default emotion. "Sounded as if something important was on your mind."

"It was. *Is*." As anxious as he was to have this conversation, he regretted not taking time earlier in his stay to explore and get a personal look at the Hibiscus Bay Resort.

He knew what it looked like on paper. The guest capacity; the number of employees; how it had surpassed projected earnings the past three years, mainly due to Mano Iokepa taking over as the hands-on manager of operations.

But stepping inside the surprisingly affordable resort that brought the tropical setting of the islands all the way inside was an experience unto itself. Between the living walls of plant life and the gleaming polished-wood floors and counters, the lush comfy chairs and settees arranged around various miniature waterfalls and flora displays, he couldn't have imagined feeling even more in a tropical paradise than he already had. But time had started slipping away from him well before Sydney had said goodbye to him yesterday.

Time that seemed to stalk him even as he attempted to ignore it.

Which explained his quick maneuvering

through the Hibiscus Bay Resort lobby on his way to Southern Seas, its one and only restaurant.

"I understand Hibiscus Bay used to have another quick service place to eat." Theo nearly sighed in relief as Mano poured him coffee out of the silver carafe on the table. Gone was the beach-friendly guy Theo had met days before. Instead, with his suit and tie covering his tattoos and the steely-eyed glare he'd fixed on Theo, it was clear Mano was in full businessman hotel-manager mode.

"It was one of the first changes I made when I took over the day-to-day operations. The resort is only part of Nalani. Granted, a large part," he added with a sly smirk. "But I thought it's important that we encourage our guests to explore the entire town and spend their money at local businesses." He sat back as their server approached. "Just my usual, thanks, Turi," he said to the middle-aged man wearing a simply pattered Hawaiian shirt and pressed beige slacks. "Theo?"

"What would you recommend?" Theo asked the server, who looked pleased to be consulted.

"The macadamia nut pancakes are a kitchen specialty."

"Turi's wife happens to be our head chef," Mano added with a teasing smile at the server. "But he's not wrong."

Theo nodded in approval. "That sounds great, thanks."

"Yes, sir."

"So." Mano eyed Theo with an almost unreadable expression. "I take it you want to discuss GVI's offer to buy Ohana Odysseys."

"In a way." Considering the scene at Hula Chicken last night, he wasn't the least bit surprised Mano had heard. Heck, by now he assumed the entire town was aware. "She's turning down the offer. In case you hadn't heard that."

Mano inclined his head. "There's very little I don't hear about in Nalani."

Probably because the man had an almost royal air about him. Theo had seen the way people were around Mano, as if he were part superhero, part town guardian and adviser. It wasn't, Theo supposed, a bad reputation to have.

"That must put you in an interesting position," Mano said. "Having been sent out here to close the deal."

"As far as I thought, I was here to do a financial evaluation. In hindsight, I now suspect I was wrong." Now it was his turn to eye Mano. "I never had cause to peek into the past of GVI. To the time before I started working for them. I see now I should have. If only to get a better idea of their business practices and history."

"A business's history should, in my opinion, always be a determining factor when attempting to secure your future." Mano pointed to the woven basket filled with the sweet Hawaiian bread Theo now found himself addicted to. "My first job was as a busboy in this very restaurant when I was sixteen. Of course, it wasn't the same as it is now, but starting at ground level provided me multiple avenues of education."

"Now you run the entire resort. It's an impressive rise to the top."

"It was a necessary one," Mano said. "Not without its sacrifices, of course. Hawai'i is special. Nalani, in my estimation, even more so. It was important for someone who understands—the islands, our traditions, our way of life—to be in charge. And to keep our history in mind. Remy understood that as well. It's probably why he wanted to bring partners in who understand the importance of keeping our ideals and way of life intact."

"And you don't think GVI will do that?" Theo asked, concerned.

"I do not. Not from what I've seen to date about how they operate. Their bulldozers will push out communities and businesses that may be small but mean a great deal to those of us who live here, raise our kids here, retire here. Change is inevitable, but there are other solutions to keeping Nalani viable and competitive in island tourism."

"You know about the emails Sydney's brother planned to send before he died."

"I received one," Mano confirmed. "Granted, mine was a different offer than the rest. He was hoping for a partnership, not only with me personally but for Ohana and Hibiscus Bay to join forces and expand. Remy had been exploring the possibility of franchising Ohana Odysseys and wanted a strong partner to back him up."

"There it is." Theo shook his head, swallowing a rush of anger along with the sweet, soft bread.

"There what is?" Mano asked.

"The missing piece to the puzzle I've been working all night." He wasn't sure if he felt irritated at himself for not seeing this earlier or felt like one seriously duped pawn. "I couldn't figure out why GVI had made such an outrageously generous offer to Sydney for Ohana. Now I know."

Mano tilted his head. "Define *outrageously generous*."

Theo rattled off the number, receiving a look of surprise.

"I would say your assessment is correct. That is a more-than-generous offer."

"How close is it to the one they made for Hibiscus Bay five years ago?"

Mano's lips twitched. His body relaxed, as if Theo had passed some sort of test.

"It just never made sense to me," Theo went on like he'd been asked a question. "Why this little tour company, in a town probably half of the tourists coming to the islands have never heard of. It wasn't just that they were interested—of course they would be. Remy Calvert built an amazing community-supported business based on one thing Hawai'i is never short on. It was the ferocity they applied to their desire to purchase. It's because it got them closer to what they really want: the Hibiscus Bay."

"Keep going," Mano said as Turi delivered their meals. "You've almost got it."

Theo's mind raced as he looked down at the stack of golden pancakes topped with crumbled macadamia nuts and a sprinkling of fresh-shaved coconut. What else was there for GVI to want? The main resort, the number one tour company…

"Nalani," Theo muttered to himself before meeting Mano's dark-eyed gaze. "They want Nalani."

"You're almost as smart as Sydney said," Mano said as he dug into what Theo recognized as a more elegant version of loco moco, the breakfast they'd had the other morning in town. "The only reason GVI didn't succeed in buying Hibiscus the first time was because the shareholders couldn't agree. Fortunately, I'd recently purchased enough of a stake to keep the sale from being approved the second time around. I thought at the time they'd be back. I should have anticipated an end run at some point. Never occurred to me they'd use Remy's death as an in."

Theo wanted to argue the point, but he couldn't.

"How much trouble are they in? GVI?" Mano asked just as Theo took his first bite of what had to be the best pancakes he'd ever had in his life. They tasted like every good thing about the islands.

"A lot," he said after he swallowed. "If I say any more, I'd be violating my nondisclosure agreement. But suffice it to say, they need this deal to go through."

"Sydney turning them down won't go over well."

"No, it won't. That's one reason I wanted to meet with you. Sydney might find herself in trouble in the future. I thought maybe making you aware could help to protect her."

"Why can't you protect her?"

"First off? I feel pretty safe in saying Sydney wouldn't want either of us protecting her."

Mano grinned and gave an approving nod.

"That said, I'll do what I can once I'm back home. But even with this new promotion they've promised me, I don't know how effective I'll be, especially once Sydney officially turns down the offer. They could even fire me for incompetence."

"I doubt that'll happen," Mano said. "You've proven yourself to be a good foot soldier. They won't want to lose that."

"That doesn't sound like a compliment." But he didn't wait for a response. "You were Remy's best friend. You've been on the receiving end of GVI's interest in the past. You care about this town, probably more than anyone else I've met. Makes sense you'd be the one to keep an eye out. For both Sydney and Nalani."

"So you're warning me, then walking away."

Theo frowned. "Better than me keeping my mouth shut before I leave."

"I'm beginning to think Sydney's wrong about you." Mano sat back and picked up his coffee. "Maybe you aren't as smart as she thinks you are."

"What's that supposed to mean?"

"It means you need to take a look at the entire equation before you attempt to solve it, Abacus."

Theo's cheeks went hot. "Okay, that's something only Sydney—"

"I am thrilled Sydney's decided not to sell. I'm even happier she's going to stay in Nalani. Honestly? I don't think she ever should have left, but sometimes we have to leave a place before we learn it's where we truly belong. When is your flight?"

"Ah." Theo glanced at his watch. "At four."

"Good." Mano resumed eating. "That should give you plenty of time to recalculate your solution. Maybe then you'll come to a different result."

"SHOULD BE AN amazing birthday party," Keane said from behind Sydney as she stood on the back porch of Ohana Odysseys and watched a group begin to carry in the picnic tables for Leora's first birthday luau.

The beach teemed with locals and tourists curiously watching the assembly of a town celebration. But no one, it seemed, was more excited than the toddler racing around in a teeny-tiny orange crop top and sagging diaper. With her jet-black curls and her big brown eyes, Leora Nalatu was the promise of the future, all tied up in old tradition and new exuberance while her parents did their best to keep her out of the way.

Poles were being hammered into the sand. Strings of lights were being stretched across and accented with bright pink and orange paper lanterns. Nearby, the puffing, rising smoke from the in-ground imu oven sent aromatic wafts of anticipation that promised a succulent roasted pig for the evening's festivities. In a few short hours, they'd be focused on a little girl whose parents had gone to extraordinary lengths to have her.

Sydney glanced to her left, envisioning the small white cottage at the other end of the beach. A cottage that, from here on, would hold only the memories of the man she'd never told she loved.

"She knows it's a special day," Sydney said and smiled through a sheen of tears as

Leora's father scooped her into his arms and sent his daughter squealing in delight. "I don't think I've ever made so much macaroni salad before."

"Well, you might have a little less than you did before I left."

Sydney looked back at him as he rested a hand on the top tip of the familiar blue surfboard. "You didn't."

"I just ate one bowl." He patted his very firm stomach. "I needed some energy to surf on. Is it okay that I use this?"

"Remy's board?" The shift of conversation brought forgiveness on the salad. "It's completely okay. In fact, keep it. He'd want you to have it. If only to make sure it sees some actual wave-riding success."

Keane's laugh nearly broke her heart. "He always believed he was better than he was out there. Mano and I used to call him *the wipeout king*. Not that he ever knew."

"Oh, he knew." She swiped at the solitary tear that escaped her control. "He wore it as a badge of honor. Also, he figured it made you feel better. *Reverse training*, he called it. You always tried to show off around him."

"There weren't a lot of people I was eager to impress," Keane said. "He was the best friend I ever had." He slung an arm around her shoulders and tugged her close. "The best friend any of us ever had."

She wrapped her arms around Keane and squeezed, feeling safe, for perhaps the first time, to finally let go. "I miss him so much it hurts."

"I know." Keane pressed a kiss to the top of her head. "I do, too. I spent a lot of time being angry with him for not telling us he'd been sick. But there's no point in being mad. Not when we've got this incredible future ahead of us."

"Ohana," she whispered.

"The future's all we have, Syd. And we never know how long that's going to be for. It'd be a shame not to embrace everything it offered."

Sydney pulled her head back and looked up at him. "You aren't suggesting we get married or something, are you?"

Keane laughed so hard his entire body vibrated. "Perish the thought. I just thought it was interesting this morning that you never once mentioned Theo in your plans for Ohana."

"Why would I?" Her throat felt too tight to swallow. "He's got his life back on the mainland, and I've got mine here."

"Remy used to worry about you, you know. About being alone out there in South Carolina."

"I don't need anyone to take care of me," Sydney said sourly.

"Not talking about that, although I reserve the right to argue the point." That earned him a gentle slap on the chest. "No, he worried you'd never let anyone in. Especially after you lost your parents. He worried about your heart."

"Yeah, well, he went all soft after falling for Tehani."

"He did," Keane said. "But that was because he knew what he'd found was special. I've never seen you with anyone the way you are with Theo Fairfax. You're, I don't know, lighter? Happier?" He gave her another hard squeeze. "Softer. I just think it would have been nice to see where it might have led."

"I belong here, Keane. Theo doesn't. For crying out loud, I couldn't even convince him to wear a pair of flip-flops! He wouldn't even walk out on the beach!"

"Everyone has their learning curve," Keane said with a chuckle. "He needs acclimating, and I can see why it was taking a while."

"Why are you pushing this so hard? Knowing him, he's probably already on his way to the airport. And his flight doesn't leave until four."

"Seriously?"

"If he's ten minutes early, he's late. Which is what this conversation is, Keane. Too late." And even if it wasn't, how could she possibly ask Theo to abandon his dreams in favor of the one she'd finally found for herself?

HANDS IN THE pockets of his khaki slacks, Theo stood in the open doorway of the beach cottage and looked out over the porch rail to the water. The heat of the day had hit with familiar ferocity, but it was a ferocity he'd come not only to expect but appreciate.

Despite his pseudo-acclimation to the climate of the islands, he was back in uniform. Back in the strangle-hold button-down, tightly-tied tie outfit that up until a few days ago had acted as part security blanket. Before arriving in Nalani, he'd known who he was. Or at least, he thought he did. A man who strived to meet expectations, not exceed them. A man who had his future mapped out in precise, solitary steps up the professional ladder. A man who—until he'd stepped foot on this beautiful, peaceful island—had no inclination to even think about love or where he might find it.

Love was indefinable. An anomaly he assumed would pass him by because he wouldn't recognize it when he saw it. As it turned out, he was right. He hadn't seen it.

He'd felt it.

All the way down to his number-crunching core.

Now his bag was packed, the cottage tidied to the point no one would ever know he'd been here. He glanced down at the movement out of the corner of his eye. "You'll know I was here, though, won't you, Noodles?"

The gecko scampered up one of the post railings and skittered over to him, stopped and looked up at him, then out at the water. "I'm betting you're just worrying where your next meal will come from. Don't worry." He stepped closer and, moving slowly, touched a fingertip to the top of the gecko's head. It was softer than expected, a little rough and pulsing with life. "I left a note for Sydney to leave some food out for you. She won't let you starve."

The little lizard's body inflated a bit, as if taking in a deep breath.

Overhead, the afternoon clouds began to race, a little earlier than normal—at least the normal Theo had become used to. As the sky darkened, the waves pushed farther up on shore, and for the first time, Theo found himself tempted by their teasing.

Impulse was something new for him. Something Sydney had unlocked, he decided as he considered some of the things he'd done that he would have never have expected of himself. Before he let himself dismiss the idea, he toed off the sneakers he'd finally broken in, reached down and yanked off his socks. Grabbing hold of the porch post, he took a step forward.

And sank his left foot ankle-deep into the sand.

The odd, cool sensation brought a smile

to his lips as he let go and lowered his other foot. He scrunched his toes, feeling the sand sift through as he lifted one foot and took another step. And another and another until he reached the edge of the shoreline. Tiny white streams of bubbles dotted the sand, indicating where the tide found its limits.

*So close*, he thought. But as the gentle lapping wave approached, he backed away. Too much temptation. Taking that final step forward might just make it impossible to leave.

And he had to leave. He had obligations. A job. If only to keep his ears open to protect Sydney. He turned, looked up at the cottage even as he saw the familiar young man heading down the winding path to the porch.

"Hey, brah! You ready to go?"

Hori's typical enthusiasm sobered him. This wasn't his place. As much as he might want for it to be, it simply wasn't.

Theo made his way back up the beach, stomping his bare feet on the bottom step before brushing off the last of the sand and putting his socks and shoes back on. He ignored how tight they felt. How heavy and clumsy.

Ducking inside, he picked up his garment bag, his laptop case and his jacket.

He looked back to the porch, but Noodles was gone. "At least Sydney said goodbye." With one final glance at the little house that had felt like a home, he pulled the door shut and followed Hori to his cab.

## CHAPTER TWELVE

"LOOK AT THOSE KIDS, dancing in the rain."

Perched on the edge of one of the dozens of logs that had been dragged from beneath Blue Moon's porch for the luau, Sydney swiped the rain off her face. Tehani joined her.

Dancing Leora and her friends had expanded to a cast of dozens. The luau attendees had begun trickling down to the beach over the past few hours. On arrival, they loaded the buffet tables with bowls and aluminum trays filled to the brim with island goodness, family recipes and the promise that no one in Nalani would go hungry.

"Pretty soon you'll have one of those dancing around yourself." It was something that brought a genuinely happy smile to her face and her heart. Something of her brother that would continue. Even better, she'd be here to be a part of it.

A makeshift stage had been set up near the thirty-something picnic tables scattered about the upper portion of Nalani beach and soon the band would start playing.

"You donning your skirt this evening, or am I on my own?" Sydney asked as Tehani stretched out her bare legs.

"I haven't decided." T lifted her face to the sky just as the rain subsided. "But I have it in my bag." She grabbed hold of Sydney's hand and squeezed. "I'm so happy you're staying. So happy you'll be here for the baby."

Sydney smiled. "Yeah, well, might be the only shot I have at one of those, so be prepared. He or she is going to be incredibly spoiled by their auntie."

"Remy would have been an amazing father," T whispered. "I wish I'd known sooner. I wish I could have told him. Maybe…"

"Maybe what?"

Tehani shrugged. "Sometimes I wonder if maybe he'd known, he'd have had a new reason to live. Silly, right?"

Was it? Sydney didn't know. "We all have to live with our regrets, I guess."

"No, Sydney. We don't."

Sydney sighed. "Don't tell me. You've been talking to Keane." Leora and her fellow toddlers dive-bombed into the sand before scrambling back to their feet. She looked up at the sky. In a matter of minutes, his plane would take off and she could finally, hopefully, move on.

"What regrets will you have about Theo?"

"None that matter," Sydney lied.

"Did you tell him you love him?"

Sydney's head snapped around. "How did you—"

"I loved your brother from almost the instant we met." Tehani squeezed her hand. "Do you really think I wouldn't see it in someone else I love?"

"He's…a mainlander."

"You say that as if it's a bad thing," Tehani scolded. "He gave you the opportunity to see Nalani through his eyes. You saw us as he did. I truly believe that's part of what convinced you to stay. Had Theo never come to the island, you would have left us."

"You don't know that."

"You may have come to understand that this is where you belong, but Theo opened your eyes. I can see where that would make him difficult to resist. And you changed him, too. He got into a helicopter for you."

Sydney grinned. "He did do that, didn't he?"

"Silly men, always wanting to impress the woman they've fallen for. He had breakfast with Mano."

"He did?" Sydney thought back. "That was Mano's last-minute meeting?"

"Mmm." Tehani nodded. "Theo warned him about GVI's real plans. It wasn't going to stop with Ohana, Sydney. They want all of Nalani for whatever reason, and there's little doubt they'd want all of us out. He thought Mano should be aware in case they approached you again or pushed back at your refusal to sell."

"He didn't tell me any of that," Sydney said.

"From what Mano said, Theo only discovered it last night. Mano didn't go into details, but the way I understood it, Theo might have gone poking into areas of the business he shouldn't have. In any case, it was you he was thinking about."

"And Nalani." Her heart swelled with

newfound affection and more than a little gratitude.

"He's a good man. Misguided in his employment, perhaps," Tehani criticized. "But nonetheless, I think he's a good man. Even after you walked away, he thought of you first. That's a man worthy of the truth, don't you think?"

Uncertainty swirled inside her like an afternoon storm. "What do I say to him, T? That I love him? What good will that do? It'll only complicate things. I don't want him being forced to give up what he loves just to make a go of things with me."

"What makes you think he'd feel forced?" Tehani released her hand and patted her knee before standing up. "Maybe he's just waiting to know that door of possibility is open. Regrets can be the most difficult part of life, Sydney. I have enough for both of us. Don't carry your own. You lose nothing by telling him the truth."

As the clouds parted and the sun burned off the remnants of the storm, Sydney sat there—the ocean on one side, the pending celebration on the other—and watched Tehani move off to scoop up the birthday girl into her arms.

She clung to the log, fingers digging into the damp wood as if anchoring herself to resolve. Hope and Sydney had parted ways years before. Hope was what someone clung to when there was nothing else left. Was that why she'd felt as if she had been adrift the past few years? Out there, all alone on the mainland, knowing something was missing but not wanting to dig deep enough into her own soul to discover what it might be?

Hope could be debilitating. Defeating. And yet, even now as she sat in the damp remnants of a tropical afternoon cloudburst, she could feel it building inside her, forcing her to ask the one question she'd refused to: What if?

"T?" she called out and shot to her feet as Tehani spun around. She had no other words, only the desperate desire to try to turn her life around one more time.

With Leora cradled in her arms, T smiled and nodded. "Go."

She didn't wait to be told twice. Sydney kicked off her sandals and hurried down to the shore. Running as fast as she could in the flat, damp sand, she sped toward the cottage and, hopefully, to Theo.

"GOTTA SAY, we're gonna miss you around here, brah." Hori had one arm slung across the back of the passenger seat as he drove toward the Hilo airport. "You're costing me a small bundle, though, leaving like this. Maru was sure you'd be staying. I even put money on it."

"You bet on whether I'd stay in Nalani or not?" Theo wasn't certain what shocked him more: that Hori was so reckless with his finances or that he himself was worthy of such attention.

"Nah, brah. Nothing to do with Nalani." Hori glanced back, his smile accentuating his round cheeks. "Sydney. Maru said she saw you two walking on the beach at sunset. One thing we know is to listen to Maru. Now I'm gonna be out fifty big ones."

"I'm sorry for your loss," Theo said with far more humor than he felt. "I thought Maru made malasadas, not predictions."

"Ha! Then you weren't here long enough. Maru, she's our guiding star, ya know? Ain't much of anything goes on in Nalani without her knowing about it beforehand."

"Maybe she should have paid closer attention to Remy Calvert, then."

Hori's smile faded. "Nothing saying she didn't. Couple weeks before he died, she talked to him. Don't know what was said, but I do know she wasn't happy with his take on the conversation. 'Wasted moments,' she said to me after. 'Wasted moments and possibilities.' Not sure there's anything worse."

It struck him as a very island thing to say.

"Now me?" Hori said and snapped right back into overly cheery mode. "I take that advice to heart. I do what I want, when I want, and embrace every moment. One reason I drive this cab, yah? Keeps me on the pulse of things. I get to meet all sorts. Like you, for instance. You don't even look like the guy who arrived here last week. Got yourself some sun, some female attention—and I heard you even helped rescue those two kids up at Hamakua. That's what I'd call a real island adventure."

"It has been that." Theo could see the turnoff for the airport coming up. But the knots that had begun forming in his stomach the second he'd taken his feet out of the sand tightened. "Appreciate the hospitality, Hori. From everyone in Nalani."

"Our pleasure, brah. That's why we're here, right? To give a Big Island welcome and make you never want to go home." His laugh echoed through the cab. "Of course, that's not logical. Everyone has to go home at some point. Just makes me glad I'm already there, ya know what I'm sayin'?"

He did know. But why didn't it feel right?

Hori continued chattering until they pulled up to his departure gate. Moving as if in slow motion, he climbed out of the car and accepted his bags from Hori before handing over his fare, plus a generous tip. "You'd best be getting back, Hori. The luau's probably already started."

"You're my last fare, brah. On my way now." Hori stepped onto the sidewalk and slapped a hand on Theo's shoulder. "Safe travels, my friend. Maybe one day we'll see you again." He moved off to talk to one of the cabbies who had pulled up behind him.

*One day, maybe.* Theo gave him a distracted nod, pulled his phone out of his pocket and tapped open his airline app to access his ticket. Dazed, foggy, he made his way inside, bag slung over his shoulder that felt far too confined in his navy blazer.

Blaring over the loudspeaker, the announcements about keeping bags close and gate changes sounded through the airport. He made his way to security, half glancing at his phone as he waited to pass through.

"Sir?" The uniformed agent waved at him. "Place your bags on the belt, please, and walk on through."

"Right." Theo slid his thumb under the strap. But he didn't remove it.

"Sir?" the agent said. "Are you all right?"

"No." He looked at the older man and shook his head. "No, I'm not all right at all." It was so clear to him now. What waited for him in San Francisco wasn't a life. It was an existence. He'd had a life here, in Nalani. With Sydney. And, okay, maybe he was seeing and feeling things that weren't entirely there, but they could be. Maybe.

If he just took a chance.

"I just need to take the chance," he told himself as he yanked himself out of line and ran back to the sliding glass doors. He scanned the street, heart pounding, and spotted Hori's cab caught in the exiting traffic.

He nearly dropped his phone as he raced to the car and slammed his hand on the trunk just as Hori began to move. The cab jerked to a stop, and Theo pulled open the door.

"What's the matter, brah? Forgot something?"

"Yeah." He jumped in and slammed the door behind him. "I forgot everything. Take me back to Nalani. We've got a luau to get to. But I'll need to make one quick stop first."

"You got it, brah." Hori knocked an open palm against the steering wheel. "Just got my fifty bucks back."

SHE WAS TOO LATE.

The house was dark. The curtains drawn. The door closed.

He was already gone.

Lungs burning, feet scraped from the sand, Sydney hadn't stopped until she reached the cottage at the far end of town. The cottage she would forever call Theo's because he was all she could envision as she looked at the structure now.

Sydney bent over, planted her hands on her thighs and tried to catch her breath. When she headed up the beach, she could swear she saw ghostly bare-footed prints guiding her. The bubble that had been building inside her burst.

This was why she didn't hope. She shouldn't have waited for Tehani's not-so-subtle lecture. She should have listened to Keane. If she had, she'd have been earlier. She'd have caught Theo before he'd left and...

"And what?" She slugged her way through the sand to the porch and sat down on the top step. "What would you have done? Told him you loved him? What would that have done? Asked him to stay? That wouldn't have been fair, would it?" She sighed, knocked her head against the porch post as a familiar little green-and-gold-speckled lizard emerged from a knothole in the porch plank. "So that's where you live, is it, Noodles?"

Noodles approached, hesitantly at first, then came close enough for her to hold her hand out. He stepped into her palm, and she raised him up. "You changed him, you know," she told the house gecko. "Maybe both of us did, and that's a good thing." But it didn't erase the sadness that she could have done—could have *had*—more. "I waited too long. I gave in to the fear. Didn't want to think I needed anyone. Now look where I am." She sighed. "I'm sitting all alone, talking to a lizard."

Noodles's head twitched before he turned and leaped out of her grasp. But not to run away, she realized as she saw a second lizard—a smaller lizard—poke its head out of the same knothole Noodles had climbed out of. Noodles glanced back, and Sydney took his expression as a desire for approval.

"Did you get yourself a girl lizard, Noodles?" She shifted and leaned on her forearms, staying still as the second lizard joined Noodles on the porch. "Hello, there. Are you his ohana?" It took her a moment to realize she was actually waiting for an answer. "There it is. The first step toward transforming into Haki. Next up, a menehune manhunt."

The distant sound of an engine's roar echoed. She glanced up as a plane arced up and into the sky. The tears burned, but she kept them in check as she watched it disappear into the clouds. "Well, at least one of us gets a happily-ever-after," she choked out. "Take care of her, Noodles."

Instead of heading back into town down the hill, she decided to take the long way, back down the beach and through the evening tide that had always brought her some peace. And hoped, by the time she got back to the luau, she'd have found some way to mend her broken heart.

IT WASN'T JUST one stop Theo had to make— it was two, but as they were both in town, he sent Hori on his way to the luau. Just as he was climbing out of the cab, bags tangled around his arms and hands, he saw the doors of Luanda's slide close.

"No, wait!" He dove forward, startling the employee. "I need to pick up a few things. I'll be really quick. Please. It's important."

"All right, brah." The teenager waved him in. "But be quick. The party's already started."

"Right. The party. Do you know if Shani's shop is still open?"

"Dunno."

"Would you go check for me? If she's still

there, just tell her I need that quilt she was going to ship for me. The sunset one. She'll know what I mean."

"Brah, you okay? You look a little *wild*."

"I feel wild!" Theo shouted, and the teen jumped. "I think maybe I can totally do this island-life thing."

"Okay, brah, I'll go get Shani." Mumbling under his breath, he left and Theo was alone in the dimly lit general store.

*Trust*, Theo thought, *is in abundance on the islands.* The kid had actually trusted him alone in this store. He dumped his bags on the floor and hurried over to the clothing section. Minutes later, he'd found what he was looking for and was just wiggling his feet into a pair of simple black flip-flops when the store's doors slid open again.

"Theo?" Shani's suspicious voice had him standing up straight. "You in here?"

"Yes, Shani. I'm back here." He waited a moment until the woman appeared, and he held out his arms to show off his new attire. "Is this luau appropriate?"

Shani, her tattooed arms hugging a tissue-wrapped bundle against her chest looked at him with concern. "It is," she said slowly as she walked toward him, then circled him. "Aren't you supposed to be on a plane?"

"Should be? Yes. Supposed to be? No." He turned and looked in the mirror, cringing at his less-than-tan legs sticking out of the beige board shorts. "Boy, this is a look, huh?" He plucked at the collar of the red-and-green floral shirt. "It's Christmas came early."

"See, Shani?" Koho said from behind a rack of shirts. "*Wild*."

"I'm thinking more like, determined," Shani mumbled, but it only made Theo smile wilder. It was then that she blinked, seemingly out of her stupor. "You're staying."

"I hope so," Theo said. "If Sydney wants me to. I mean, I don't know, do I? I'm actually leaping before looking, and I don't know, it feels kind of amazing. Freeing, even."

*"Kuokoa ana,"* Shani said, with a smile. "Freeing. You wanted this, too?"

"Yes. I thought a gesture of affection might get things off on the right foot with Sydney. I had bought it for me, so I wouldn't forget, but now…" He took a deep breath and let it out slowly. "Now I know it was meant for her."

"He going to pay for all that, Shani?" Koho asked.

"Yes," Theo announced. "Yes, I am." He dropped down and dug into his discarded jacket pocket and pulled out a good number of bills. "This should cover it."

"Too much, brah," Koho said and pushed some bills back at him. Theo gathered up his clothes and returned to his bags, shoving and stuffing them inside. That left only his sneakers. "I should go to the cottage. Stash all this until I know—"

"Here." Shani placed the package in his arms and picked up his bags. "I'll keep all this in the store for you. Just let me know when you want to pick it up."

"I can do that." Theo nodded. "Mahalo. *Mahalo*, Koho."

"Mahalo, brah."

Theo left the store and made his way down the street to the path that would take him to the beach. He could live with that. Might take him a while to get there, though, as he tripped a few times, attempting to adjust to the flip-flops. How did people walk in these things? Even before he made it half-way down Pulelehua, he heard the music, the ukulele-led sound of the islands that until now, he hadn't realized soothed his soul.

Laughter and a buzzing happiness made their way through the trees and over the rooftops as people finished work for the day. Closed signs were flipped around in shop windows, and lights went out as he passed. The town was shutting down for one very simple reason: they had a birthday to celebrate.

Arms clutching the package, he began to doubt he was doing the right thing. Such a public display—the last thing he wanted was to embarrass her, but stopping now didn't seem possible. His entire being had been awakened. If he was going to get shot down, may as well make a spectacle of himself and earn a reputation. Could be a good way to start his new life in Nalani.

While he'd known most of the town had planned to turn up, the size of the crowd and revelers caught him off-guard. He came up short at the end of the path, a bit overwhelmed at where to start.

Buffet tables had been laid out, and across

the way—behind the band—white smoke plumed up and scented the air with salty, roasted meat.

"Theo!" Keane seemed to pop out of nowhere beside him, slung an arm around his shoulder and toasted him with a beer. "Aloha! Thought you'd be on a plane, brah."

"Realized I'd left something important behind."

Keane's eyes sharpened for a moment before he glanced away and took a long slug of his drink. "You hurt her, I'll hunt you down. You feel me?"

"No hunting will be necessary," Theo said, finally feeling smart enough to interpret teasing. Teasing that wasn't *entirely* teasing, at least. "Where is she?"

"Took off a while ago. Said she'd be back. Tehani probably knows. Hey, T!" he bellowed over the growing crowd. "She's over there by the band. Getting ready for the hula."

"Nice. Okay, I'll just—"

"Open bar, down by the tables," Keane gestured off to the left. "Help yourself."

"Right." Alcohol was not on the top of his list at the moment. He made his way through the crowd that was making its way over to the imu pit, where traditionally clad locals were getting ready to pull the pig out of the underground oven where it had been cooking since early this morning.

He finally wiggled his way through toward the stage, where Tehani was helping a little girl tie up the sides of her sarong.

"Tehani."

Tehani glanced up, eyes going wide before she shot to her feet. "Theo! What are you doing here?"

He lifted the wrapped package, which was beginning to tear at the edges. "I have something for Sydney. Where is she?"

"What about your flight?"

"I missed it."

"Ah. Going to reschedule, then?"

"No idea." He offered a weak smile. "Depends on whether she accepts the gift."

She reached up and caught his head in her hands, drew him down until she pressed her forehead against his. "Aloha, malihini. I was right." She took a deep breath and stepped back. "You are a good man. She's there." She pointed over his shoulder. "Be easy, brah," she said when he stepped back to look. "She went to find you."

"Did she?" His voice cracked, and he wasn't ashamed. Not one little bit.

"Go. While everyone's distracted. Oh, and take this." She plucked a solitary hibiscus flower off a nearby plant.

"What's this for?" he asked as he accepted it.

"She'll let you know." She gave him a gentle push and from then on, he didn't see anyone but Sydney. He slid the flower into the front pocket of his new board shorts.

His clumsy footing had him kicking off the flip-flops and sinking his feet into the sand as he made his way toward her. She was still down the beach a ways, kicking her feet in the surf as she approached the luau. At some point, he just stopped and watched as she came closer, closer. Closer still.

Never in his life had he seen a more beautiful sight than that of Sydney Calvert, a knee-length skirt tied around her waist in the same bright orange-and-gold-speckled pattern as the two-piece swimsuit she wore. Her hair was down, blown by the breeze as she turned and moved as elegantly as a dolphin spinning in the water.

He knew the moment she'd spotted him, and even from a distance, he saw the confusion on her face.

She looked up at the sky, turning as she propelled toward him. He still couldn't move. Not even as she raced to him, her face a mingling of shock, confusion and joy. "Your flight left almost an hour ago!"

"I know." He felt his lips twitch.

"You aren't on it."

"No." He shook his head. This was already going better than he'd hoped. "I'm not."

"You didn't leave." She looked as if she couldn't—didn't—believe it.

"I couldn't." He shrugged. "You're here."

She looked him up and down. "I almost don't recognize you. I can see actual legs. And..." She gently pushed him back. "You're barefoot! In the sand!"

"You make me want to do unpredictable things," he teased. "Things out of my comfort zone. I can't believe how good it feels. How...free."

She gasped, tears exploding into her eyes

as she covered her mouth with one hand. "I didn't think I'd ever see you again."

He could hear the emotion in her voice and could only hope it matched what he felt blooming inside him. "I—"

"No!" She reached up, pressed her fingers against his lips for a brief moment. "No, let me say this first. Because I should have before. I love you." She exhaled and nearly doubled over. "Oh, that feels good to say. I love you, Theo Fairfax."

"I'm happy to hear it, Sydney Calvert," he said with false solemnity. "Because it so happens, I love you, too."

"Okay." She nodded and planted her hands on her hips. "So what does this mean? Where do we go from here?"

"Well, first, I should probably look into getting a job."

"Why?"

"Because I sent in my letter of resignation on my ride back to Nalani. Should be effective as soon as my supervisor opens the attachment."

"You quit your job? For me?"

"And for me," he quickly countered. "That job was sucking the life out of me. I just didn't see that until I met you." He offered the package. "I'm hoping you'll accept this. As a token of the future I'd like to make with you. It's a promise of sorts, I suppose. And a thank-you."

"Oooh, I love presents." She bounced on her heels as she ripped open the tissue and unfolded the quilt. "Theo," she whispered, looking at the intricately sewn collection of colors. "I've never seen anything—was this in Shani's store?"

"She brought it out of the back before anyone else saw it. I didn't realize then, but I knew it was yours. Afterglow," he said as she drew the quilt up and out of the sand. "I never would have seen it that first night without you."

"Theo Fairfax." She shook her head and hugged it to her chest. "You are, without a doubt, the most unexpected, wonderful, spectacular thing that has ever happened to me." She kept the quilt over one arm as she stepped into his.

When he tilted her chin up to kiss her, as their lips met, everything other than her— missed flights, lost jobs, changed dreams— they all faded with the setting sun.

"Tehani said to give you this." He pulled the semi-crushed flower out of his pocket, offered it palm up. "She said you'd tell me what it means?"

She caught his hand in hers, lifting the sturdy bloom and gently placed it behind her left ear. "It means I'm spoken for," she said as she slid her fingers between his and lifted her face for another kiss. "Now. And forever."

\* \* \* \* \*

*Don't miss the next installment of the brand-new miniseries coming soon from acclaimed author Anna J. Stewart and Harlequin Heartwarming!*
*For more feel-good romances visit www.Harlequin.com today!*

# Get 4 FREE REWARDS!

**We'll send you 2 FREE Books plus 2 FREE Mystery Gifts.**

**FREE**
Value Over
**$20**

Both the **Love Inspired®** and **Love Inspired® Suspense** series feature compelling novels filled with inspirational romance, faith, forgiveness and hope.

---

**YES!** Please send me 2 FREE novels from the Love Inspired or Love Inspired Suspense series and my 2 FREE gifts (gifts are worth about $10 retail). After receiving them, if I don't wish to receive any more books, I can return the shipping statement marked "cancel." If I don't cancel, I will receive 6 brand-new Love Inspired Larger-Print books or Love Inspired Suspense Larger-Print books every month and be billed just $6.49 each in the U.S. or $6.74 each in Canada. That is a savings of at least 16% off the cover price. It's quite a bargain! Shipping and handling is just 50¢ per book in the U.S. and $1.25 per book in Canada.* I understand that accepting the 2 free books and gifts places me under no obligation to buy anything. I can always return a shipment and cancel at any time by calling the number below. The free books and gifts are mine to keep no matter what I decide.

Choose one: ☐ **Love Inspired**
Larger-Print
(122/322 IDN GRHK)

☐ **Love Inspired Suspense**
Larger-Print
(107/307 IDN GRHK)

Name (please print)

Address                                                                                          Apt. #

City                                    State/Province                          Zip/Postal Code

**Email:** Please check this box ☐ if you would like to receive newsletters and promotional emails from Harlequin Enterprises ULC and its affiliates. You can unsubscribe anytime.

**Mail to the Harlequin Reader Service:**
**IN U.S.A.:** P.O. Box 1341, Buffalo, NY 14240-8531
**IN CANADA:** P.O. Box 603, Fort Erie, Ontario L2A 5X3

**Want to try 2 free books from another series! Call 1-800-873-8635 or visit www.ReaderService.com.**

*Terms and prices subject to change without notice. Prices do not include sales taxes, which will be charged (if applicable) based on your state or country of residence. Canadian residents will be charged applicable taxes. Offer not valid in Quebec. This offer is limited to one order per household. Books received may not be as shown. Not valid for current subscribers to the Love Inspired or Love Inspired Suspense series. All orders subject to approval. Credit or debit balances in a customer's account(s) may be offset by any other outstanding balance owed by or to the customer. Please allow 4 to 6 weeks for delivery. Offer available while quantities last.

**Your Privacy**—Your information is being collected by Harlequin Enterprises ULC, operating as Harlequin Reader Service. For a complete summary of the information we collect, how we use this information and to whom it is disclosed, please visit our privacy notice located at corporate.harlequin.com/privacy-notice. From time to time we may also exchange your personal information with reputable third parties. If you wish to opt out of this sharing of your personal information, please visit readerservice.com/consumerchoice or call 1-800-873-8635. **Notice to California Residents**—Under California law, you have specific rights to control and access your data. For more information on these rights and how to exercise them, visit corporate.harlequin.com/california-privacy.

LIRLIS22R3

# THE NORA ROBERTS COLLECTION

**Get to the heart of happily-ever-after in these Nora Roberts classics! Immerse yourself in the beauty of love by picking up this incredible collection written by, legendary author, Nora Roberts!**

**YES!** Please send me the **Nora Roberts Collection**. Each book in this collection is 40% off the retail price! There are a total of 4 shipments in this collection. The shipments are yours for the low, members-only discount price of $23.96 U.S./$31.16 CDN. each, plus $1.99 U.S./$4.99 CDN. for shipping and handling. If I do not cancel, I will continue to receive four books a month for three more months. I'll pay just $23.96 U.S./$31.16 CDN., plus $1.99 U.S./$4.99 CDN. for shipping and handling per shipment.* I can always return a shipment and cancel at any time.

☐ 274 2595          ☐ 474 2595

Name (please print)

Address                                                                 Apt. #

City                          State/Province                    Zip/Postal Code

### Mail to the **Harlequin Reader Service:**
**IN U.S.A.:** P.O. Box 1341, Buffalo, NY 14240-8531
**IN CANADA:** P.O. Box 603, Fort Erie, Ontario L2A 5X3

NORA2022

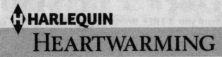
## #475 A COWBOY SUMMER

*Flaming Sky Ranch* • by Mary Anne Wilson

Rodeo star Cooper Donovan can handle bucking broncs, but not die-hard fans. His family's ranch is the perfect hideout—until he finds pediatrician McKenna Walker already there. Sharing the ranch for a week is one thing—falling for her is another!

## #476 A SINGLE DAD IN AMISH COUNTRY

*The Butternut Amish B&B* • by Patricia Johns

Hazel Dobbs has been waiting years for her dream job of being a pilot. But when she's with groundskeeper Joe Carter and his adorable daughter, it's her heart that's soaring...right over Amish country!

## #477 FALLING FOR THE COWBOY DOC

*Three Springs, Texas* • by Cari Lynn Webb

Surgeon Grant Sloan doesn't plan on staying in Three Springs, Texas—he's working there only temporarily. Even though his time in town is limited, he just can't stay away from rodeo cowgirl Maggie Orr.

## #478 THE FIREFIGHTER'S FAMILY SECRET

*Bachelor Cowboys* • by Lisa Childs

After breaking off her engagement, Doctor Livvy Lemmon is permanently anti-romance. Then she meets firefighter Colton Cassidy—he's handsome and kind, and it's impossible not to fall for him. But after losing herself so completely before, can she trust her heart again?

# HARLEQUIN
## PLUS

Try the best multimedia subscription service for romance readers like you!

---

## Read, Watch and Play.

Experience the easiest way to get the romance content you crave.

Start your **FREE TRIAL** at
<u>www.harlequinplus.com/freetrial</u>.